Also by Julia Brannan

HISTORICAL FICTION

The Jacobite Chronicles
Book One: Mask of Duplicity
Book Two: The Mask Revealed
Book Three: The Gathering Storm
Book Four: The Storm Breaks
Book Five: Pursuit of Princes
Book Six: Tides of Fortune

Jacobite Chronicles Stories
The Whore's Tale: Sarah
The Eccentric's Tale: Harriet
The Ladies' Tale: Caroline & Philippa
The Highlander's Tale: Alex

CONTEMPORARY FICTION

A Seventy-Five Percent Solution

Dealing In Treason

A Jacobite Chronicles Novella

Julia Brannan

Copyright© 2022 by Julia Brannan

Julia Brannan has asserted her right to be identified as the author of this work under the Copyright, Designs and Patents Act 1988

All rights reserved. No part of this publication may be reproduced, distributed, or transmitted in any form or by any means, including photocopying, recording, or other electronic or mechanical methods, without the prior written permission of the publisher, except in the case of brief quotations embodied in critical reviews and certain other non-commercial uses permitted by copyright law.

DISCLAIMER

This novel is a work of fiction, and except in the case of historical fact, any resemblance to actual persons, living or dead, is purely coincidental

Formatting by Polgarus Studio

Cover design by najlaqamberdesigns.com

NOTE TO READERS

This novella fills in a gap in Mask Of Duplicity from February-June 1743, looking at what Alex MacGregor and his clansmen were doing while the other characters were in London. Because of this, if you haven't already, I'd advise you to read Mask of Duplicity before starting this book. It will be a lot more enjoyable if you do!

ACKNOWLEDGEMENTS

First of all I'd like to thank all the people who helped me with my research for this book, both directly and indirectly. First of all fellow author and all-round lovely person Helen Hollick, partly for writing a very interesting and readable non-fiction book about smuggling, as well as wonderful fiction, and partly for her support. Thank you also to John Millar, an expert in tall ships and sailing, who helped me in my research for Tides of Fortune, and was kind enough to come to my assistance again for this book.

Thanks also to Highlanders4Hire, for putting on a fascinating and extremely educational display of Highland fighting skills and for their endless patience in explaining various aspects of weaponry and tactics. And thank you too to fellow author Maggie Craig for hosting them, and for the wonderful conversation we had about all things historical and Jacobite. It was a fabulous day, and I learnt an enormous amount which will help me in future novels!

I'd also like to thank Steve Williams for sending me numerous articles and videos of historical information, in the hope that some of it will be useful to me. It is, and it saves me a lot of time which would otherwise be spent searching for such titbits of information!

Thanks to the long-suffering Mary Brady, friend and first critic, who reads my chapters as I write them, critiques them for me and reassures me that I can actually write stuff people will want to read, and to my beta readers Angela, Claire, Susan, Jason and Alyson for their valued and honest opinions. I can't stress how important you are!

My gratitude also to fellow author Kym Grosso, who over the years has given me the benefit of her experience in the minefield of indie publishing. I value her friendship enormously and am so sorry that her first experience of Scotland was blighted by the dreaded Covid. I'm really hoping she'll return soon and give me a chance to show her how beautiful my country is!

A big thank you also to Diana Gabaldon, who wrote a fabulous review for my books, and who is a kind, supportive, and very interesting person!

I also wanted to thank Inverness Outlanders for welcoming me into their group and for introducing me to so many fascinating people who share my love of Jacobite and Scottish history. I really appreciate your support of me and my books, and look forward to many more interesting meetings with you!

And thanks as always go to Jason at Polgarus Studio for doing an excellent job of formatting my books, and to the talented and very patient Najla Qamber, who does all my covers, puts up with my lack of artistic ability, and still manages to somehow understand exactly what I want my covers to look like!

On a personal level this year has been a difficult one, and I'd just like to take the opportunity to thank Susan, Lise, Mandy, Arne, and Bob and Dolores for your wonderful friendship and support, both emotional and practical. I love you all more than you can imagine.

And finally to all my wonderful readers, who not only buy my books, but take the time and effort to give me feedback, to review them on Amazon, Audible, Goodreads, and Bookbub and recommend me to others, by word of mouth and on social media —thank you so much. You keep me going on those dark days when I'd rather do anything than stare at a blank screen for hours while my brain turns to mush…you are amazing! Without all of you I would be nothing, and I appreciate you more than you know.

ABOUT THE AUTHOR

Julia has been a voracious reader since childhood, using books to escape the miseries of a turbulent adolescence. After leaving university with a degree in English Language and Literature, she spent her twenties trying to be a sensible and responsible person, even going so far as to work for the Civil Service for six years.

Then she gave up trying to conform, resigned her well-paid but boring job and resolved to spend the rest of her life living as she wanted to, not as others would like her to. She has since had a variety of jobs, including telesales, Post Office clerk, primary school teacher, and painter and gilder.

In her spare time she is still a voracious reader, and enjoys keeping fit, exploring the beautiful countryside around her home, and travelling the world. Life hasn't always been good, but it has rarely been boring. Until recently she lived in the beautiful Brecon Beacons in Wales, but in June 2019 she moved to Scotland, and now lives in a log cabin in rural Aberdeenshire, a perfect place to write in!

A few years ago she decided that rather than just escape into other people's books, she would quite like to create some of her own and so combined her passion for history and literature to write the Jacobite Chronicles. She's now writing the side stories of some of the minor characters, and is researching for her next series, The Road to Rebellion, which will go back to the start of the whole Jacobite movement.

People seem to enjoy reading her books as much as she enjoys writing them, so now, apart from a tiny amount of editing work, she is a full-time writer. She has plunged into the contemporary genre too, but her first love will always be historical fiction.

CHAPTER ONE

Kent, England, February 1743

When Alex woke up for the final time on this restless night, it was still dark. True, the shutters were tightly closed, not only against the light but against the storm which still raged outside, but there was also no sound of movement in the building, no voices, no creaking of floorboards as people moved about. As this was a tavern, if it was anywhere near the approach of dawn people would be stirring.

In spite of the chair wedged firmly under the doorknob, the fact that he carried no valuables, and having the small, sparsely furnished, but clean room to himself, this was the fifth time he'd been roused from his light and fitful slumber, and this time he did not turn over and attempt to go back to sleep as he had earlier, realising it was a lost cause. He was alone in a building full of strangers, strangers who might bear him ill-will depending on their opinion of the man he'd killed on the previous day, and the only person between him and their vengeance was Gabriel Foley, their leader, another stranger. Or, being fair, a relative stranger, following their meeting last night.

He stretched out in the unexpectedly comfortable bed. Events yesterday had moved at such a frenetic pace that he hadn't had the luxury of time to contemplate his next move. Instead he had acted on instinct, as he often did. His instincts rarely failed him, but now he *did* have time to think, he realised how insane his urge to ride through the night alone to confess to the leader of a notorious smuggling gang that he had just murdered one of his men had been. If he'd had more time to think, had known then what he knew now about his victim, he would never have done it. He had never met Foley before, had had no idea what manner of man he was, had known only that he was trustworthy as a dealer, and that his occupation meant he must be both courageous and ruthless. It was honour not sense that had driven him, and, in view of how it had turned out, he was not sorry to be here. But that did not mean that, given a similar situation, he would repeat his reckless action. It was Angus who was the reckless brother, not him. He could not afford to be reckless; as chieftain of the Loch Lomond MacGregors, the safety and wellbeing of the clan rested on his shoulders.

Angus would have moved the weapons from Joshua White's cellar, that was certain. But Alex had no idea whether he'd disposed of the smuggler's body as well, or what he'd done with the two servants who'd been locked in the pantry. On his way home he would take a brief detour through Stockwell to find out.

He sighed. He was sorry that he'd been forced to take the fool's life, but he could not have let the man live, even though the information he'd thought to blackmail Angus with had been false. Sir Anthony Peters was not Angus's sponsor as Joshua had believed after spying on him and seeing Angus entering a tavern in Covent Garden, then Sir Anthony leaving a short while later. He had assumed they were having a meeting about bringing illicit goods into the country. He'd been wrong, but in spite of Joshua's treachery Alex would have thought twice before killing him, if all they'd been smuggling into the country was tea, brandy or tobacco.

Half the nobility was involved in the free trade, as smuggling was called. At the very least they bought goods at prices so low they must have been brought in illicitly. At the most they financed whole expeditions, raking in a tidy profit, and knowing that the risk of them being arrested was minimal. All the risk was taken by the people under whose roof Alex was now lying –the men and women who sailed the ships across the Channel, who brought the goods into the country, and the others, often poor labourers glad of the extra cash, who carried the cargo from the ships to safety. You could not be arrested for smuggling unless you were actually caught in the act of doing so, or with items on your person that could be proved to be contraband.

No, Sir Anthony would not be seen dead doing manual labour,

doing anything that might soil his outrageously expensive silk and velvet clothes. The thought of the effeminate baronet riding across the country in a storm, or hauling casks of brandy up a cliff made Alex smile. He would have the vapours if so much as a drop of wine spilt on him!

But Alex and his men were not bringing innocent commodities into the country. They were bringing weapons. Weapons with which they hoped one day to eject the Elector of Hanover from the throne of Great Britain and restore the rightful king, James Stuart. If Sir Anthony was suspected of being a Jacobite, and an active one, he would be arrested, baronet or not, and brutally interrogated to reveal the names of his associates. And for that reason Alex had no regrets about killing Joshua White. He would kill *anyone* who threatened either his clansmen or his friends. And by spying on him Joshua had threatened everyone Alex held dear. He could not have been allowed to live.

Alex had assumed that Gabriel Foley would feel the same way about his own gang, if for different reasons. And that was why he had taken the chance of riding alone to the coastal inn, and now he was very glad that he had, for his instincts had been right. He was all the more sure of it now, as after their interview Gabriel had returned all his weapons to him, a gesture of trust. And no one had attempted to enter his room during the night, another good sign.

His musing was interrupted now by the creak of a door opening below, followed by the sound of voices, although he could not make out the words. He lay for another few minutes, listening to the rain and the homely noises of the tavern, and then he yawned and sat up, swinging his legs out of bed and taking the few steps over to the window.

Opening the shutters brought a blast of fresh, sea-scented air into the room, peppered with sleet. Outside it was still dark, although if he looked to the right he could discern a slight lightening of the sky in the east. Alex leaned his elbows on the sill and breathed deeply as he watched a sleepy stable boy make his way across the yard to tend the horses. Although he could hear the relentless sound of the sea crashing on the shore, could smell the bracing briny tang of it on the air, when he leaned out of the window to look down the steeply sloping street on which the tavern stood, which led down to the water, he could see only darkness.

He stood there for a few minutes, letting the fresh air wake him and the icy rain wash his face. He was reminded of home, although the current stormy crashing of the sea was a far cry from the gentle susurration of Loch Lomond against its shingle shore. The fact that it *did* remind him told him just how homesick he was. He hated the life he was forced to live now, the falseness, the duplicity, the sedentary nature of his days, which drove him, by nature an active man, to distraction.

He remembered the last time he had crossed the ocean on his return from Paris, his excitement on seeing Scotland again after so many years, his impatience to set foot on the soil of his homeland and the giddy exhilaration when he had, followed rapidly by guilt that he could feel so happy, when his father was dead and the responsibility of the whole clan now rested on his young shoulders. Even so, his joy at being home had tempered his grief, and he had realised then just how very homesick he had been, through all the long and eventful years he'd been away.

He felt the same way now, even though he had only been away for some eighteen months and had his brothers with him, and Iain and Maggie too. Even so, the yearning to be in his homeland, where everyone spoke his tongue, everything was familiar, and he did not have to pretend to be anyone other than himself washed over him, filling him with a longing for home so strong it threatened to unman him.

He turned from the window then, closing it firmly, before rubbing his hands across his wet face briskly in an attempt to banish the weakness. He would not see Scotland for some time yet, and must accept it. His work here was too important. Slipping his feet into his shoes and his weapons into his belt, he brought his mind back to the present, the tasks of the day ahead. If the stable hands were up, then he could be on his way. He had a long ride and a lot to do. The sooner he set off the better. He pulled the chair from under the doorknob and opened the door.

"Ah! Mr Abernathy! Good morning! I hope you slept well," came the greeting from the room directly opposite his. Its door was open, revealing Gabriel Foley sitting at his table, exactly as he had been during their interview the night before, the only difference being that instead of a bottle of claret, the table now sported several plates of food and a pitcher of ale.

"Good morning, Mr Foley," Alex replied. "I slept a lot better than I would have done had I had to ride through the storm last night."

"Good. Although it seems you'll have to ride through it today, as it shows no sign of abating."

"I've ridden through a lot worse," Alex observed. "Thank ye for your hospitality though. Yesterday was…eventful, and the chance to rest was much appreciated. I wish ye a good breakfast, sir." He turned then, intending to make his way downstairs.

"Would you care to break your own fast, before you go?" Foley asked.

Alex hesitated, torn between eagerness to be on his way and the pleadings of an empty stomach, which had not seen food since the previous morning.

"Are you riding to Stockwell today, Mr Abernathy?" Gabriel continued.

"I intend to, aye. I need to make sure that White's body is removed, and I also locked two of his servants in a wee pantry. Mr White didna seem to be a popular man, so I doubt he has many visitors. I'd no' have the servants die there, should they no' be found."

Gabriel smiled.

"In that case, if you have no objections I will ride with you, along with a few of my men. We also have things to remove from his cellar, and can deal with White's remains at the same time."

Alex deliberated for a moment, then turned from the stair and went into Gabriel's room, sitting down in the same chair he'd occupied the previous night.

"Help yourself," Foley said. "We have a long ride ahead, and you had nothing to eat last night, which was remiss of me. In fact you need not go to Stockwell, if it's out of your way. My men will release the servants, and a word from me will ensure they cause no trouble for me, or for you. Am I right in assuming you will be heading for London?"

"Why d'ye ask?" Alex said, causing Gabriel to laugh at his instinctive caution, a trait they both shared.

"Merely because it's the largest city in the kingdom, so a likely place for you to live. If you are, then we can ride together for part of the way, at least. If, however, you live in the opposite direction entirely, then I would ask you to close the door. In fact, close the door anyway. I have a proposition to put to you, and on second thought we might as well discuss it civilly over food and ale, rather than shouting it while riding through a howling storm."

"What manner of proposition?" Alex asked, freezing in the act of taking a kidney from a dish to add to the bacon he'd already put on his plate.

"One that you can say yes or no to, without any objection from me. I ask only that should you decline you say nothing of it to anyone at all. You seem a trustworthy man, so I have no particular fear that you will break your word, once given. It's an endeavour that I think you might find both interesting and profitable to you. And you would certainly be solving a problem for me, too."

Alex continued selecting his breakfast, thinking as he did. Then he stood, and moving to the door closed it firmly before returning to his seat.

"Tell me of your proposition, Mr Foley. If I refuse, I'll tell no one. If I accept I'll tell only those who might need to ken. Does that satisfy you?"

"It does," Foley replied, pouring ale into a tankard and pushing it across the table to his guest.

Alex raised the tankard by way of thanks, then drank deeply and waited for Gabriel to begin.

CHAPTER TWO

London, England

Once Alex had finished relating the events of the previous evening and this morning, his four companions fell silent for a moment, taking in what they'd been told. There was a lot to take in.

"Ye're no' seriously thinking on doing this, are ye?" the only female member of the group asked, after the silence had stretched on for a time.

Alex ran his fingers through his hair.

"I am. After all, if I hadna killed his man, Foley wouldna need my help," he replied, without meeting Maggie's sceptical gaze.

"If ye hadna killed his man, all of us, Foley included, would likely be in prison now," Maggie's husband Iain pointed out dryly.

"Aye, well. Even so," Alex commented, reddening a little.

"I'm thinking it's a bonny idea," Angus put in enthusiastically. "When do we leave?"

"Ye would think that, ye wee loon," Maggie said. "For myself, I'm glad ye killed the wee gomerel, but I'm no' wanting ye all to drown for it."

"Thank ye for getting rid of the body, Angus," Alex said quickly, before Angus could respond hotly, as he was clearly about to do. "I didna expect ye to do that."

"Nae problem. When I'd finished putting the guns and swords in the cart it was nearly dark, and wi' the weather coming in there wasna a soul on the street," Angus explained. "So I wrapped the body in yon flowery material and put it in wi' the weapons. I figured that if I was caught wi' fifty muskets and broadswords, a body wouldna make much difference. He's buried in a wee bit of woodland off the road a few miles out of town."

"I'm glad ye didna bury the cloth, though," Maggie said. "It's awfu' pretty."

"Aye. I cut the bloodied piece away, but there's still a good deal of it," Angus said. "I was thinking we could sell it, maybe, buy some more weapons for the cause?"

Alex glanced at Maggie then, saw the look of longing on her face.

"Are ye wanting a wee bit, Maggie?" he asked. "Ye could make a fine gown from it. It's chiné silk."

"What? Have ye run daft, man?" she replied. "What would I do wi' such a thing? It'd be wasted on me."

"No it wouldna!" her husband protested. "Although I canna think when ye'd be able to wear it."

"Ye could wear it sitting in yon drawing room of an evening," Angus said, Maggie's earlier insult forgotten.

"Ah, no, it'd be a waste," she replied wistfully.

Alex came to a decision.

"Maggie, this house is meant to have a whole pack of servants, but ye do everything yourself," he said.

"I've Iain's help, and the rest of ye, when ye're no' about your other work," Maggie protested.

"Aye. But ye still work long hours, lassie. Ye deserve it. There's plenty in the roll, and it didna cost us anything. Foley didna mention it was missing when he was moving his own goods out of White's cellar, and he would have done, for that's an awfu' costly roll o' silk. So I'm thinking it was bought by White himself. Ye take enough to make yerself a gown, and I'll make good use of the rest." He raised a hand then, seeing her about to object again. "And when it's made, I'll pay for you and Iain to go to Ranelagh Gardens one day, and then to the theatre. Christ knows, ye both deserve it. Dinna argue wi' your chieftain."

"Just say aye, Maggie," Duncan put in now. "We can all see ye want to. And ye do deserve it."

"Do I no' deserve it too?" Angus said. "For moving all the evidence, and burying yon smuggler?"

"Ye're wanting a silk gown too, are ye?" Alex asked, making everyone laugh, including Angus.

"A day at Ranelagh, I was thinking," he replied.

"Ye'd as well just go direct to the whorehouse as waste good money on the entrance fee, for ye'd spend your time there looking for a whore anyway," Iain commented.

"Ye're no' trying to bribe me into agreeing to yon stupit venture, are ye?" Maggie asked suspiciously.

"No. I ken well I'd be wasting my time, for ye're a stubborn wee lassie," Alex said, omitting to add that he partly agreed with her view of the prospective venture. He was too aware of his desperate need to do something wild, active, dangerous, something to counteract the stultifying tedium of his current life. And to have reason to set foot in Scotland again, however briefly. It was clouding his judgement, and he knew it. But if his brothers and Iain were in favour, he'd feel justified in agreeing to it. "It's a thank you for all your work. We dinna thank ye enough. So, then," he added, turning to the men, "we ken Maggie's view. What do the rest of ye think? I thought to get your views before I talk to the men, for I'm no' decided."

"So the idea is to take the weapons back across the Channel to France, buy more, and some other things, then sail direct to Burghead, unload the weapons there, and take a cargo of whisky back to France?" Duncan asked.

"Aye, that's about it," Alex agreed. "Then we come back to Kent from there. Foley doesna want any more to do wi' White's men. If he was an informant, it doesna say much for the calibre of his men."

"And ye killt their leader, so they may be all the more inclined to peach on ye, if they find out it was you," Duncan added.

"Aye. Which means Foley's in need of men, for his others are across the sea in Schiedam at the minute, buying a cargo of Geneva."

"Does he ken we're no' sailors?" Duncan asked. "I dinna think rowing a boat across the loch to fish will count for verra much, somehow."

"Aye, I tellt him that. But he doesna need experienced sailors. He needs strong men who are no' afraid of hard work or danger, and who he can trust."

"It doesna matter how hard we work, if we dinna ken which way we're going, or how to move yon sails up and down when the wind changes," Iain pointed out.

"Gabriel kens the route well, he said. And we'll no' need to fash ourselves about sails, for the boat willna have any. It's a type of rowing boat," Alex clarified.

A moment's profound silence fell as the group absorbed this sentence.

"A *rowing* boat?" Iain said incredulously. "Yon Foley man's thinking to *row* to France?"

"Holy Mother of God," Maggie commented. "Well, I'll be a fine-looking widow, if I can finish my gown in time for your funerals. At least there's that."

"It's no' a rowing boat like yon wee things we use to go out fishing on the loch," Alex explained. "It's much bigger. Gabriel tellt me it has twelve oars on each side, and a man only pulls one oar. He uses them often, for they're faster than any revenue cutter, and they havena a mast or sail, so they're no' so easy to see on the ocean."

"What if the weather turns?" Iain asked.

"I dinna ken, in truth. I'd think that any boat would be in danger if the weather turns. But if they're as fast as Gabriel says, then we'd be on the ocean for a lot less time, which has to count for something."

"That's still an awfu' long time, if we're to row to France, then Scotland, France again, then back here," Iain said.

"Ah. No, we're only to row to France. He's a big cargo there, which we'll help to load on a sailing ship, then his men in Calais will sail it to Scotland, where we'll unload our part. Then we'll go back to France wi' the whisky he buys in Elgin, and we'll row the wee boat back across to England. If we do it," Alex added.

"So what will yon Gabriel do while we're taking the weapons home?" Iain asked. "It's an awfu' long way from Elgin."

"No' as long as it is from London," Alex countered. "We'll no' be taking the weapons home. I was thinking to ask you, Angus, to ride away home and take the other men up to Burghead, and wait for us there. I'll take the laddies who are already here to Gabriel."

"I'm no' riding to Scotland!" Angus cried. "I'm coming wi' you. It sounds awfu' exciting. And I've never been to France!"

"Ye canna come, Angus," Duncan said. "Alex has the right of it."

"Why? I ken I'm the youngest, but I'm strong. I can row a boat as well as any of ye!"

"I ken that. But ye couldna even sit in a boat when the loch was as still as a millpond without puking. Ye'd be useless. And miserable," Duncan replied.

"I was just a wee bairn then," Angus protested. "I'm a man grown now. I've outgrown that. I want to come."

"I'd rather Iain rode to Scotland on a horse than row across the sea in a wee boat," Maggie said before Duncan could comment further. Angus grinned.

"Before we look at who does what, d'ye trust this Gabriel laddie, Alex?" Duncan asked. "Or d'ye think he's spinning ye a yarn so ye'll agree to help him?"

This was a good question, so Alex thought before answering.

"Aye, I think he's trustworthy. He treated me very fairly, and once he'd tellt me the details of the venture, he didna press me for an answer. In fact he tellt me to go away and think on it, but no' for long, as we need to sail next week, and that he'd understand if I didna wish to do it. He's a hard man, I'm thinking, but a fair one. We'll benefit too, for we can buy more weapons in France, and it'll be quicker and safer to get them home by ship and then across our own country, than to ride through England wi' them in a coach."

"And ye're wanting some excitement, for ye're awful bored wi' all this," Duncan said, waving his arm around the luxuriously furnished drawing-room they were all sitting in, and getting to the heart of the matter. He knew his brother well.

"Aye. I'll no deny it. It would feel wonderful to be doing something real –physical, I mean. And to see Scotland again, even if it's only from the sea. But if ye all agree wi' Maggie that it's a stupit venture, then I'll tell the man no," Alex said candidly. "I've done the trip north in the coach before, after all, and never been caught. It doesna signify which way the weapons get home, as long as they do."

"Aye, but there'll be more weapons if ye do this, and it isna just yourself, Alex. All of ye are restless. I ken that, for I'm restless myself," Maggie said. "I've no' changed my mind about it. I still think it's stupit. Our whole lives here are stupit and dangerous, are they no'? But we're all here, even so. So dinna let me stop ye, if ye all want to go. Ye're all men of action, and if rowing a boat across the sea doesna get rid of your energy and calm ye all, nothing will."

"I'm happy to ride home and tell the others, if Angus wants to see France," Iain said. "Will ye come wi' me, Maggie?"

"I'll think on it, if ye do it, aye," Maggie said.

"Are we doing it, Alex?" Angus asked enthusiastically.

There was silence again, while Alex tamped down the excitement he felt at the idea of being directly involved in a run for arms, pushing it to one side so he could make a sensible decision.

"Aye," he said after such a long pause that Angus now looked about to explode with impatience. "I'm thinking we'll do it."

Angus leapt up at this, with a triumphant cry.

"I need to talk wi' the other men who are here first, though," Alex continued, before Angus could bombard him with questions. "I didna promise Foley a set number of men, just tellt him I'd let him know in two days how many I could provide. If I agreed. If anyone doesna want to do it, I'll no' compel them to. And now, if it's all the same to you, I'm away to my bed, for it's been a busy two days, and I'm tired. We can talk more on it in the morning, wi' the others."

CHAPTER THREE

They talked more on it in the morning with the other clansmen who were currently in London and staying in various cheap lodgings around the town. All of them were equally enthusiastic about doing something out of the ordinary. The ordinary for them in February (if they were in Scotland) was to make any repairs to their cottages that needed doing, mend any equipment, and then pass the long winter evenings telling tales, singing and drinking. There wasn't even the concern of watching out for redcoats descending on them from Inversnaid, for no British soldier would engage in such a suicidal venture in the depths of a Scottish winter. So a bit of excitement would be welcome, and it would give them a wonderful tale to relate for winters to come, even more interesting than tales of London, as outlandish as some of its sights were to men who'd lived their whole lives in the Highlands of Scotland.

So they agreed the venture was to go ahead, and next day Alex sent his two brothers to Gabriel Foley with a message confirming their participation in the venture. He sent Angus because his excitement and continuous volley of trivial questions was driving Alex mad, and Duncan because he wanted to get his middle brother's opinion of the man. Duncan was an excellent judge of character and his opinion of Foley would not be influenced by his desire for adventure, as Alex knew his was.

Kent coast, England, March 1743

The group of men stood near the edge of the cliff, looking over it at a narrow strip of beach below them against which the waves gently lapped. Unconcerned by both the sheer drop and the sudden gusts of wind that could well assist him in descending the cliff by the fastest route, Gabriel walked to the edge and pointed straight down, forcing all the Highlanders to follow his example in order to see what he was pointing at. Pulled up close to the foot of the cliff was a boat, which looked very tiny from this height.

"So that's what we'll use to row across. Abernathy tells me that most of you have rowed a small boat before, but on a lake, not the sea," Gabriel said, "So I thought to spend today practising, both rowing and following commands, because rowing on the sea is very different to a lake, as I'm sure you can imagine. Once we're at sea everyone will need to work together, and you'll need to obey my commands immediately, for we could all drown if you don't."

"Or be caught by the revenue men," Duncan commented.

"That's possible, but we'd have to be really incompetent for a revenue cutter to catch us, as we'll move a lot faster than they can, and we don't need the wind as they do," Gabriel replied. "Which is why we need a day to train you. Abernathy says you're all strong and used to hard work, which is good. And it's clear you've all got a good head for heights," he added, grinning at them as they all teetered on the edge of the cliff.

General laughter greeted this.

"Ye havena been to Scotland, I'm thinking," Dougal said.

"No, though I've heard about it," Gabriel said, tactfully omitting to elaborate on exactly what he'd been told about his companions' homeland.

"Much of it's mountainous," Alex explained, "Wi' steep drops like this, and wi' mist and rain too. We're none of us feart by a landscape."

"Will we have to bring yon barrels and muskets up the cliff?" Jamie asked.

"No, we're taking the guns to Burghead, no' here," Angus said. "There are no cliffs there. And the whisky's going to France."

"That's true," Gabriel agreed. "But we never sail with an empty ship, if we can avoid it. We'll be bringing goods back from

France with us. But not to this part of the shore, although we do move goods up such cliffs at times. The boat's kept here because it can only be seen if you stand right on the edge of the cliff as we are now and look down, which no one would normally do. And you'll see when we're down on the beach that the rocks mean it can't be seen from a ship at sea either. It's illegal to own a galley with more than four oars now. That one has twenty-four."

"Could we no' be seen while we're practising though?" Alex asked. "We dinna want to be chased before we ken how to manoeuvre the boat."

"We could, but it's quite isolated here. No one is likely to just pass by while we're rowing up and down the coastline. Even so, a couple of my men will stay up here to look out and if anyone comes, by land or sea, they'll warn us and we'll head round the bay out of sight and hide the boat. We've a number of places to do that. Let's make a start then," he said.

The men, a mixture of Alex's clansmen and Gabriel's gang members, followed him along a steep narrow track leading down to the beach. Once there they dragged the boat out to the water's edge, and Gabriel organised the men so that there were an equal number of inexperienced and experienced rowers on each side, after which they pushed out to sea and the lessons commenced.

It was a dull, overcast day and very cold, although the cliffs looming to their side at least cut out the wind chill. After a short while of rowing up and down the coast slowly just to learn how to work well together, Gabriel ordered them to pick up speed, until they were rowing at the rate they'd need to keep up if they were to cross the channel to France in the five or six hours they needed to.

"Once you're used to that, I'll start to teach you what you need to do to turn left or right, or to stop capsizing in a rough sea," Gabriel shouted to them from his position at the helm.

As they settled into the rhythm and started to pick up speed, the exhilaration of a new experience, a new *physical* experience coursed through Alex's blood. He could feel his powerful muscles bunching and relaxing as he pulled against the sea, the salt spray on his lips and the wind tousling his hair, and laughed for the pure joy of feeling free for the first time in months, of doing something dangerous but worthwhile.

That was an illusion. He knew that even as he revelled in it. He was no more or less free here than in a gilded drawing room in London –he had made most of his life choices freely, governed only by his conscience and loyalties. And this work was neither more nor less dangerous than his current sedentary occupation in London. But it *felt* so, because physical danger was what he was accustomed to, what he'd been brought up to accept as a normal part of being a MacGregor, a Highlander.

He glanced at Duncan, who was sitting to his left. They exchanged a smile and Alex knew that he was not the only one feeling like this. Duncan too was loving being out in nature again, away from the artificiality of the town.

Duncan, who hated crowds with a passion, hated the noise and filth of cities more than either of his brothers, had been in London for far too long, Alex realised. *I must find a reason to send him home soon,* he thought. *Give him some respite from the hell of the capital.*

He couldn't see Angus's reaction, as his youngest brother was sitting behind him, and he couldn't look back without losing the rhythm. He would ache tonight, he knew that, but his heart was singing.

When they got to the end of the bay, Gabriel told them to stop rowing for a minute. They all did, taking the opportunity to stretch their arms and legs.

"Are you unwell?" Gabriel asked. For a moment Alex thought the question was directed at him and was about to answer that he felt quite the opposite, when he realised that the man was looking behind him. He turned, and instantly knew who Gabriel was addressing.

"Christ, man, are ye all right?" Alex asked his youngest brother, who was deathly pale.

"Aye, nae bother," Angus replied, yawning. "I'm just a wee bit tired."

"You drank a lot last night," one of Gabriel's men observed. "I've never seen a man take so much and still be standing at the end of the night." As this sentence was said in a tone of awe rather than scorn, no offence was taken by any of the MacGregors.

"Aye, I'm thinking that must be it," Angus said, seizing the reason he'd just been given. "I've a wee pain in my head too. It'll pass."

Alex and Duncan exchanged a look. Angus had always been totally unaffected by drink. Neither of them had ever seen him even tipsy, let alone drunk. And he never suffered from any after effects, no matter how much he'd imbibed the night before. Alex leaned toward him.

"Are ye thinking it's the seasickness ye've got?" he asked quietly.

Angus shook his head, then winced.

"No. I canna mind that so well, for I was a bairn. I remember I was sick, that's all. But I tellt ye, I've outgrown it. I'm well," he added in a louder voice, his last words directed at Gabriel.

The smuggler eyed him doubtfully for a minute, then nodded. "Right. Let's turn her. Once more back along the cliffs, and then we'll start the commands."

They turned the boat and rowed back along the bay, much faster and more smoothly than before. They were really getting into the way of it now. When they had, Gabriel had them pull up on the beach and sit in the shelter of the cliff, so he could explain the commands without having to shout against the wind.

"You've the seasickness," he said to Angus as they all made their way across the sand.

"No, I havena. I just drank a wee bit too much last night," Angus insisted angrily.

"I'm sure you did. But I've been at sea my whole life, and I know the difference between crapulence and seasickness. You're showing *all* the signs. You're white, you're sweating but I'll wager you feel cold, and you're breathing fast."

"Of course I am!" Angus shouted. "I've just rowed yon boat up and down for an hour!"

"You're irritable too," Gabriel added calmly. "Is he always so?" he asked the Scotsmen.

"No, he isna," Alex replied. "We've all just rowed the boat, man, and ye're the youngest of us, but we're no puffing like ye are. And ye look dreadful. Are ye feeling sick?"

"No, I'm no' feeling sick. Will ye just leave me be," Angus cried, before proving himself a liar instantly by bending over and vomiting copiously on the sand. "I'm well," he insisted weakly once he'd finished retching, wiping his mouth with his sleeve.

Alex and Gabriel exchanged a look, and then Gabriel sighed.

"Sit down. I'll explain the commands and what you need to do when you hear them, and then we'll row along the coast once more. When we do, keep your eye on the horizon the whole time. Don't look at the oar, or the man in front of you. That might make you feel better," he added doubtfully.

They sat down, leaning back against the foot of the cliff while Gabriel explained the commands.

"When we're at sea I'll have to shout the commands, so I don't want to have to do it more than once, if possible," he said. "For the rest of the day we'll practice the different manoeuvres. You'll likely not remember them all now, so when we're out on the water, I'll explain any you're not sure of again. First, then. When we're just rowing, if I say 'easy', that means row *very* slowly. 'Handsomely' is slowly, 'cheerly' at mid-speed, and 'smartly' means quickly. When we go back out, the first thing I'll do is show you how slowly easy is, and so on. When we've practised that for a while, then we'll do a few other things. So, if I shout 'steady', that means just keep doing exactly what you're doing at that moment…"

He continued explaining the commands, while the members of his own gang sat quietly but inattentively, for they were already familiar with all of them, and the Highlanders paid rapt attention. When he'd finished, Gabriel looked around.

"There's no better way to learn than by doing it," he said then. "We're all rested now, so let's make a start. You'll be glad to know that the barmaid at the Swan is a fine cook, and I've asked her to lay on a spread for us all later, because you'll be hungry, I'm sure!"

This last statement made everyone smile, even Angus, who was still sweating and pale, although his nausea had lessened a little. They all got up, and headed back to the boat.

"Eyes on the horizon," Gabriel reminded Angus as they sat down and he moved to the helm. "Right then. Before we set off, let's practice holding the oars in the different positions."

He was a good teacher, Alex thought, as he held his oar upright, then horizontally, as instructed. His voice carried well too, which would be vital once they were out on the open ocean. At least two of them would remember all the commands, for both he and Angus had exceptional memories. Duncan would have learnt most of them, and the others would make up for memory in willingness to learn. They were all very capable, he thought with pride, and would give a good account of themselves. He had no doubt of that. As they lowered the oars again and prepared to set off, he sent up a silent prayer that Angus would now be recovered of his seasickness.

By the time they'd rowed up and down the coast once more they were all familiar with the various speeds required, and with the important 'hold water' command, which was a way of slowing the boat when at speed, but which could cause injury to the oarsman if done wrongly. And it was also very clear that Angus, although he'd followed Foley's advice and had stared fixedly at the horizon the whole time, was very unwell, in spite of his protestations to the contrary.

"I'm sorry," Gabriel said, and meant it. "But I don't see that we can take you with us. You might well recover, in time. But we can't take that chance. I need all of you to be strong and capable, and the seasickness is a terrible thing."

"It isna your doing, laddie," Alex added quickly, seeing Angus was about to argue again. "We all ken ye've the courage and the ability to do this. I wouldna have brought ye along had I thought otherwise. But ye canna row for hours like ye are now."

"It'll get worse, I think, too," Gabriel said. "I've seen it many a time. If it does, not only will you be incapable of doing anything, but you'll want to die, really you will. It's a terrible thing. Bad enough if you can just lie down in a cabin, but if you have to work, and hard…no. I'm truly sorry."

They had pulled in to shore again, the three men walking away from the boat together so that the others wouldn't hear what they said, although it was pretty obvious to everyone what was going on.

"But ye'll be a man short then," Angus said desperately. "I'll be better than no one at all, surely?"

"Ye always were thrawn," Alex said, frustrated. "Obstinate," he added to Gabriel, realising the Englishman wouldn't know the meaning of the Scottish word. "When are ye thinking to leave?"

"We need to practice tomorrow, to get you all accustomed to the rowing and commands, then we should leave the next day, unless the weather turns. But I think it won't. Why?"

"Give me a minute," Alex said. Gabriel nodded, and headed back to the boat.

Alex and Angus walked back to the place where they'd all sat to listen to the commands.

"When ye're recovered, I want ye to ride back to London and send Iain in your place," Alex said, once Angus had finished his second bout of retching and was sitting on the sand, green-faced and sweating. "Ye must see the sense of it. I ken how much ye want to see France, but ye canna do this. Maybe one day we'll go on a ship, together, and ye'll no' feel as sick on such a huge vessel."

Angus looked at him sceptically.

"When are *we* likely to go on a ship?" he said. "We havena the means."

"Sir Anthony has though," Alex said. "Maybe he'll take ye as his manservant, do one of they 'Grand Tours' the nobles do to pass the time."

Angus laughed, in spite of the waves of sickness and fatigue that were shuddering through him.

"Ye can still be useful. Ye can ride up to Scotland instead of Iain, gather the rest of the clansmen, and take them up to Burghead to meet us when we come in with the arms," Alex added.

"I dinna think Maggie'll be wanting to go to Scotland wi' me," Angus said.

"Aye, well, it canna be helped. She can sew her fine dress instead, and look after the house. I'll make it up to her. I'm sorry, man. It isna your fault. But ye must see the sense in it."

Angus nodded, sadly. There was no point in protesting any further. If he did, Alex would assert his right as chieftain and command him to take Iain's place. And in any case, Alex was right. At this moment, young and strong as he was, Angus doubted he could even walk back up the cliff path, let alone row across the ocean.

Instead he sat on the sand and watched disconsolately as Alex made his way back to the boat, as they set off. He watched them row in a somewhat zigzag manner along the coastline, as Gabriel taught them the commands that would turn a boat to the left or right. And when at long last the boat disappeared round the edge of the bay, he lay down and closed his eyes, giving in to the sickness now he was sure no one could observe him do so.

He felt absolutely dreadful.

CHAPTER FOUR

It was dark by the time the men arrived back at Gabriel Foley's current headquarters, the Swan Inn, tired and aching but feeling a bit more confident about their ability to row across the English Channel. None of the MacGregors had been surprised that Angus was not waiting for them on the beach when they returned, but they did expect him to be at the tavern.

"No, he's not here," the cheerful, rosy-cheeked landlady told Alex when he enquired about his missing brother. "Rode out a couple of hours ago, I reckon. Looked awful peaked, he did. I asked him if he wanted to lie down for a while, said I'd bring him some food up to his room. But he said it was nothing some fresh air wouldn't cure, and he had an urgent errand to do. Asked me to make up a parcel of food for him to eat on the way."

"I'm thinking he'll have recovered quickly," Duncan said when Alex relayed the message back to him. "He did when he was a bairn, anyway. He wouldna have been capable of riding if he hadna."

He had a point.

"Aye, but I'm worried that he might have gone even if he *was* still feeling sick, because he didna want to be here when we all returned. He was awfu' shamed by what he saw as his weakness," Alex said.

"He'll recover his temper quickly enough. He doesna let anything fash him for long."

This was true. And seasickness wasn't fatal. He'd be all right. And the quicker Iain arrived the better, because he might be able to get in a little practice with the other men before they set off for France.

"He's a good man," Duncan continued, causing Alex to frown in puzzlement. "No' Angus. Yon Foley man," he clarified.

"Aye, I ken that. Ye tellt me that when ye first met him."

"I did. But what I said was that he *seemed* like a good man. Now I'm more certain of it. No' just because of the way he was with ye after ye killed his man, but he was tactful wi' Angus too. Tried to make him feel better about the sickness. Most men wouldna be so considerate, and especially a hard man such as himself."

"It clearly didna work, his tactfulness," Alex said ruefully.

"That's because Angus is young, and cares too much what others think of him," Duncan replied. "He's no' sure of his manhood yet. When he is, he'll no' be so sensitive. Ye were like that yourself. Ye grew out of it a wee bit earlier than he's doing, but then he hasna had the hardships that ye did."

"That *we* did," Alex corrected.

Duncan smiled.

"Shall we away in and join the others before they eat everything?" he said by way of reply.

In the event there was plenty of food, as the landlady had a lot of experience in feeding smugglers and knew what hungry work it was to row or sail for hours, then usually unload a whole cargo in record time, often in the dark. When everyone was full they set to drinking and telling tales of various smuggling escapades, careful not to let slip any information that an exciseman might be able to use, as there were strangers among them. Soon the atmosphere became rowdy, but in a friendly way.

Really they were not much different to Highlanders in this way, Alex thought, except in the subject of their boasting. With them it was ingenious and humorous ways they'd dodged the excisemen, or succeeded in carrying illicit goods across inhospitable territory; with Highlanders it would be how they'd reived cattle from under the noses of other clans, or of brave deeds in battles with hostile clans.

The other MacGregors felt the same way, and soon they were sharing their own stories, relaxing as they acknowledged that, although Sasannachs, the smugglers had much in common with them.

"Your man Jim has gone home then, I take it?" Gabriel said

when Alex sat down next to him in a corner of the room, having just replenished his ale tankard. All the men had given false names to Foley's men, as the smugglers no doubt had too. When you lived such lives as they all did, trust had to be earned, and the less others knew about you the better.

"Aye. He should be home by now, and once John kens he's to replace him, he'll waste no time. I'm thinking he might be here by morning. I'm hoping so, for then he can learn the commands wi' us all when we go out again." Alex yawned and rolled his shoulders to release his muscles, which were tightening. This was ridiculous.

If I stay in London much longer I'll lose all my strength, he thought. He must find a way to stay in peak condition. A surreptitious way, for he could never be seen to be fit and active in public. His hands had got soft over the last months too, and he had a blister across each palm. His men would never let him live it down, but he'd have to wear gloves for the rowing tomorrow, as he wouldn't be able to row for hours then lift and carry heavy crates if his hands were raw and bloody. He wished Angus had been able to stay long enough to join in the good-natured mockery of the clan chieftain. It might have made him feel better about his perceived weakness.

"I'm still thinking we'll lose a day, though," Gabriel said, cutting into his thoughts. "I can't risk taking an untrained man out."

"I'm no' thinking that'll be a problem. John used to live near the sea, and he used to go sea fishing. He's more experience of the ocean than any of us," Alex reassured Gabriel, who nodded.

"It's good to see your men and mine getting along well," Gabriel observed. "That'll help more than anything, if we should run into any difficulties."

He'd spoken too soon, for minutes later the mood in the centre of the room suddenly changed, causing both Gabriel and Alex to pause their conversation in order to discover the reason for the sudden quiet.

"I only spoke the truth!" a young yellow-haired member of Gabriel's crew said indignantly. He had taken Angus's place in the boat that afternoon. "We've wasted a day rowing up and down the bloody coast, when we could have been having fun."

"Aye, and so did I when I tellt ye that yon 'useless lump' as ye called him, is my brother, and I'll no' have ye speak ill of him when he isna here to answer ye," Duncan replied calmly, so calmly that neither Gabriel nor Alex would have heard him had the silence in the room not deepened as more people became aware of the incipient argument.

"It's not my fault he ran away, is it?" the blond man persisted. "If he was here I'd tell him to his face."

"But he isna," Duncan pointed out. "I am, though, if ye're wanting to discuss your last remark further wi' me."

Gabriel sat back. The man Murdo seemed a peaceable fellow, and showed no sign of rising to Tom's provocative statement. This would come to nothing. Tom was all bluster. He would soon calm down, particularly when his temper wasn't being stoked.

"So, if John arrives—" he began, then stopped as Alex leapt to his feet, having seen Duncan shift position on the bench to free his right arm, and knowing what that meant.

"Stop your man now, before he speaks another word," he said urgently to Gabriel, and then was striding across the room to intercept his other clansmen and stop whatever happened between his brother and the wee loon becoming a general brawl. If it did, no one would be rowing anywhere tomorrow.

"Well, what else was he doing? He clearly didn't have the balls—"

"Tom!" Gabriel's deep voice roared across the room, stopping his red-faced gang member in his tracks. "Outside. Now."

The man reddened, bit his lip, but did not hesitate to obey his leader, heading for the door. Gabriel stood and looked across his men, his expression cold, implacable. When he saw that none of them would meet his eye, he nodded.

"See that you stay so," he said, in a normal voice now. "These are our guests, and good men. If you shame me, you'll answer for it." Then he turned and followed the unfortunate Tom out of the tavern door.

"I'd have taken it outside too, just myself and the laddie," Duncan said when Alex approached him, once he'd had a quiet word with the other MacGregors. "Ye ken that. And he willna be rowing to France in any case."

"Aye, I do ken that, which is why I didna come to ye directly," Alex replied, sitting down next to him on the bench. "But I'm thinking his friends wouldna take kindly to us killing another of their number."

"Och, I wouldna have killed the man," Duncan said. "But aye, ye've the right of it. Better so, for we'll likely be needing them at our backs, if the weather turns on the ocean. I'll no' have anyone insulting An..Jim though. He's no coward, as yon wee gomerel was implying."

"I ken that. Gabriel kens it too, and I'm reasonably certain yon wee gomerel is learning that, right now," Alex said, looking to the door and grinning.

Duncan laughed.

"Aye. Foley's a wee bit like yourself, a natural leader," he commented.

Whatever Tom learnt the others never found out, for he didn't return to the tavern that night, nor any other night while the MacGregors were around. Gabriel, however, did, a few minutes later, wearing an expression which told everyone in the room that the matter was over, and that there would not be a repeat of such behaviour.

Slowly the conversation started up again, stilted at first, then more relaxed as time passed and both the Scots and English realised that the other side was not going to force them into any violent action.

It was just one fool, and that fool had been dealt with. Not worth spoiling a good evening for. A good adventure for.

Half an hour later it was as though nothing had happened. True, the two groups were holding a contest, and each side was determined to win. But as it was a singing contest, with much laughing as the songs grew increasingly bawdy, there was no danger of any more animosity.

"That was well done," Alex said to Gabriel later.

"I note you didn't go to calm the Murdo fellow first," Gabriel said.

"No. He never loses control of himself," Alex replied, dismissing the one time when his brother *had* lost control, with disastrous consequences. That had been understandable, though. "But if your men had sided wi' yon Tom, the others would have made a fight of it, for if ye insult one of us, ye insult us all. I dinna ken if Tom realised that, but ye need to. Neither of us want ill-feeling between us. It's in our interest to work well together." He failed to add that if that had happened, the likely result would have been that none of Gabriel's men would have been doing anything for a long time, if ever. It would not be tactful to make such a statement, even if it were true.

Gabriel was a hard man and his men were undoubtedly hard men, too. But they were not Highlanders, had not been trained as warriors from infanthood, had not had to fight for everything they owned. Having said that, once at sea the smugglers would have the advantage, knowing the ocean as his men did not.

He would have a word with them later, tell them that if anyone else was stupid enough to say anything against Angus, or in fact against any of them, not to react, but to come to him first. And he would tell them why, so they did not feel unmanned by having to do such a thing.

He sat back, yawned, rolled his shoulders again, and drank, deeply. He would go to bed soon. The unaccustomed exercise and fresh air had tired him. God, but he was getting soft. He examined his palms, the deep welts running horizontally across both of them.

Gloves. He would never hear the end of it, to his dying day.

CHAPTER FIVE

London, England

Several minutes passed after the caller had first knocked before a footman, dressed immaculately in emerald green livery, complete with supercilious facial expression, finally opened the door.

"Christ, man, what the hell are ye doing, chapping at the door like that?" Iain said crossly on identifying the visitor.

"It was locked. Were ye wanting me to break it down?" Angus said equally crossly, pushing past Iain to get out of the pouring rain.

"No, but ye could have gone to the back door. Ye ken I dinna wear all this shite," he said, waving a hand down his silk-clad torso, "when Sir Anthony's no' at home."

"Is that why ye were so long answering?" Angus asked, taking his dripping wet coat off and hanging it over the banister.

"Aye. What's amiss? We were no' expecting ye for weeks! We're in the drawing room," he added, seeing Angus head in the direction of the kitchen. "There's a good fire there. Ye'll be dry in no time."

When they entered the drawing room, Maggie, who was lying drowsily on the sofa, glass of claret on the spindly-legged table next to her, looked round and then, seeing Angus, sat up.

"What's amiss?" she asked in unconscious echo of her husband.

"Nothing," Angus replied, grabbing the wine bottle on his way to the hearth. "Well, nothing wi' Alex and the others." He took a hearty swig of wine and then wiped his hand across his mouth, before replacing the bottle on the table and setting to work peeling off his sodden breeches and stockings. That done he threw himself into a chair opposite the others, Iain having similarly disrobed, so that both men were now wearing only knee-length shirts.

"Alex wants ye to ride to him as quickly as ye can, for ye'll be needed to row to France after all," Angus explained. "He's wanting ye to practice wi' the others tomorrow if ye can, for there's commands and the like to learn."

"Who's going to ride to Scotland, then?" Iain asked

"Why? Who's injured?" Maggie asked at the same time.

"No one's injured," Angus replied, flushing. "I'll ride to Scotland, and take the men up to Burghead."

After a few moments of silence in which Maggie and Iain waited for more information and Angus wondered how little he could get away with revealing, he sighed. Iain would find out anyway, the moment he reached the others.

"I got the sea malady after all," he muttered to the fire. "I canna row to France."

Iain nodded.

"I'll leave directly then," he said. "I'll away and pack a few things, then saddle the horse."

"I'll put some food together for ye," Maggie said, jumping up.

"No need. It's only a few hours' ride."

"Even so. The weather's fierce, and I doubt ye'll be fed if ye arrive in the middle of the night," she said. "I'll bring ye something too," she added to the shamefaced Angus.

* * *

It was over an hour before she returned to the drawing room, partly because there had been a good deal to do, this change of plan having come at such short notice, but also because she'd taken her time about it, knowing she wouldn't see Iain for weeks, maybe would never…

No, she wouldn't think about that. No good in tempting fate. Hopefully Angus at least would be warm, dry, and have cheered up by now.

But when she opened the door and walked in, carrying a platter full of assorted meats and bread, she saw immediately that this had hit him hard, for he was staring moodily into the fire and would not meet her eye as she placed the platter on the table. Nor did he dive into the food with relish, as he normally would. The wine bottle was, however, empty.

She quenched a guttering candle, replaced it with a new one, fetched another bottle from Sir Anthony's stock, then sat down on the sofa.

"Are ye thinking it's my fault that my hair's red? Something I should be shamed about?" she asked.

"What?" Angus asked, shocked out of his gloomy contemplation by this nonsensical question. "No, of course it isna. Ye were born wi' it, were ye no'?"

"I was. No more is it your fault ye've the seasickness. Ye just have it, from God, as I have this," she said, pointing to the mass of auburn waves currently falling loosely over her shoulders. "Ye didna choose it. I asked Iain about it, for I've never been on the sea and canna imagine it making ye ill, and he tellt me it's a fearsome thing."

"Aye, it is," Angus agreed, turning away from the fire now.

"He said it makes ye wish ye were dead, your bones turn to water, and ye puke your inside out."

"How does he ken that?" Angus asked.

"He tellt me he had it himself, just the once, on a very rough sea, and that most have it then, but he saw other men wi' it too, even on calm water. Kenneth, for one."

"*Kenneth?*" Angus said. "I've seen Kenneth row across the loch many a time. He doesna have what I had."

"No' on the loch, but they went sea fishing together once, and he was well until they were out on the ocean and stopped the boat to fish, then he got awfu' sick, Iain said, even though it wasna very choppy, just a wee bit. Iain had to row back, wi' Kenneth clinging to the sides of the boat and puking like a wee bairn."

"I canna imagine him behaving so. He's…well, ye ken what he is." Angus said. Kenneth was a giant of a man, fearless in battle, with the strength of ten men. *Nothing* frightened him. "I didna ken he had the sea sickness."

"No, well, ye wouldna, for Kenneth felt much as you do now about it, and for the same stupit reason. Iain promised no' to tell anyone. Until now."

Angus nodded.

"That was kind of him. I still feel awfu' bad, though. I ken I was sick as a bairn, but I didna remember *how* bad it was. I thought I'd outgrown it. I'm thinking the others will think I'm afeart of a wee bit o' water. And I'm awfu' sorry for you, too."

"So, ye're going to call Kenneth a coward when ye get home, are ye? If ye are, I'll need to be sewing yon fancy silk gown quicker than I thought, for your wake."

Angus laughed at that, and reached across for a roll.

"I'm no' *that* daft," he said.

"But daft enough to think Alex'll believe ye a coward because of something ye canna do anything about? When ye cut yersel, it doesna stop bleeding because ye wish it would, does it?"

"No, of course it doesna."

"Well, then. This is the same, I'm thinking. No' a thing ye can fight off. And ye're still doing something useful, taking the other men up to Burghead. Why are ye sorry for me?"

"Ye were wanting to ride up wi' Iain, were ye no'? I ken how much ye're missing Scotland."

"Aye," she said. "I am, missing it awfu' bad. But I'm thinking it's better if I dinna go, no' until I can stay for a wee while, at least, for it would be awfu' difficult to leave again, once I was there. Better to stay here. I'm accustomed to it now." She wrinkled her nose, showing just how accustomed she was to it and making Angus laugh, although his eyes were still troubled. "If I wanted to go, I could come wi' you, in any case," she added.

"Aye, ye'd be welcome to. But ye said ye didna want him to row across the sea."

"I did, for I'm thinking it's a dangerous thing. But I kent when I married a Highlander, and then he joined wi' the MacGregors, that everything he did would be dangerous."

She did *not* mention that if Iain had ridden to Scotland she would have gone with him, not only because she was missing Scotland, but because since they'd married they'd never been apart for more than a few days, and when they were she missed him terribly, a deep gnawing ache that did not lessen with time. How she would manage for weeks without him, she had no idea.

She did not voice that, because although Angus was young and in general carefree, he was also loving, and would take it badly if she did, and he could do no more about that than he could about his sea sickness.

She would cope with it, as she had coped with many things, and would no doubt cope with many more. Because she had to.

And because such a feeling, unlike seasickness, could at least be concealed from others, if not banished.

Angus would be fine after a good night's sleep, she reasoned. And if he *was* still sad, she would give him a list of jobs to do tomorrow to take his mind off it and make him feel useful, for in a house of this size with so few servants due to necessity, there were *always* jobs to be done.

* * *

When Iain arrived at the Swan Inn it was after midnight and not only the tavern but the whole street was in darkness. He sighed. It would not endear him to this Foley man's gang if he woke them all up by hammering on the door. If he'd been wearing his *fèileadh mór,* he wouldn't have hesitated to wrap himself up in it and sleep outside. It had finally stopped raining too.

But he was in England, so was wearing woollen breeches and a leather jerkin, with a coat that had seen better days over the top of it. And his horse was sweating and needed to be stabled, for he'd ridden her hard. So he would have to wake someone.

He led the horse round the back of the inn, figuring it would be better to waken the stable hands than the smugglers. Once she was cared for, he'd curl up in a corner somewhere and get a few hours rest before everyone woke up.

However, when he opened the stable door he was greeted by an angry man with a pistol, who it seemed had not been told to expect a stranger in the middle of the night, and who was not convinced by Iain's tale, the result of which was that the residents of the tavern were woken up anyway. After a sleepy Alex and Gabriel had both confirmed that yes, John was expected, and this ruffianly-looking specimen was indeed said John, Iain was allowed to lead his mare into a stall. If he'd hoped the stable hand might offer to take care of her, he was disappointed. The disgruntled man threw himself down in the hay, pulled his threadbare blanket round him and was instantly asleep.

By the time Iain had wiped the horse down with some straw, let her have a drink at the trough, found and filled a bucket with water to put in her stall, and then had got her settled with some hay, before finding a spot to lie down himself, he only managed to snatch what seemed to be a few minutes' sleep before he was woken by the noises of a busy tavern rousing itself.

He threw some icy water on his face to wake himself up, removed the bits of hay sticking to his clothes and hair, and then presented himself to his now fully awake chieftain, who was just sitting down at a scrubbed wooden table with a number of familiar faces and some strangers, to have breakfast.

"Christ, man, ye look like ye havena slept at all," Alex said by way of greeting.

"Aye, well, I had to look to Whitefoot first," Iain explained.

"Gabriel, when will we be leaving to practice the rowing?"

"Not for another hour. Let's say two hours," Gabriel amended on seeing the new arrival's heavy lids. "I take it Jim arrived at night, and you'd been awake all day?"

"Aye, that's the sum of it," Iain said, yawning. "He tellt me I'd be wanted here this morning to learn some commands and suchlike. I'll be good when I'm on the water and moving."

"Take some food wi' ye, and away to my bed for a couple of hours," Alex said in his chieftain's voice. "Ye'll be needing to remember all manner of new things and ye canna do that if you're sleepy. Here, I'll show ye where to go." He grabbed an assortment of foodstuffs off the platters on the table and then walked out of the room, leaving Iain no choice but to follow him.

"Dinna argue, man," Alex said once they were in the bedroom, on the floor of which a number of pallets were lying. "It's no' just the commands. Ye need your wits about ye, so ye'll remember I'm Abernathy, you're John, and all the aliases of the others. And no' to give away any information that might be useful to others later, when we're all drinking together. I ken ye're accustomed to that, wi' the life we have now, but ye dinna go out drinking and holding singing competitions wi' all yon noble loons Sir Anthony mixes wi', ye being his coachman and beneath contempt to them. It's easier to let something slip here."

"Do ye no' trust yon Gabriel, then?" Iain asked.

"Aye. As far as he trusts me. But I've found in the last year that it's safer no' to trust *anyone*. Except our own, that is. Which is why I'm standing here blethering wi' ye, instead o' rotting on a gibbet somewhere." He grinned. "Get some sleep. I'll wake ye."

Alex was right. He was, after all, an expert in duplicity. And Iain would never forgive himself if he let something slip that might threaten the lives of his adopted clan. He lay down, and got some sleep.

* * *

Later, he was very glad he'd snatched the two hours of sleep, because it had been a gruelling day both physically and mentally. But by the end of it he had learnt the commands needed, had settled into the way of rowing with twenty-three other people rather than just one as he was used to, and, as far as he knew, had not let anything incriminating slip.

That last part had not been difficult in the end due to the fact that Iain was a taciturn man by nature anyway, and had taken Alex's warning to heart. The main risk was in calling someone by their real name, the most likely mistake to make, as they all knew. As a result virtually all the MacGregors addressed each other as 'man', whilst pointing to indicate which man they were currently referring to. They would laugh about this later, once they were alone.

However, at the moment they were getting great amusement out of the fact that their chieftain had worn gloves all day while rowing, the only man who had. He had borne their unmerciful ribbing about lily-white soft hands and questions about which lotions he used to keep them so pale with good grace. Everyone knew why his hands were not currently as hardened by manual labour as theirs were, and everyone knew that in a fight they would want him at their right-hand side, wearing gloves or not. The days when Alex had felt insecure in his chieftainship were long past, and he took the jokes of his clansmen in good part.

Over supper, Gabriel outlined the plan for the first day, which was to carry the muskets and swords already brought into the country by Joshua White, the smuggler Alex had killed, down to the beach they'd been at today, load them on the boat, and then head straight for Calais.

"We'll carry the goods down before dawn, and then set off just as the sky starts to lighten," Gabriel said.

"Would we no' be safer leaving at night?" Duncan asked.

"You're not experienced enough yet for that. And if we row by day and a sudden storm rises, I'll be able to see the clouds coming in, and see the waves as well as hear them, which gives more time to prepare before it hits us. At night I can only listen for them, which makes it a lot more dangerous, even when the whole crew's experienced. And we're rowing, with no mast or sail, so there's little chance of us being seen by a revenue cutter. It would be better if it were campaigning season when there's virtually no risk of being caught by the revenue at sea, as most of them are navy men and are off getting themselves killed then, for George."

"Hopefully. Not as many of them to be revenue men next winter then," another man said, to general laughter.

Gabriel grinned.

"It's no real problem anyway, because the local exciseman, Andrew, has a great fondness for the cognac, which we provide for him at a very reasonable price. In return he's found his sight failing badly on days when we're heading down to the coast. Or up from it. No, normally we could leave in broad daylight, announcing ourselves with a fanfare of trumpets and be in no danger."

"So why are we no' doing that then?" Dougal asked.

"Because we're carrying weapons, no' tea or brandy," Alex put in. "And that's treason."

Gabriel nodded.

"It is. Even if we're caught red-handed with tea and suchlike and come to court, we're unlikely to be convicted, because almost everyone in the area is involved in the free trade to some extent, and they couldn't find a jury that would convict us. But treason is a completely different thing. So it's not worth taking any risk we don't have to take. When we take the weapons to Burghead we'll be in a ship, so can sail at night with no problems. And we'll row back here from Calais with a less dangerous cargo. So, I want none of you in your cups tonight, for it'll be a long hard day tomorrow and you all need to be well-rested and sober. My men know that already," he continued in an aside to Alex, "and I'm not trying to insult yours by stating what might be obvious to them. But I'd rather insult them than risk their lives."

Alex smiled.

"No offence taken, man. I'd be doing the same if I was leading ye all into a clan battle, which I'm thinking ye havena any experience of," he said.

"Ha! No, I haven't," Gabriel admitted. "And if I ever am in one, I wouldn't want to be facing you across the field. Your men have never rowed like that before, and not one of them has made even the slightest murmur of complaint. And none of them seem even slightly worried about tomorrow."

This was true. In fact, they all looked quite the opposite, to be relishing the idea of doing something different. The risks involved hadn't even registered with them, so accustomed were they to danger.

"No," Alex said. "They're good men. I wouldna have brought them otherwise. Highland life accustoms ye to danger. If anything *does* arise, though, I'll be looking to you to tell me the best way to deal with it. And my men will take orders from you, for I've tellt them to. Unless I tell them directly no' to, for their first allegiance is to me. But I canna see any reason why I'd need to do that."

"No," said Foley. "We're all in this together, after all. But I'm relieved that they'll take orders directly from me, for it could be that we'll not have time for me to tell you, and then you tell them, as it were. I think we'll be a good team for this venture," he added.

"Aye. I'm thinking that too," Alex agreed, and meant it. And he would learn a new skill, which was always a good thing when you had no idea what the future might bring, and what skills you might need to survive it.

CHAPTER SIX

Calais, France, March 1743

By the time they finally arrived at the ramshackle building in the fisherman's area of Calais, which Gabriel told the Highlanders was his French headquarters, all of the MacGregors were completely exhausted, although you would not have known it to look at them, as for a Highlander to admit to any physical weakness, unless life-threatening, was unthinkable. So while Foley's gang members chatted about how much more tiring it was to row than sail across the English Channel, and how heavy the crates of weapons were that they'd carried to the tavern they were now sprawled in drinking tankards of ale, the Highlanders remained taciturn. Indeed anyone watching would have thought the tartan-clad men had done nothing more strenuous than take a casual stroll along the seafront all day. Well, apart from the fact that they were drenched to the skin and their hair stiff with brine, with white salty streaks forming on their kilts as they dried in the warmth of the L-shaped room that comprised the ground floor of the tavern.

When the men had assembled on the beach early that morning, which now seemed to them like weeks ago, the bemused Englishmen had watched as the Scots had all stripped to their shirts before producing great lengths of patterned cloth, in which they had then artfully wrapped themselves, before folding the discarded breeches and stockings into their small packs.

"What the hell are you doing?" Gabriel asked, as bemused as his men.

"We didna want to wear this to leave the inn," Alex explained. "We dinna want to advertise that we're Highlanders, for the English believe all Highlanders to be savages and Jacobites, do they no'?"

"Something of that order, yes," Gabriel admitted. "I can understand that. But why do you want to wear something that barely covers you, rather than warm breeches and a jacket? It'll be very cold on the journey, and you'll likely be wet for much of it."

"Aye, that's exactly the reason we're wearing the *féileadh mór*," Duncan said. "For it's awfu' adaptable, ye ken." By way of proving this, he pulled the long length of kilt currently falling from his waist at the back up, firstly round his shoulders, then over his head, and then draped it over his shoulder, pinning it to his shirt with a pewter brooch.

"And at night," Dougal added, "ye can take it off, and wrap yourself in it entirely to sleep in the heather without being seen. And when it's wet, it keeps ye warm."

Gabriel looked doubtfully at the exotic attire.

"I'm not sure I'd feel warm with my legs bare like that," he said. "To say nothing of the other bits. Don't they get chafed in the wet?"

"I think they'd shrivel up entirely in the cold!" another man commented, to general laughter.

"Aye, maybe if you're a Sasannach," Dougal replied. "But we Highlanders are well endowed by way of compensation for the Scottish weather. How would we occupy ourselves on dark winter nights, if the means of doing so couldna be found?"

This dry comment had resulted in a tirade of jovially insulting comments, all of which were taken in good part by both sides. Both Alex and Gabriel joined in, relieved that yesterday's hostile incident had now been replaced by good-humoured ribbing. It boded well for the trip.

After this, to Alex's great relief, Gabriel had handed out leather gloves to both his own men and the Highlanders, telling the latter that he always instructed *all* his men to wear them for such a long journey.

"It doesn't matter how accustomed your hands are to the rowing, or other heavy work," he explained to the reluctant Scots, "you can still get a splinter from the oar, or a packing case. Or the salt water can split your hands. If that happens you can't stop to tend it, and if your hand is badly injured, which it would be after seven hours of constant rowing, you'll be no good to me or your team mates. I've seen it too many times. Trust me about this. I'm not insulting you, nor am I implying your hands are soft. We won't be staying in Calais for more than a few days, and there'll be a lot of heavy work to do in that time. And on the ship to Scotland. There'll be no time for healing."

As his own men had already donned the gloves without a murmur and Alex did likewise, the rest had followed suit, ruefully accepting that there would be no more jokes at Alex's expense tonight.

They had then loaded the crates of weapons into the boats and set off, by which time the sky could be seen to be lightening in the east, even through the mist that blanketed the sea.

"I'm hoping we'll have fair weather the whole way," Gabriel, who had taken the helm, told Alex, who was sitting close to him. "It looks promising, if we row quickly, and as your men make up in strength and determination for what they lack in experience, I see no reason why we shouldn't. We've a good team, I think."

"Aye, I think so too," Alex said. "Your men have a similar outlook on life to mine, although our lives are very different in most ways."

Gabriel smiled.

"That's what being outcasts does to you. And we are, even if half the country depends on us for affordable luxuries. And even necessities, when there's a war on. On a clear day," he continued conversationally, "you can see Calais from where we are now. If you stand on the beach at Dover, you can see it from the shore at times. If it's clear in Calais when we're there, I'll show you."

They continued then, establishing a smooth fluid rhythm after a time, as the sun rose and the mist slowly cleared, upon which they could indeed see Calais, which did not seem *too* far away, although it didn't seem much closer after another hour of hard rowing, which told them its apparent nearness was an illusion.

When Gabriel assessed they were half way across, and as the sea was indeed remarkably calm, they stopped for a few minutes to drink, and eat some salt pork and biscuit, which Gabriel had brought with him in a waxed leather bag. After that they continued, partly because they wanted to arrive as quickly as possible while the weather held, and partly because once they weren't working they grew cold very quickly. The Englishmen had looked on somewhat enviously as the Highlanders had pulled their plaids up over their heads to shelter themselves and their meal from the salt spray and brisk cold wind.

"Now if I could wear my breeches *and* that, I might think on it," Gabriel said.

"The breeches are the worst of it," Alex replied. "Your men said earlier about the chafing, but there's nothing chafes more than breeches, when ye're used to the freedom of the *fèileadh mòr*. And when they're wet, it's worse."

"I'll take your word for it," Gabriel answered. "At least breeches give you support, shall we say?"

* * *

In the end they made it to Calais without incident, to the relief of everyone, landing slightly east of the main part of town, in the area where the fishermen pulled their boats onto the shore and where they would be unlikely to be noticed.

"It's not far to *Le Chat D'Or,* where we can store the weapons until we've got the rest to take to Scotland, and where we can eat our fill and get warm. There's a good-sized room upstairs where all your men can sleep, if that suits you. There'll be a fire lit in there, so it'll be warm by the time you've eaten," Gabriel said as they pulled the boat up the sand.

"You won't be needing a fire, if you're used to sleeping in the Scottish winter in a petticoat!" Alan, one of the older gang members joked.

"We dinna *need* a fire," Alex replied, "but if there's one waiting for us, we'll no' refuse it. I willna, in any case." Another way in which he was growing soft, he'd realised as they'd been travelling. The wind had felt colder than any in the mountains, and as he knew through common sense and the attitude of his men that this wasn't true, could only assume that sitting in heated rooms and sleeping in soft feather beds for months had made him more vulnerable to the cold. Christ! He couldn't be the chieftain if he was soft in body *and* mind! True, he could still hide it well enough that his clansmen had no idea he felt painfully chilled, but for most of his life he hadn't even *noticed* the cold unless it was extreme. When this trip was over, he would have to find a way to address these side-effects of his current lifestyle.

"That was a good journey," Iain said, breaking into his gloomy thoughts. "I'd forgotten how much I miss the sea. But it's good to be on land safely too."

"There's a lot more sea to come yet," Gabriel said. "I daresay you'll have your fill of it by the end."

"I'm sure I will. But at the minute it's bringing back good memories of when I was a boy, sea fishing wi' my da," Iain added.

After they'd eaten and drank their fill and the weapons were safely hidden in the cellar behind a load of barrels, the MacGregors were shown upstairs to their room, which was indeed lovely and warm.

"Is there a river nearby?" Duncan asked the man who'd showed them to the room.

"A river? Why on earth would you want a river at this time of night? Haven't you been wet enough all day?" the man asked.

"I'm no' used to my hair being stiff like this, and the salt's making my skin itchy. I'm wanting to wash it off before I sleep," Duncan explained.

"Ah! I'm so used to it, it doesn't bother me any more, but I remember feeling that way, when I was a boy. There's a pump at the back. You can use that if you want," he said.

As everyone suddenly realised they felt the same way, they all went out to wash, which resulted in a good deal of horseplay, with all of them ending up as wet as they had been on the ocean.

Watching them, Alex felt a great sense of pride. Not one of them had mentioned how tired they were, or how much their muscles were aching from the unaccustomed labour. Rowing a boat for seven hours used different muscles to those needed to wield a sword, or any of the other tasks Highlanders habitually did. Alex knew that, because he could feel every muscle in his upper body, and he was not the only one, in spite of his months of relative inactivity. He could tell only because he knew his men well, could see the tell-tale signs of pain in their eyes or carriage as they moved about the room or shifted the boxes etc. But not one of Foley's men would have any idea of their discomfort.

After washing his hair and body, Duncan picked up his *fèileadh mór* and washed the salt out of that, too.

"I was after thinking," he said conversationally to Alex as he wrung it out, "I saw a church tower as we rowed past the town. It seemed a fine church, and I thought, as tomorrow is Sunday, I'd away to Mass. So I'm no' wanting my clothes streaked wi' salt if I do."

The horseplay stopped as everyone suddenly realised that they were in a Catholic land now, and not only could they wear the *féileadh mór* in public if they wanted, as there were many exiled Highlanders both here and in Paris, but they could go to Mass too. In a proper church. Openly. None of them, with the exception of Alex, had ever done that.

"Oh, that would be a wondrous thing," Dougal breathed. "I'll come wi' ye."

And so it was that the next morning the wondrous fortress-like Church of Our Lady was besieged (if peacefully) by twelve MacGregor clansmen, resplendent in their tartan kilts, bareheaded, hair brushed and neatly tied back. They looked at the soaring roof, the statues, and the carvings of the glorious high altar with awe and reverence, before enjoying what for all of them would be the highlight of the whole trip, so wonderful was it to be able to take communion openly and joyously, with no fear of reprisals. It was a long time since any of them had celebrated Mass at all, and when they had it had been in the chieftain's home or the cave on the mountain above Loch Lomond. Most of them had never been in a Catholic church in their lives, and this was *such* a glorious one, full of people who all believed as they did!

After Mass they decided to take a stroll around the town, partly because Gabriel had not told them they were needed for any manual labour, and partly because they didn't want the magical quality of the day to end.

"After all," Jamie pointed out, "we'll likely never be in France again, so it would be a shame no' to see a wee bit of it, to tell the others about when we're home again."

This was true. Next winter would fly by, filled as it would be with exotic tales of London, of the sea crossing, and of the wonders of France! As they hadn't eaten since they'd decided to go to Mass, as you had to fast before communion, their first task was to find a street vendor who sold food, after which they broke their fast with a dish of fish marinated in wine and herbs, which was both delicious and very different to anything they'd eaten before, which added to the magic of the day.

They were now all feeling very light-hearted and festive as they walked around the town, commenting on the wonders of the architecture; the Gate of Calais, the citadel with its impressive walls and gates patrolled by soldiers, and the docks with its mass of sailing ships. Then they walked along the coast a little way, wanting to see if Gabriel had been exaggerating when he said you could see the cliffs of Dover from here on a clear day. It *was* a clear day, bright and sunny with a warmth in the air which hinted of spring and raised the MacGregors' spirits even higher.

Gabriel had not been exaggerating, they discovered. They could indeed clearly see the land mass of Kent, the white chalk cliffs of Dover brilliant in the sunlight.

"I didna ken that France was so near to England," Iain said. "That'll be good if Louis does decide to support James when he makes his next attempt to take the crown."

"I'm thinking Charles is more likely to do it," Alex put in. "For James isna of the temperament, and he's no' a young man any more."

"France hasna got any closer to England in the last fifty years, but the French king hasna got off his arse and landed troops in all that time, so I wouldna count on him doing it now," Duncan commented dryly.

"I canna believe it took us seven hours to row across from there," Dougal said in awe. "It doesna seem that far away. Ye'd think ye could swim to it easily, would ye no'?"

"Ye can try if ye want, but I was chilled enough rowing across in yon wee boat, without swimming across it. I canna imagine anyone choosing to do such a thing," Iain replied.

"Aye, and Maggie would kill ye for being a loon, should ye survive it," Alex added, to general laughter. It was a lovely day, just the kind of day he and his men had needed; a relaxed and happy day, without a care in the world. That was an illusion, but it *felt* that way right now, which was what mattered.

When they finally returned to *Le Chat D'Or* it was nearly dark, and they entered to find a drinking and arm-wrestling contest under way, the smuggler gang seemingly in as high spirits as the MacGregors were, albeit for different reasons.

"Ah, here you are!" Alan shouted as they entered. "We wondered when you'd come back. Now we can have a proper contest, lads! England against Scotland!"

Whether he meant a drinking or an arm-wrestling contest was unclear, but in any case the MacGregors accepted this challenge readily, and a fierce but good-natured battle on both fronts commenced.

"Dinna tell me we're to sail across to Scotland tomorrow," Alex said later to Gabriel, having just won his latest contest, against a much smaller man who hadn't stood a chance and probably wouldn't have even attempted to beat Alex had he been less drunk. "I'm thinking none of us will be fit to do anything in the morning."

"No. You worked hard yesterday, and although the muskets are here, I'm expecting the swords to arrive tomorrow. They're coming from Germany. There are a few swordsmiths there whose work is very good, and very consistent. It'll be worth the wait to have them. And I'm waiting on other things too. But we should start loading the ship tomorrow. Afternoon," he added, glancing round the room with a smile.

"We walked down to the dock today, to see if we could see Dover as ye said," Alex admitted.

"You didn't believe me then," Gabriel said without rancour.

"We didna ken if ye were jesting wi' us, no, for it's the sort of thing we'd do to raw men ourselves." He sat down opposite the smuggler leader, and drained his tankard. "I'm glad I agreed to do this," he said. "The men are enjoying it. They're none of them city dwellers, and it's good to see them happy and relaxed."

"If any of them ever want to take up the free trade, I'd be happy to take them on," Gabriel offered.

"I doubt they'd go that far. But I'll tell them, for that's fine praise. I dinna think ye're a man who'd say such a thing and no' be sincere," Alex told him.

"But you think I'm a man who'd tell you you could see Dover from Calais, and not be sincere!" Gabriel retorted.

Alex laughed then.

"Aye, because I would do that. But I wouldna tell a man I'd employ him in jest, and I'm thinking ye're a man of my own way of thinking, to some extent."

"I am indeed. Your good health, sir," Gabriel agreed, raising his tankard.

"*Slàinte mhath*," Alex said in response, raising his own.

It had been a good day. Hopefully God would look after them for the rest of the trip, now they had taken communion for the first time in years.

Yes, it had been a *very* good day indeed.

CHAPTER SEVEN

London, England

"Christ, man, ye're no' going to Scotland dressed like that!" Maggie exclaimed when Angus appeared at the foot of the stairs.

"Why, would ye prefer I wear my *fèileadh mòr*?" he asked, adjusting a black patch carefully over his left eye in the hall mirror.

"Ye couldna attract more attention if ye did, that's certain," she replied dryly. This was probably true, dressed as he was in scarlet velvet breeches, black greatcoat, a long black wig of a style fashionable some sixty years previously, an extravagant hat with an ostrich feather stuck in the brim, and the aforesaid eyepatch. Although it was also true that the kind of attention he'd attract would be less hostile than that he could expect were he to wear the traditional Highland clothing in the capital city of England.

"I'll no' be wearing this to ride the whole way, just until I'm away from London," Angus said in an attempt at reassuring her. "I've worn it before when I've no' wanted to be recognised, I thought ye kent that."

"I kent ye wore some manner of outlandish garb, but no' such a one as that!" she retorted, waving a disparaging hand at him.

"Aye, well, I'm thinking wi' this I look formidable, and no one will be likely to accost me. They havena before, anyway," Angus said. "When I'm a good way outside the city I'll change into yon sober outfit Alex bought for me."

"Angus, ye'd look formidable dressed in your sark," Maggie said. "Ye're taller and broader than any man I've seen in London, excepting Alex, and ye carry weapons as though ye ken how to use them. Which ye do. Dinna let this sea malady make ye feel less of a man."

Angus flushed scarlet, which told Maggie that she'd hit the nail on the head.

"I'm no' wearing it for that reason," he protested. She looked at him wryly. "I'm no' wearing it *only* for that reason," he amended after an uncomfortable moment. "Since we discovered yon Joshua mannie was spying on us, I dinna feel as safe as I did before."

"Ye felt *safe* before?" she laughed. "None of us are safe, wi' what we're doing. I'll no' feel safe until I'm home, sitting by the lochside at sunset, with Iain beside me." This last was said so plaintively that Angus reached out impulsively and pulled her into a fierce embrace. She relaxed into it for a moment then pulled away, swiping tears away from her eyes angrily, annoyed at her momentary lapse of control. That could wait until she was alone.

"They'll all come back safe, I'm sure. That Foley man is verra good at the free trade, and wi' boats and suchlike," Angus said sympathetically. "I ken how ye feel about being home again. I'm longing for that myself. Except I dinna want Iain sitting beside me," he added, making her laugh. "No, I feel safe enough going out to do normal errands that ye'd expect a servant to do. But we didna ken we were being followed. It isna easy to spot someone following ye when there are people *everywhere*. A lot of people ken Jim, Sir Anthony's manservant, though. If Anthony's suspected, then they'll be watching me. And as I'm no' going on a normal errand, I'd rather no one kent I was riding north."

He had a point, she had to admit, so she gave in.

"Be careful, even so," she said, following him as he made his way to the kitchen, intending to leave by the back door. His horse was ready, his saddlebag packed with everything he'd need for the long trip, which, as he was a Highlander, was very little. "Ye dinna want to be arrested when Sir Anthony isna here to rescue ye."

Angus responded with a snort of derision, then made an elaborate bow, removing his hat and waving it in front of her face with a great flourish before replacing it. She stood on tiptoe to adjust it so it shaded his face, and then, as impulsively as he'd embraced her, she kissed him on the cheek.

"I love ye, ye wee gomerel," she said. "Dinna take any risks, and come back to us safely."

She watched him ride down the long garden, leaping the horse over the low wall and then setting off at a gallop across the fields. He would re-emerge onto the road a few streets away and then head north to the village of Hampstead. Hopefully once there he'd change out of that ridiculous costume into something less ostentatious.

She closed the door and went back into the kitchen, where she bustled about for a while. Not because there was anything that needed doing desperately; she would after all be on her own in the house for a few weeks now, but because she was restless, worrying about her husband, about Alex, and all the other MacGregors. It was true there was safety in numbers, and a group of MacGregors were more capable than most of dealing with anything life threw at them. But the sea was an unpredictable, ruthless creature, an enemy about which they knew little.

She had never been on the sea herself, although she had seen it during the time she'd lived in Edinburgh, and Iain had told her about his watery adventures when he'd lived with his birth clan in the north-east of the country. No matter how well you could wield a sword and targe though, you would be no match for a storm on the ocean. In a rowing boat.

And then Angus. Of all the MacGregors to ride alone through the country, Angus was the last she would choose. Not because he was less courageous or less proficient with weapons than his fellow clansmen, but because he was so youthful, so reckless, so careless of consequences. And so caring and affectionate. One day, if he ever settled down, he would make some lassie a wonderful husband. If he lived that long.

She shook her head to clear it of all these gloomy imaginings, then sat down at the table and looked around the immaculate kitchen, wondering what she could do to occupy both her body and her mind. She could start work on her new gown. That would be a formidable task, for although she had sewn her own clothes before, she had never attempted to make anything as complicated as a formal gown. No. She was not ready to tackle that, not yet. In a day or two, when she felt more settled perhaps, and could concentrate better.

Although she had often been alone in the house for a few hours at a time, she had never been alone for weeks before. Knowing that was now to be the case changed the whole atmosphere. Instead of relishing a little peace and time to herself as she usually did when all the men were out, she now dreaded the lonely abyss that stretched before her, and felt the house, empty and cold, looming over her malevolently.

This was ridiculous. Right. She would clean the whole house. Every room, every closet, starting in the attic rooms and working her way down. That would keep her occupied for weeks, if she was thorough. And in the evenings she would begin her dress. Sir Anthony had some wee dolls somewhere, dressed in the latest fashions, which he said had come from Paris and were sent to wealthy people who wanted to see what an expensive costume would look like before ordering it. She would find them, and decide what manner of dress she wanted. Or rather, what manner of dress she might be capable of making.

Decided, she stood, and set about gathering together the implements needed to clean the attic rooms. It was what clanswomen did to calm their nerves when men were away at battle. This was no different, except that the clanswomen supported each other, singing and chatting while working, whilst she was on her own. But she would not think of that.

* * *

As Maggie had assumed, Angus did indeed emerge some distance away, on Mortimer Street, far enough from the house that no one would think him to have anything to do with Sir Anthony. He stopped at the corner of Titchfield Street, checked for the tenth time whether all his weapons were instantly accessible should he have need of them, then deliberated as to whether to ride along a back lane or a main thoroughfare in order to get to Tottenham Court Road, which would then take him north.

"Good day to you, sir!" a voice came from behind him. "Are you lost? Can I be of any assistance?"

Angus turned in the saddle, assessing the man who was approaching him. Middle-aged, well-dressed, round, podgy face. Two bulging saddlebags. Almost certainly a businessman of some kind then, a merchant perhaps. Unlikely to be a threat. He smiled, waiting until the man drew level with him.

"Thank ye, but no, I'm riding north and deliberating which route to take, is all," Angus replied.

"Ah, then we are well met, for I too am riding north, as far as Hampstead! If you are taking the same direction, perhaps we could ride together? There is safety in numbers, you know!" the man suggested.

This was true, although Angus doubted he would be any safer in the company of this particular man, who, it was clear to his expert eye, was no fighter of any sort, his sword being clearly for decorative purposes only, and his red face and corpulent figure displaying more fondness for food and drink than activity of any kind. But he would be alone for most of the way north, and it would look strange if he declined the kind invitation and then ended up following the man to Hampstead anyway.

"I am indeed travelling to Hampstead," Angus said. "I see no reason why we shouldna make the journey together. James Mortimer at your service," he added, plucking the surname from the street he was currently on.

They turned right and set off along Titchfield Street, Angus rightly assessing that this was not a man who would want to gallop along muddy rutted tracks.

"Benjamin Highmore, at your service, sir," the man replied. "I confess I am not accustomed to travelling outside of this fair city, and will be glad of some company. You are going to Hampstead on business, Mr Mortimer?" Highmore asked.

"No. Mine is a social visit," Angus replied vaguely. "Are ye on business yourself?"

To his amusement, Mr Highmore looked around theatrically to make sure no one else was in earshot, which was somewhat ridiculous, as this was London; there were people *everywhere*, but as the two of them were moving rather than in a tavern or coffeehouse, and mounted rather than walking, he could have bellowed his reason for visiting Hampstead without any passers-by being any the wiser.

"In truth, sir, I am on a…let me say…a mission on behalf of our dear king, in the hope of relieving the burden laid upon his shoulders," Mr Highmore stated hesitantly, pulling his horse close enough to Angus that he could smell the man's last meal, which had contained a plentiful supply of garlic and onions.

"Are ye? That's verra loyal of ye, I'm sure," Angus replied.

"I am a loyal Englishman, sir, as I am sure you also are.

Although your accent is not from these parts, if I am correct."

"Indeed ye are," Angus agreed. Unlike his brother, he had no ability to mimic other accents. The only attempt he had ever made to adopt an English accent had been greeted with hilarity by Alex, who had told him that merely saying 'yes' instead of 'aye' was not enough to convince even the most simple-minded fool that he was anything other than a Scot. Even so, it seemed that here was such a fool. "Have ye ever visited Newcastle? It's a town in the north of England," he added. If the man had, then he would find another English town to be from.

"I have not. Is that where you are from?" Mr Highmore asked.

"It is indeed. Although I have not seen my home town for a long time," Angus added, thinking he might as well speak the truth when possible.

They had now reached Oxford Street and were threading their way through the crowds of shoppers, careful to avoid the recklessly driven hackney cabs that would veer out suddenly into the carriageway to grab a fare, so Mr Highmore's act of loyalty remained a mystery until they finally reached Tottenham Court Road, where the thoroughfare became less congested.

"I will admit to you sir, that I am most excited to be both assisting His Dear Majesty in the war, while also hoping to make a profit for myself. It is a very safe venture, I'm assured."

"I'm intrigued," Angus said, who wasn't, having neither the funds nor the inclination to invest in anything that might benefit the Elector. But his prattle would pass the time. "Perhaps I might make an investment myself, if it's a safe one and helping the cause."

"Ah! You see, as soon as I set eyes on you, I saw you as a true patriot, sir! It is certain that our king will soon be leaving these shores to lead his brave troops, many of whom are already in Germany. And of course at such a time, our free land is in danger from that parcel of traitors who seek to overthrow him in favour of that lickspittle Pretender, who would have us all in thrall to Rome in an instant! Why, he is not even of royal blood! Everyone knows that he was smuggled into the birthing chamber in a warming pan, and was certainly some servant's brat!" Mr Highmore's voice rose as he warmed to his subject now, clearly very passionate in his views.

"So, what is this loyal venture? Please, dinna keep me waiting. I ke…know the history of the Stuarts myself, as does any well-read man," Angus said, feeling his temper rise at this slanderous tirade about the rightful King of Great Britain, and hoping to shut the man up.

"Ah. Well, I have here a goodly sum of gold, which is why I was reluctant to ride alone, in case of footpads or highwaymen. So many of them are Jacobite scum, sir, and I had hoped to meet with a loyal companion. I think no one will accost us now, for, if I may say, you have a most formidable appearance, sir! I mean no offence, of course!"

"None taken," Angus said, thinking Maggie had been right in her assessment of his costume, and maybe of him too. Being seasick did not make him weak. He smiled and Mr Highmore, seeing it, was reassured.

"So, in Hampstead is a group of loyal men who wish to buy arms and train men to fight, not in Europe, but in London, if it becomes necessary. They intend to guard the city, and prevent any attempt by the Pretender to seize an opportunity while our land is vulnerable. I am assisting them to purchase these arms! Is that not a noble undertaking?"

"It is indeed," replied Angus, trying not to look at the bulging saddlebags, which until now he had assumed were loaded with all the ridiculous fripperies Sasannachs thought essential for even the shortest trip. "It's always noble to do all ye can to support your king. But I'm no' sure how ye think this will make a profit for ye. No' that that's important, of course. But ye did say it was a safe and profitable venture."

"Ah, of course. Well these men are borrowing the gold from me, at a very low interest. But of course when His Majesty returns from his venture he will be appraised of our loyalty, for one of our group has the ear of the king and has no doubt His Majesty will be suitably generous in his gratitude! So who knows what might happen?"

Who knew indeed? *Dear God,* thought Angus, *but this man is a loon.* Even if the venture was a genuine one, which he doubted given the amount of fraudsters in London looking for such gullible men as the one he was now accompanying, it was highly unlikely that the Elector, who was not renowned for his generosity even to those who *did* perform a useful service, would reward a group of overweight merchants for parading around London ineptly armed with muskets.

"Well, it's a most interesting proposition, that's certain," Angus said. It was. Not as interesting as the proposition that was now entering his head, though.

No, he mustn't. He'd told both Alex and Maggie that he wouldn't take any risks. Even so, those saddlebags looked *very* full.

"I'm glad you think so," Highmore replied. "If you're interested in making a contribution, I'd be happy to introduce you to my friends. Will you be staying in Hampstead for long?"

"No, I'll be visiting my acquaintance and then returning immediately," Angus said. "And I'm no' carrying money, in any case."

"Ah, I understand. But if you change your mind, do contact me…I will give you my address before we part company."

"Aye, I will, of course," Angus replied, remembering too late that he should have said yes rather than aye. Although hadn't Alex told him that northern English people said 'aye' too? It didn't matter. Not with this man.

"I was reading recently about the parcel of rogues from North Britain, the savages who see this Pretender as one of their own, him being a Papist as are they all. Superstitious, and no doubt in league with the Devil! Who knows what wild and unnatural practices they get up to in their mountain hovels? I've been told that if they're hungry, which they always are as they will not do an honest day's work, they have even been known to slaughter and roast their own children! And these are the…the…beasts that the Pretender will call upon to ravage this fair land, in the hopes of returning us all to the Pope and damnation! Even if there were no profit to be had, this is certainly a worthy way to invest a sum of money, if you have it to spare!"

Oh, to hell with not taking risks. He wasn't going to listen to this insulting rubbish all the way to Hampstead. He glanced around while the man continued his tirade, working himself up into a righteous frenzy now. No, there weren't many people on the road, but enough. However…hadn't he said he wasn't accustomed to travelling outside the city? And the distant clouds were certainly dark enough for rain to be likely.

"D'ye see yon rainclouds, sir?" Angus said, cutting into the man's comments about the bestial behaviour of the Highlanders, which had now moved on to the various creatures they were willing to copulate with. "We're riding into a downpour, unless we can be under shelter before it arrives."

Mr Highmore looked anxiously over to the left, where Angus was pointing.

"Ah. You are certainly right, although I see no way of arriving in Hampstead before the storm is on us," the man said worriedly.

"No, but I'm familiar with the route, having visited my acquaintance on several occasions, and I'd suggest we take the track ahead on the left. I wouldna suggest it if we were on foot or in a coach, for it's a wee bit muddy and narrow, but as we're riding that'll no' be a problem. There's a wee bothy…a wee hut that we can certainly reach before the rain, and can shelter there until it passes. And if we carry on along the track, it's actually a shorter route to our destination!"

They had now reached the lane, which was indeed narrow, but not muddy at the moment, the weather being dry. They stopped. Mr Highmore looked up at the clouds again. Angus remained silent. It was now down to the man to decide his own fate.

"Well, then. It would be foolish to ride through a rainstorm, if we don't need to," Highmore murmured. "We could catch our death of cold." And so saying, he turned his horse down the track, and in doing so made Angus's decision for him.

He rode behind Highmore until they were both out of sight and earshot of the main route north, and then, having reached a wider part of the track, and after ensuring that no one was either following them or heading their way, Angus rode to the left side of his companion, drew his dirk and hit him smartly on the side of the head with the hilt, rendering him unconscious.

As insulting as the man had been about his people, Angus had no desire to kill such an innocent, or even injure him any more than was absolutely necessary, so he grabbed the man's coat, pulling him over across his own horse while grabbing the other horse's reins to stop it bolting. Then he dismounted and lowered the unconscious man to the ground, checking to make sure he was still breathing but not likely to revive immediately.

By the time the man started to recover consciousness a minute or two later, Angus had unstrapped the saddlebags from Highmore's chestnut mare, cut a number of strips from the bottom of his shirt, bound the man's hands behind his back, and was securing his legs. Seeing that he was now regaining what sense he had, Angus pulled him into a sitting position against the low stone wall at one side of the track, and then took out the flask of ale Maggie had given him, holding it to the man's lips so he could drink and revive a little. Then he gagged his victim securely with some more strips of linen.

Certain that Highmore was going nowhere and could not shout for help, Angus now examined the saddlebags. They had felt solid as he'd lifted them off the mare, but he had no intention of taking the man's clothing and useless fripperies with him. He opened the first one, took out one of the many leather pouches it contained and looked inside.

"Holy Mother of God," he muttered on seeing the gold coins within, and discovering that all the other leather bags inside had similar contents. He drew the string on the pouch and replaced it, then sat back on his heels, wiping his hand across his face in disbelief.

Angus looked across at his unfortunate companion, who was staring at him, his eyes bulging with terror, and felt a momentary twinge of pity for him. Only a twinge. Not enough to restore him to his fortune, but enough to give him *some* comfort.

"Ye've no need to fear, man," he said. "I'm no' going to kill ye. And I've tied ye well, but ye'll no' die here, for the track's used by the farmworkers and there'll be a goodly number of them along in a few hours, who I'm certain will release ye. And," he added wryly, glancing up at the sky, "ye'll no' be wet, for although they're rainclouds they're moving away, no' toward us. It's true I'm taking your gold, but the lesson I'm teaching ye's worth that, I'm thinking. For there are no' many men who would do as I'm doing, if ye trusted them on first meeting and tellt them ye were carrying a goodly sum of money –and then let them take ye down a lonely track. I canna believe ye havena been robbed before, if ye always behave so. Many a man…no, most men would kill ye without a thought for such a sum as this. So think of it as payment for a good lesson, for if ye heed it ye'll no' end wi' your throat cut in an alley somewhere. Indeed, ye should have an armed guard wi' ye if ye ever think of travelling wi' such an amount of gold again."

He stood then, discarded the clothing and other paraphernalia that Mr Highmore no doubt deemed essential for a short trip and Angus considered superfluous for a four-hundred-mile ride. After putting his own change of clothing, bag of grain for the horse and the food Maggie had packed in the space he'd made, he tied the saddlebags across his own horse.

"I'll be away home to London, then," he said, leaping back into the saddle. "I wish ye a good day, and a long life."

He turned then and galloped back along the track, which had not been a short cut of any sort, and continued on his way north, at a much faster pace than he had taken until now. He had intended to buy food at towns and villages along the way, and maybe even stay in a room if the weather was fierce, as he needed to look respectable as he travelled north, as though he could afford the horse he was riding.

Now the deed was done, he realised that he should have thought more before committing it. Not because he thought for one moment he would be identified as the robber. Any description Highmore gave to the authorities would be pointless once he'd disposed of this ridiculous outfit he was wearing, which he would do at the earliest opportunity.

He was not sure how much money he was carrying, but it was a lot. And he could not take it back to London, because if he did Maggie would give him hell, and Alex, when he returned from the sea trip and found out, would be incandescent with rage at his recklessness. Angus shuddered at the thought of what he might do.

Which meant he now had to take this huge amount of gold all the way to Scotland without being himself robbed and killed by the various highwaymen and footpads who operated along the highways. So although he could now afford to stay in a palace if he wanted to, ironically he would have to forego all luxuries. He would have to avoid all well-travelled roads and centres of population, sleep in the open in impractical Sasannach clothes, and make the food Maggie had given him last for the whole journey unless he could forage. In March.

And when he got to Scotland, he would need to get the gold up to the cave above Loch Lomond and hide it without being seen. Because he was then taking the clansmen up to Burghead, where they would meet with the chieftain and would be certain to tell him about the gold, if they knew of it.

Angus sighed. Should they find out, he would never be able to dispute the fact that he was reckless again. But it was worth it, he told himself. Partly because he had stopped the money from being used by Hanoverians, if the unlikely militia scheme had been genuine, and if not, he had stopped an innocent, if very stupid man being murdered. But mainly because this money could be put to good use, either buying weapons for the cause or ensuring that the MacGregors would not starve for years to come, no matter how bad the harvest. And when a bad harvest happened and he then revealed what he'd done, Alex would surely be grateful to him for saving the clan, and that would override any anger at his impulsive deed.

Yes. It *had* been worthwhile, Angus told himself. It would be no great hardship to avoid people and sleep under hedges. He had merely seized an opportunity when it had presented itself to him. That was sensible, not reckless. Not reckless at all.

He rode on, whistling to himself. Alex, Iain and Maggie were right. Being seasick did not make you less of a man. He had just proved that.

CHAPTER EIGHT

Scotland, March 1743

By the time Angus saw the waters of Loch Lomond sparkling through the trees in the cold sunlight, he was so relieved that he sank to his knees on the ground and thanked God for getting him home safely.

He had slept in a woodland in the icy torrential rain the night he'd robbed Mr Highmore of his gold, and the following morning when he woke up, drenched to the skin, he had thought again about his resolution the previous day never to travel on a road or stay at an inn. Not because he was drenched to the skin and cold, although he was both those things. Nor was it because he had only one bag of oatmeal to see him home, over four hundred miles away.

No, it was because if he rode across country the whole way rather than on the road it would take him a *lot* longer to get home, particularly as he was not familiar with the landscape of England as he was with Scotland. And as well as the likelihood of getting lost, at least temporarily, there was also the fact that his horse would not be able to travel as far each day if she was not stabled at night with a good feed. He might be able to live on a bag of oatmeal for twelve days, but his horse could not.

And time was of the essence. Because when Alex and the others arrived at Burghead, the rest of the clansmen would need to be waiting for them. Gabriel had told him that if everything went favourably they should be there in three weeks. True, he had then added that if they were it would be a miracle, but even so Angus wanted to impress the brother he aspired to be like one day, and turning up a few days after the ship full of arms sailed in would not achieve that. Once he had reached home, the men would have to prepare, and it would take a few days to travel up the country to Burghead. So he could not waste days wandering aimlessly around the English countryside.

He should be in no more danger travelling on the roads and sleeping in inns with the gold than without it, he realised, now he was thinking rationally. After all, the gold was not particularly heavy. Nor did it actually take up much space, except in his head. After he'd counted it last night and realised he had over thirty years' worth of footman's or craftsman's wages with him, it had suddenly taken on immense dimensions in his mind, and he'd imagined that everyone who saw him would somehow know that he was carrying a fortune and would have no qualms about killing him to relieve him of it, or of informing the authorities in the hope of a reward when he was arrested, which he certainly would be.

Whilst it was true that if anyone *did* find out what was in his bag his life would be worth nothing, in fact, providing he never let the bag out of his sight there was no reason why anyone should actually discover its contents. He would simply arrive at the inns late in the evening and leave early in the morning. That way he could eat whatever was available when he got there and go to bed immediately afterwards, which would minimise the amount of time he had to watch over his baggage to ensure no one tried to ascertain its contents.

Yes, that would work. Then he could ride along the roads in comparative safety. Although alone he was well armed, and, as Maggie had said, not only knew how to use those arms but looked as though he did. And he was a good horseman too.

Having reassured himself, he had made a small meal from his bag of oatmeal, pouring some into a small wooden bowl and then waiting for the rain to provide sufficient water for him to make it into a nutritious paste. Then he had removed all the bits of vegetation from his clothes, smoothed and tied back his hair, and generally made himself as respectable-looking as he could. He needed to appear wealthy enough to either own a horse or be able to afford to rent one. But everyone riding in this weather would be drenched, so he should not appear *too* disreputable.

DEALING IN TREASON

He'd repacked his saddlebags, mounted his horse and headed to the roadway, feeling optimistic once more.

* * *

After that all had gone well for several days. Several tedious, but safe days. Angus was a gregarious, sociable young man, the opposite of the middle brother Duncan. Alex should have chosen Duncan to make this trip rather than him, he thought. Duncan relished being in the open air in all weathers, and loved his own company. He would have *chosen* to sleep outdoors, no matter the weather, rather than have to make small talk with fellow travellers in the inns.

Having said that, Iain was not unlike Duncan in that respect and Alex had in fact initially chosen him to make the ride home, until Angus's ineptness had changed everything. Angus sighed. In truth he wouldn't mind the long days of riding, if he didn't need to be constantly on the alert. It was very tiring to maintain a high level of awareness to ensure no one was riding up behind him with evil intent. Normally he would be with others, and they would take turns to be vigilant. It would also have been less tedious if he'd been able to arrive at an inn at dusk, then enjoy a hearty meal in convivial company.

But of course he could not do that, partly because he needed to ride the full distance his horse could reasonably manage each day, and partly because if he clung fervently to his bags throughout a whole evening in a busy tavern it might arouse suspicion that he had something worth stealing.

So he had arrived after dark, had eaten his meal in the bedroom he shared with several other travellers and then had settled down to sleep, putting his saddlebag under his head as a pillow. That would not attract undue attention, as theft in the night from an untended bag was a very common occurrence. He usually awoke before dawn, left the room silently and was on the road before the occupants of the inn were stirring.

This pattern had continued until he'd arrived at Durham, by which time he was starting to relax a little. No one had accosted him, or threatened him in even the slightest way. He had told anyone who asked that he was heading to Glasgow as quickly as possible, as his mother was gravely ill and unlikely to live for much longer. He felt no guilt about this lie, nor was he tempting fate, as his mother had died many years before, and it had given a good reason for him arriving late at the inns and leaving early.

That night in Durham he had shared the room with just three other men, all sleeping on pallets on the floor. But the pallets had been blissfully free of bugs and he had been tired, so had fallen asleep as soon as his head hit his saddlebag pillow.

He had no idea how long he'd been asleep when his 'pillow' suddenly moved. Only very slightly, but he was alone and a Highlander, and it was inbred in them to sleep lightly and be immediately alert if woken. Their lives could depend on it.

So he had woken instantly, but apart from gripping his dirk, which was next to him under the blanket, he had given no sign that he was awake. Instead he had opened his eyes just enough to see that the room was pitch black, the shutters closed and all the lights quenched. So he had closed them again, and had listened instead.

The man had frozen when the bag had moved, waiting to see if his victim had been disturbed. Angus could sense his closeness, could hear him breathing very softly, trying to make the least noise possible. Behind him, near the window, another sleeper was breathing deeply, his nose whistling slightly. So the thief was one of the two men between him and the door. They had not been together, so Angus did not need to worry about anyone coming to his friend's rescue when he acted.

He lay still, breathing deeply, normally, waiting. It seemed like hours before the man finally relaxed, believing Angus to still be asleep. Knowing he would be unable to open the flap of the bag without waking his victim, very slowly the thief slipped his fingers inside the top of the bag, no doubt hoping to slide something out and then return to bed.

Angus waited until the man's hand was almost certainly far enough into the bag that it would be difficult for him to withdraw it once his victim moved, and then in one fluid movement he shot his left hand out of the bed, grabbing a fistful of the man's shirt and twisting it, pulling the man toward him and placing the cold metal of his dirk where he estimated the throat to be. It was difficult to be sure which body part he hit in the total darkness, but Angus knew it was bare skin, because the man squealed then froze instantly, making no attempt to free himself, which he almost certainly would have done had he thought Angus to be wielding anything other than a deadly weapon. Behind them the window sleeper snorted, then returned to his whistling breath.

"No' this man, laddie," Angus murmured, his tone almost conversational. "And no' any other in this inn, either. Ye'll be leaving now, I'm thinking."

He felt the man nod, and then the whistler snorted again, and this time woke.

"What's going on?" he asked sleepily.

There was a tense silence for a few seconds. Angus could feel the man trembling in his grip, but did not remove the dirk, or loosen his grip. Not yet.

"I'm sorry," the thief said shakily. "I need to leave now. I didn't want to waken anyone. I'll be gone in a moment."

Angus released the man then sat up, knife at the ready, listening as the man fumbled noisily around, trying to locate his belongings in the darkness.

"Oh, for God's sake," the whistling man said. "You're making enough noise to waken the dead. Here. I'll open the shutter so you can see. It's a full moon tonight."

Ignoring the other man's objections he stood, flinging the shutters open and flooding the room with pale silver light. Angus, now sitting up apparently innocently, no sign of a weapon, met the thief's eyes, committing his face to memory, and then he smiled coldly and nodded his head slightly. The thief blanched, understanding the gesture.

Once he'd left the room, closing the door quietly behind him, the whistler stood and closed the shutters again.

"Bloody fool," he said. "If he intended to leave in the middle of the night he should have slept in the stable, not woken honest travellers crashing about like that." Then he lay down, his breathing becoming deep and regular almost immediately.

Angus had lain awake for a little longer, listening intently until he heard the tavern door below close, and then he pulled the bag further under his head and went back to sleep.

Angus was certain that the unlucky thief had had no idea what he was carrying. No doubt he'd successfully tried this trick at many taverns, waiting until the darkest part of the night when exhausted men were most deeply asleep, before stealing whatever came to hand, which he would hope to trade for food or a room the next night. Certainly by moonlight he had looked very poor, his face gaunt, his clothes ragged. Not the sort of man who would normally be able to afford to stay at decent inns with clean beds.

Even so, after that Angus did not stay at inns any more, reckoning that he couldn't take the chance. If the man had been accomplished and ruthless he could have slipped the knife between Angus's ribs while he slept and made off with the gold. After all, inept as he was, he had managed to get close enough to touch the bag without rousing him, to Angus's shame. He was no pampered man, used to comfort and safety. The mere sound of the man getting up from his pallet should have woken him, and the fact that it had not shocked Angus to the core.

Now he understood Alex's concerns that his current lifestyle was making him soft. Because the same must be happening to him, and he had not realised it until this minute, thinking that because his role in London kept him far more active than Alex's did, that he need not worry on that score. He had not thought that his survival instinct was becoming dull. But it seemed it was.

So, because he was not sure how to remedy that and still needed to sleep every night, for the rest of the journey home he had slept outdoors, in woodlands, under hedges, anywhere where he was certain he would not be disturbed by people. Before he left the tavern he bought enough grain to feed his horse for what he estimated would be the rest of the journey, and enough food for himself. Because if he was going to sleep in the open, after a few days he would not look respectable enough to own a horse. And if he was arrested on suspicion of having stolen a horse and the gold discovered, he would certainly hang. It was just not worth it.

* * *

Which meant that the thankful prayer he uttered on seeing Loch Lomond had been one of the most sincere of his life so far. The journey to Burghead would be great fun, in the company of his fellow clansmen. He laughed out loud with relief, and then his smile faded as he realised that he was not home yet, nor was he safe. Firstly he had to get the gold into the cave halfway up the mountain above the MacGregor settlement without anyone seeing him.

He would need to make sure his horse was safely hobbled in a remote spot, and then would wait until the middle of the night before he made his way, silently and stealthily, up to the cave. He had absolutely no chance of doing that from the lochside without being observed by someone, no matter the time, for the clan always had a member looking out for either redcoats or hostile clans.

Which meant he would have to go up the mountain from the other side, and then descend to the cave. In the pitch black, silently and stealthily. In breeches, frockcoat, stockings and shoes with hard slippery soles. Normally he'd discard the shoes and stockings and go up the mountain barefoot. But he had been wearing stupid shoes for months now. No doubt his feet were as soft as his survival instincts. And there was gorse on the mountain. A lot of gorse. Very prickly gorse. Maybe he should just ride the damn horse openly into the settlement now, then sneak up to the cave later.

No. The chances of him doing that without someone noticing him carrying a ten-pound bag up the mountain were negligible. And if they did see him, then Alex would, definitely, learn about it. Angus would do a lot more than sneak up a gorse-covered mountain in the dead of night to avoid his brother's anger. To avoid his disapproval.

In that moment he sincerely wished he'd left Mr Highmore to have his gold stolen by someone else. But it was too late now.

He sighed, and turned his horse away from the loch.

* * *

"What the hell are ye doing here?" Simon, sitting outside his sweetheart's house asked when Angus rode into the settlement the following morning.

"That's a fine greeting, and me riding all the way from London to invite ye to a wee stramash," Angus said crossly. He had had a horrendous night and was in a horrible mood as a result. All the more so because the situation was all of his own making, so he couldn't blame anyone else for it.

"Jesus Christ, Angus, what's amiss? Ye look dreadful!" Janet cried, having come to the door on hearing Simon's comment.

"Nothing's amiss," Angus replied. "It's been a long ride, that's all. I'm tired. And hungry," he added hopefully.

"A ride? Ye look as though yon horse dragged ye behind her from London," Simon said tactlessly.

"I've ridden four hundred miles through pouring rain!" Angus shouted, causing several other MacGregors to come out of their houses. "What d'ye expect me to look like?"

"No' as though ye've crawled here through a bog and slept in a gorse bush every night, for one thing," Simon added coolly.

As this was a pretty accurate reflection of what he'd been doing last night, Angus flushed, aware that he could not admit that. Instead he would have to let them assume the horse had thrown him into a gorse bush.

"Och, leave him be, man. Can ye no' see he's fashed?" Janet said, re-emerging from the house with a bowl of something savoury-smelling and steaming. "Here, sit down and eat this. Ye'll feel better wi' a hot meal inside ye. Will I be calling the others?" she added, although there was no need, for the others were already coming across the clearing to discover the reason for the unexpected and somewhat dramatic appearance of the chieftain's youngest brother.

Angus ate, allowing the others to all congregate around him and trying to calm down. It was not their fault that he'd acted on impulse and then had to pay for that action for days. Nor was it their fault that he'd had the most uncomfortable night of his life so far, spending half of it clambering up the rain-drenched mountain in the dark, made more miserable by his ridiculous footwear which had caused him to slide rather than climb back down it after safely depositing the gold in a dark recess of the cave and covering it with stones. It was the descent that had caused Simon's comment and much of Angus's foul mood. Gorse was *very* prickly, and he was intensely uncomfortable as a result.

When he'd finished eating he put the bowl down on the floor beside him and looked around at the group of clanspeople who'd now assembled.

"Before ye tell us why ye're here, are ye wanting to change out of yon stupit outfit?" Kenneth asked. "I'm thinking ye'll no' be as prickly if ye do."

This last caused everyone to start laughing, as it summed up perfectly not only Angus's mood but the intense itchiness of most of his body. He closed his eyes for a moment, trying to see the funny side as he normally would, and in doing so realised just how bone-weary he was. This good-natured ribbing was part of what he had missed whilst he was in London. He should be giving as good as he got.

"I'm sorry," he said. "I'm awfu' tired, and a wee bit fashed, as Janet said. No' because there's anything amiss," he added quickly, seeing the change of expression on his audience's face. "I'll away home and change my clothing."

He returned a few minutes later, feeling better now he had given himself a telling-off, and had resolved to forget the last weeks, starting from when he was seasick and ending with his skid down the mountain. He also felt more himself now he was clothed in the soft warm wool of his *fèileadh mór*.

He sat then and explained the reason why he was here, omitting the fact that he had replaced Iain, who was now hopefully helping to load the boat that would sail to Scotland, if it was not already on the way.

"Yon Foley man, the smugglers' chieftain, tellt me they'd be landing near Burghead about three weeks after they left Kent, but he wasna certain, for there were a number of things that could delay them, the weather for one. That was two weeks ago, so I'm thinking we should be there beforehand, for when they sail in they'll no' be wanting to have to wait for us," Angus said.

"Where's Burghead?" Peigi asked.

"I'm thinking it's on Clan Grant's land," Alasdair said. "Is it no' near Elgin?"

"Aye, that's what Foley tellt me," Angus agreed. "He said it's a wee spit of land on the coast, but that there are a couple of other good places to land to the east of it, one wi' two caves, one of them a big one we could shelter in while we're waiting. I'm thinking that's the most likely place they'll land."

"Your da went to a gathering once wi' the Grants, where they talked about joining wi' the MacGregors," Kenneth said. "It didna come to be, though."

"Did the Grants no' fight for James in the '15?" Rory asked.

"They fought on both sides. The Highland Regiment has a lot of Grants in it, and they fight for the Elector," Alasdair said, who had fought in every Jacobite battle so far, including the first one at Killiecrankie in 1689, and was considered an authority on the subject. "But in fairness, a good number of clans fought on both sides, so whichever side won they could claim to support them."

"Is that no' a traitorous thing to do?" Angus asked, shocked.

"There's those who would say so, aye," Alasdair replied. "But no' every clan is like the MacGregors, laddie. We've nothing to lose. Many clans have lands, castles, fortunes. That makes a man think before he draws his sword for what could be a lost cause."

"It doesna seem honourable to me," Angus said.

"No, it isna. But it could seem sensible. A chief has to care for his clan. They would say they were doing that, and it would be hard to argue wi' their reasoning."

"So we'll need to be leaving the morrow?" Simon put in before Angus could argue with this, which he was clearly about to do. Alasdair was a vast source of useful information, but, being too old and infirm to fight now, was only too eager to enter into lengthy discourses, which could be very interesting when there wasn't something even more interesting beckoning on the northeast coastline.

"Aye, if we can," Angus said. He just needed one good night's sleep and another bowl of Janet's wonderful broth and he'd be ready to prove to his brothers, and to the other clansmen who'd seen him puking like a wee bairn, that he was worthy to be the chieftain's brother after all.

CHAPTER NINE

That evening the men prepared themselves, making sure that any urgent tasks or repairs the women couldn't do were done, and that their weapons were sharp. They did not expect to have to fight, but they were Highlanders and fighting was just a part of life. It was unlikely that they'd be challenged by any clans through whose lands they passed, providing they kept away from actual settlements, but it always paid to be battle-ready, just in case.

None of them had ever been to Burghead before, nor had they ever had direct dealings with smugglers, so this was an exciting adventure and cause for a good deal of conversation in the various homes in which preparations were being made. The women made bannocks and prepared bags of oatmeal, the children asked a million questions and got in the way, and then the families settled down to an evening of sitting by their hearths talking about what it might be like, compared to previous adventures. Once the children were asleep their parents could engage in a more intimate activity, made sweeter by the knowledge that they would not see each other after tonight for a few weeks.

It was in the main very pleasant, the men eager to be doing something active at the end of a long inactive winter and to be seeing their chieftain again after so many months of absence, the women glad that the restless men would be out from under their feet for a while, and on a peaceful excursion that almost certainly guaranteed they would all return home uninjured.

Only one house was an exception to this.

When Kenneth arrived home his wife was not there and had clearly not been there for some time, as the room was cold and unwelcoming. He coaxed the embers of the fire back to life, then, while he waited for a flat stone to grow hot enough to make oatcakes on, he did as the other men were doing; checked his weapons and packed the few useful items he might need on the journey. Then he sat down by the fire, melting butter and mixing oatmeal with water, before making himself a number of oatcakes.

It was while he was finishing these that his wife Jeannie finally returned, looking somewhat dishevelled, her wavy black hair tousled, her cheeks flushed.

"Ye didna need to make those," she said. "There's a broth ready. It just needs heating."

"Where have ye been, lassie?" he asked, looking up at her. "Ye've been gone for hours."

"I've been walking," she said, flushing crimson. "I often go walking, ye ken that."

"Aye, but no' when it's raining and there's chores to be done," he responded calmly.

"It didna rain for long," she retorted hotly. "And I'm sick of doing chores in this wee hovel. I canna keep it clean. It's dirty again before I've finished."

He almost pointed out that the other women seemed to have no such difficulty. But he was tired of arguments, so very tired. And she was so good at starting them. *No,* he thought, *no' the night.*

"Angus is home," he said instead. "He brought news of Alex."

"Did he?" she replied, taking off her arisaid and hanging it on a hook on the door. "What news is that? Is something amiss?"

He told her Angus's news then, about the men rowing to France, about the ship coming back with weapons.

"So we need to leave the morrow, for we dinna ken when they'll land, or exactly where Burghead is, only that it's near Elgin. It's a good way though," he said. "There's a beach wi' two caves on it nearby, Angus said, and that's where they'll likely come in."

Jeannie sat down on a stool and held her hands out to the fire to warm them. She had mud on the back of her skirt, as though she'd been sitting on the wet ground.

"And ye're going? Even though it's still winter, and ye dinna ken where the place is?" she asked. "Just because Alex has a fancy to sail the seas and visit France?"

Kenneth sat on the floor then, forgetting his latest oatcake, and looked at her, shocked.

"Aye, of course I am," he replied. "He isna just visiting France, he's bringing weapons back for us. And he's my chieftain. What d'ye expect me to do? What's amiss wi' ye?"

"There's nothing amiss wi' *me*," she spat back, refusing to meet his eye. "I'm thinking there's something amiss wi' you, though. Look at yourself! There isna a man in the clan ye couldna kill in a moment, wi' your bare hands. Everyone kens that!"

This was indeed true, and everyone did know that. Kenneth was head and shoulders taller than the tallest man, and broad, with the strength to match his size.

"Why in hell would I want to kill MacGregors?" he asked, truly perplexed.

"I dinna expect ye to kill them. But when I married ye, I did expect that ye'd challenge Alex one day. Ye taught him everything he kens about fighting, ye were like a da to him too. Ye're the only man who *could* challenge him. I've no notion why ye havena thought to. Then I could have a home wi' a stone floor, and a real hearth wi' a chimney instead of a fire in the middle of the room."

"Jeannie, we've been married for seven years and in all that time ye've never mentioned that ye wanted me to challenge Alex," Kenneth said. "If ye're fashed about something and saying such a stupit thing to start an argument, I'm no' in the mood for it."

"I'm no' saying it for that!" she shouted, although her expression made it clear she was. "And it isna stupit! I mind well when ye almost challenged his da. We all do! D'ye no' think the clan's waiting for ye to challenge his son? Everyone thinks ye're a coward because ye havena! Everyone *kens* ye're a coward, for what other reason could ye have for running after him like a wee bairn? For no' wanting to be chieftain yourself?"

In spite of his resolution to stay calm no matter what she said, he flushed at this insult. He would have killed any man who called him a coward, without a moment's regret. But this was not a man. This was a woman, the woman he called wife. The woman he loved, God help him.

"I thought ye'd ken this, as clever as ye are. There's a lot more to being a chieftain than fighting," he said after a few seconds of reining in his temper, something he was an expert at doing. "Alex is a good chieftain, as was his da before him. He can inspire loyalty, make good plans, for battle or reiving, think of all the possible problems and how to overcome them if they happen. He's caring, and he provides for us all. We couldna wish for a better man to lead us."

"He isna leading us!" Jeannie cried. "We havena seen him for over a year now. What manner of chieftain is that?"

"One who's fighting to get the proscription raised on the MacGregors. I couldna do that, lassie. I dinna *want* to do it, and even if I did, and I killed Alex, the men wouldna follow me, and they'd be right no' to. Surely ye ken that?" What the hell was wrong with her? She'd been restless for a couple of months now and increasingly hostile to him, but this…this was ridiculous.

"Aye, well, maybe ye're right. After all, a chieftain's expected to have bairns to carry on after he's gone and ye're no' even man enough to manage that, are ye? Christ, if I'd kent what ye were really like, I never would have agreed to marry ye when ye asked me," she said coldly. "We'll be too old soon to even hope for a bairn."

Kenneth closed his eyes for a moment, not wanting her to see how much she was hurting him with her vicious comments. Neither of them knew why she had not conceived in seven years of marriage. If a woman could not have children the general view was that it was her fault, but in the past, when there had been affection between them, he had comforted her when her monthly bleeds had come, had told her that she mustn't blame herself, that it could be something with him, or just God's will, which it wasn't their right to question. Never for one moment had he blamed her for the lack of the children he so desperately wanted.

"Jeannie, I dinna ken why your womb hasna quickened yet, but ye're twenty-five. We've many years ahead of us to have bairns, if we keep trying."

"I wasna talking about me, but you," she shot back. "I shouldna have married an old man. Ye tellt me no' to, and ye were right. Ye didna tell me ye were a coward and no' capable of doing your duty, though. All I can look forward to now is years of barrenness and then having to care for ye in your dotage. Christ!"

It was hopeless. She wanted a fight, he did not. So he stood and left the house, closing the door quietly on her insults, and went down to the lochside to think for a while, hoping she would calm down if left alone. He sat down on the rock near the water, staring out over the loch, feeling the tears prickle in his eyes.

How had it come to this? What had he done to make her hate him so? Every instinct told him that it was not because of the lack of children. She had never shown any interest in having them. It was him who had always loved children, had looked after all the clan's little ones from being hardly more than a child himself. Nor was it because she had expected him to challenge Alex. Alex was the best chieftain they'd ever had. The whole clan were happy with him.

No, there was something else, something that had happened in the last months to suddenly turn her against him. But she would not tell him, and he could do nothing to amend his ways unless she did.

So he sighed, and sat, and looked out over the water until it grew dark, and then he stood and made his reluctant way home, hoping she would have calmed enough for the evening to be at least bearable.

But when he arrived she had gone out again. Normally he would have been concerned, for the wind was icy and it had started to rain again. But he was too heartsore for that. She knew the land, and there were no enemies around. The redcoats at Inversnaid would not budge until the snow melted on the mountains surrounding their garrison. He coaxed the fire back to life again, then set about preparing more oatcakes. She would come home when she was too cold or wet to stay out.

* * *

"Christ, woman, don't ever sneak up on a man like that!" Harold said, after having squealed loudly enough to startle his horse. "I could have killed you!"

"I'm sorry," the woman replied, aware that in fact he had been in more danger than she was, for in spite of the fact that rather than sneaking up on him she had made no effort to tread quietly, he hadn't heard her until she was right behind him and spoke. Any Highlander, including herself, could have driven a dirk between his ribs without him being aware of their approach.

It would not be politic to point that out, though, not when she wanted something from him.

"What are you doing here, anyway? I would have been on my

way back to barracks if Caspar hadn't got a stone in his hoof," Harold continued.

"I tellt ye we couldna meet for a while now, for although my husband's a loon, he's starting to wonder why I'm away so much. But he tellt me tonight that he's away to a place called Burghead the morrow, wi' some of the other men. He'll be gone for a good while, I'm thinking, so we could meet whenever ye'd like!"

She smiled, and reaching up stroked his cheek gently, her eyes sparkling at the prospect of him making love to her again. Or fucking her, as he thought of it, although he didn't tell her that, of course. She was the one thing keeping him from insanity at the moment, bored as he was with endless days of barracks routine and evenings of soldiers' tales and card-playing, with not a whore in sight. Meeting this one had been a blessing. And such a pretty one, too. Worth stringing along, at least for now.

"How long is a good while?" he asked. "It's not easy to get out of the place without being noticed, you know. If I'm seen, then I'll not be able to meet you at all."

"I'm thinking at least two, maybe three weeks," she said. "He tellt me that Burghead's away up on the coast, near a place called Elgin, and there are two caves on the beach nearby that they can all shelter in while they're waiting on the ship. So he'll likely be waiting there a while, too."

"A ship?" Harold said, interested now. So it was not some petty thievery they were planning, or attacking another group of savages. Was the Pretender landing? My God, if he was, being able to give information like that could promote him to the stars!

Impulsively he embraced her, kissing her soundly, waiting until she softened in his arms.

"Are you cold?" he asked softly. "Shall we find a way to be warm?"

She laughed then, a beautiful silvery laugh.

"Are ye able?" she asked. "It isna so long since ye spent yourself inside me."

"Of course I am!" he snorted. "I'm not like that old man you're married to! I'm in the prime of my life. Here, let's put the blanket down again. It'll be warm from the horse too."

He busied himself pulling out the blanket he'd brought with him for their earlier meeting, laying it out on the ground under the trees, wondering how to approach the subject of the ship without arousing her suspicions. He'd fuck her first, and then ask her while she was still breathless.

He had not been lying about being capable. He *was* young and virile, and even though she was a savage's whore, she was very beautiful, and like most beautiful women just needed to be told she was, to be reassured that he loved her, that he would one day take her away from all this. Then she would let him do almost anything to her.

Her husband was most likely a gnarled, vermin-ridden, toothless thing, riddled with rheumatics, Harold thought. He was not too worried about the man coming upon them, although she seemed to be. He'd probably bored her with so many stories of his prowess fifty years ago that she actually believed he was still a threat.

Dismissing husbands and ships from his mind for a while, Harold focussed on enjoying his unexpected second helping of a very good thing. God, but she was lovely! The moment he pulled her breasts out from under her stays, felt the firm roundness of them, bent his head to her perfect nipple, he was hard as a rock.

"Aye, that's it," she gasped. "Dinna be gentle. He'll be gone in the morn, so he willna see if ye mark me a wee bit. I'm sick o' being treated like glass."

He needed no second telling, suckling harder on her nipple, then at the white firmness of her breast, bruising her as he abandoned his usual caution, feeling her stiffen and moan with mingled pain and pleasure.

And then he was reaching under her skirts, feeling how wet she was, the wanton bitch, and releasing his penis from his breeches he plunged into her without warning, causing her to arch under him in surprise. And then they both forgot everything but the rising tide of passion as he hammered into her, far more roughly than he normally did, almost as roughly as he would a genuine whore, one he'd paid for.

She seemed to like it, for she writhed under him, wrapping her legs around his body to pull him further into her. And then she cried out, and he felt his seed explode inside her.

Once he was done, he started to think again, holding her as the last of her orgasm shuddered through her.

"Is your husband sailing away on this ship, then?" he asked, when she seemed capable of listening again.

"Why d'ye ask?" she said breathlessly.

"I think you enjoyed that. I did. It was wonderful, being able to show you how much I love you, treat you as a beautiful woman should be treated, with passion. If your husband's sailing away, he'll be gone for a long time, and we can have many hours like this together."

It was all empty flattery, although he had enjoyed not having to be careful with her body. And he would enjoy another few sessions of hard fucking like that if he could. And then hopefully he'd be relieved of his duty in this Godforsaken place.

"Ah. No, the ship's bringing in swords and muskets, and maybe other things, I dinna ken. Kenneth'll be helping them unload and then bringing them back here. Well, to Stronmelochan, anyway. There's a wee cave there where they'll be storing them. So he'll no' be away for months. Christ, I wish he was! I'm tingling all over. Ye're awfu' good at the lovemaking!"

"It's a joy to be with such a lovely woman. How could I not be good!" he said automatically. Where the hell was Stronmelochan? Where was Burghead for that matter? The colonel would know. He needed to get back, to tell him. It was a shame it was not the Pretender, but even so…

"Are the swords and suchlike from Louis?" he asked.

"Louis? I dinna ken who they're from," she replied. "Who's Louis?"

"Er…a French swordmaker," Harold lied, seeing the suspicious expression on her face. "The French make the finest swords, and Louis' are the finest of them all. I would give my left arm to own such a sword!"

"Ah. I'm sorry, man. I willna see them at all. So will we meet again, while he's away?"

"I'd love to, if I can. I wish we could meet in a warm room with a fire and a bed, though," he said.

"Ye could take me with ye while he's away," she said impulsively. "I could marry ye, and look after ye in the garrison. He willna ken where I am. Then we could do this every night. Would that no' be a wondrous thing! And if ye're sent home to England, I'd go wi' ye. I've never seen England, but I'm tellt it's a fine place, wi' big houses wi' clear glass in the windows and fires wi' chimneys, so the black doesna fall on ye when it's wet! And tiles on the floors too instead of dirt! Oh, that would be fine," she said dreamily, while he was wondering what the hell she was talking about. Dirt floors? Black falling on you? What sort of hovel did she live in? He shuddered at the thought of taking such a creature home to his parents. His father would have an apoplexy! Had he told her he would? He might have done. He had promised her all sorts of nonsense.

"I would love that, sweeting," he said. "But we're not allowed to marry, and there are no women in the garrison. It would be too tempting for the men. And a woman as lovely as you…no. You wouldn't be safe there, and I couldn't bear it if anything happened to you! And you're married already."

"Well, aye. But I wouldna tell anyone that, and no one would ken, would they? I wasna married to Kenneth in a church, ye ken, nor even by a priest. So I'm thinking the pope wouldna consider it a true marriage," she commented. "I so want to live where I can have bonny gowns and ribbons in my hair, and go to see a play. Could we no' do that?"

Hell, she was a Papist! His father would definitely have an apoplexy!

"Not while I'm at the garrison," Harold said. "But we can have fun while your old husband's away. And then when I *do* go back to England," he added hastily, seeing the sulky expression forming on her face, "I'll take you with me, of course I will. That would be the safest thing, for you to leave when the whole regiment goes. Your husband wouldn't dare to stop you then! You'd be safe."

The sulk was transformed to a smile, to his relief.

"And would ye buy me a bonny gown then?" she asked.

"I'll buy you ten gowns, in silk, all in different colours, and to hell with ribbons for your hair. Only jewels will do for you! Emeralds, rubies, sapphires. They'll sparkle in those beautiful tresses, and every man will be jealous because I have such a lovely wife!" he enthused, meaning not one word of it. "But I need to go now, sweeting, and so do you, for it'll be dark soon and my colonel won't let me out of barracks for a month if he finds I'm missing. I'll try to come again in a few days."

She flung her arms around his neck and kissed him joyfully. And then she stood, helping him to fold the blanket, her lovely grey eyes sparkling with happiness, her cheeks still rosy from their lovemaking.

"I'll come here every day when the sun's high, until ye come," she said. "Oh, I'm so happy!"

She waited until he'd fastened his red military coat, until he mounted the horse, and then she melted away into the trees, turning back once as she always did, to blow him a kiss. Dutifully, he blew one back.

And then he forgot all about his ridiculous promises, all about her, except for the information she'd given him, and rode hell for leather back to the garrison. He needed to see his colonel, and tonight.

* * *

The men rose early the following morning, while it was still dark. The women and children rose too, gathering outside to see their menfolk leave. They hugged, kissed their children, listened to and gave words of advice, promised they'd take care.

Jeannie stayed in bed, her back firmly turned to Kenneth, pretending to be asleep when he told her he was leaving now. He sighed, and when he had finally gone she opened her eyes, turning on to her back and looking up at the soot-blackened roof, smiling as she contemplated what it would be like to wake up under a white plaster ceiling with a beautiful sparkly chandelier over her bed, next to a handsome soldier.

Seeing Kenneth come out of his house alone Peigi went back into hers, emerging a moment later with an extra bag of food, which she gave to her husband.

"Here," she said softly. "I'm sure that wee besom hasna made anything for Kenneth. If she hasna, tell him I gave ye too much and share it wi' him. She doesna deserve him."

"He doesna talk about what happens," Alasdair Og said, slightly awkwardly.

"Aye, I ken him well. He willna. And if he did ye wouldna tell me, which is as it should be. She'll regret it one day. He's a fine man."

"Are ye thinking of having him yerself one day?" Alasdair Og asked jokingly.

"Och, away wi' ye, man! I'm accustomed to ye now," she said, grinning. "He wouldna ask me anyway, wouldna ask any woman. She's the only woman for him. Damn loon."

Whether this last comment was directed at Kenneth or Jeannie, Alasdair Og didn't know, and didn't ask, because the men now started to say farewell to their women and prepare to leave, and he didn't want to waste his last precious moments talking about someone else's unhappy marriage, when he had a perfectly happy one of his own.

So he swept her off her feet, making her giggle, and kissed her.

And then they all left, heading down to the lochside before turning north.

CHAPTER TEN

Inversnaid Garrison, Scotland

"Are you mad?" Colonel Walker said to the somewhat dishevelled but very eager soldier standing in front of him. "When you said you wanted to see me on a matter of the utmost urgency, I thought you had news of an imminent attack on the garrison, not a ridiculous rumour! Where the hell did you hear it, anyway? What have you been up to?"

Private Morrison flushed.

"It was told to me in confidence, sir," he said, "so I can't divulge the identity of my informant. But it's very reliable."

The colonel looked at him with deep scepticism.

"So you're telling me that a 'reliable' informer wandered up to the garrison today without anyone else seeing them, just to inform you alone out of the goodness of their heart that a ship is landing on some uncertain date hundreds of miles away, with smuggled swords on board, and you expect me not only to believe that, but to send the whole garrison galloping off to capture them, leaving us unprotected? Come on man, think. Even if I believed you, which I don't, do you think I'd walk into such an obvious trap?"

Private Morrison thought about this. The colonel had a point, but if he was to tell him the real circumstances in which he'd gained the information, he'd be disciplined for sneaking out of barracks without permission, which would hardly further the promotion he was so desperate to attain.

"If you're wondering how to tell me you've been sneaking out at night to meet some doxy, don't bother. You're not the only man who does it," the colonel finally said, somewhat wearily. "I'm human. I understand how bored you all are. If I *catch* you doing it that'll be another matter, you understand. But if this is an attempt to empty the garrison to ambush it or the men leaving it for the 'sword ship', then I need to know who told you this rumour, because if we don't fall for this, they'll try to attack us in some other way. Come on man, out with it."

Private Morrison cursed silently. He should have thought this through before he approached his commanding officer. He'd been so eager to win glory for himself, so aware that if he was to succeed they needed to move fast, that he'd just assumed Colonel Walker would accept his story about meeting a man at the gates. Now he had to either abandon his dream or tell the truth and risk a flogging.

To hell with it. Nothing ventured, nothing gained.

He told the colonel about the woman he'd been meeting, about how infatuated with him she was, and the reason why she'd told him about the ship coming in at Elgin, wherever that was. The colonel listened, and then looked studious for a minute, which raised Harold Morrison's hopes that he was finally taking him seriously.

"The woman's name?" the colonel asked.

"Name? Er…Jeannie, sir," Harold replied. Why did her name matter?

"No, her surname, you fool," the colonel snapped.

"I don't know, sir. I didn't think that was important," Harold said, confused.

"You have been garrisoned at Inversnaid for three months, and you still don't know that we are surrounded by mobs of savages who are allied by their surname? Their clan name? Dear God," the colonel muttered under his breath. "The surname of this whore you've been swiving and sweet talking is crucial, man! It would tell me whether she belongs to a loyal or a rebel clan!"

"Ah. I didn't think of that, sir," Harold said shamefacedly.

"No, of course you didn't," Colonel Walker replied contemptuously.

"But is it not treason to smuggle any weapons into the country, sir? No matter which mob you belong to?" Harold ventured hopefully.

"It is. But if it's the Campbells doing it, for example, then we would be expected to turn a blind eye to it, for most of them are loyal to the king and are willing to ride out at a moment's notice to fight traitors like the Camerons or MacGregors, for example. Where did you meet her? Did she tell you where she lives?"

"No, sir. But she goes back towards the lake over there," he pointed. "Lomond, is it?"

Hmm. She could be MacGregor then. Or Buchanan, or Stewart.

"Elgin, you say?"

"Near Elgin. She said Burghead, a beach with two caves near there."

"Right. You're dismissed. Clean yourself up man, and let me think. Come back in an hour."

When the idiot had gone, Colonel Walker thought. The men were very bored and it was growing increasingly difficult to keep them in order. Floggings had increased as a result, and morale was dropping. That was why he had turned a blind eye to the men sneaking out to meet with whores or to try their hand at hunting in the local area. The colonel was in a difficult position. He was expected to keep strict order, but the men were soldiers and wanted to fight. If they had no enemy to attack and nothing to do, they would eventually attack each other. Which was now starting to happen. The last thing he wanted was a mutiny, which would reflect very badly on him.

He had been told not to antagonise the clans by attacking anyone unless absolutely necessary, but the damn Highlanders had been quiet all winter. Also the unscrupulous bastards had no idea of loyalty and would band together with rival clans at a moment's notice to attack redcoats, given a reason to. He dared not give them a reason by attacking them without provocation.

So. This could actually work in his favour, as flimsy as the evidence was. Elgin was on the other side of the country, so if it *was* the Campbells or the Gordons or some other huge clan smuggling in guns, he needed to be able to claim any attack on them was nothing to do with him. And if it was the MacGregors or some other rebel clan and his men were successful, he could claim the credit. At the least it would burn off their destructive energy and give them some experience of combat, or of what it was like to march through this horrendous country.

He thought some more, until Private Morrison reappeared, his boots polished, his uniform brushed to get rid of the mud that had adorned it previously.

"Right, Private. I've considered this, and I've decided that it's certainly worth investigating this treasonous shipment. It's likely this doxy is telling you the truth. But we cannot do this openly, you understand."

"We cannot?" Private Morrison asked.

"No. Because if it *is* a friendly clan, or a large clan, and it's known that we've attacked them, we could end up with thousands of enraged savages besieging us. We're here to keep order, as I'm sure you know, not provoke unrest. So I'm thinking to grant you and say, thirty other men, some leave. What you do on that leave is your own affair. If you're successful, then I will be most grateful, and will of course see that you're suitably rewarded for your initiative and bravery. If you're *not* successful for any of the reasons I've stated, or any other, then we'll say no more about it and you will not be disciplined in any way. It will of course give you valuable experience, which I'm sure will help you to shine in future battles, which I know you wish to do, an ambitious young man like yourself. I'm sure you will go far, and this cannot harm you," the colonel lied fluently.

Morrison flushed with pleasure.

"I won't let you down, sir, I promise!" he cried. "Who will go with me?"

"You can start proving yourself here," the colonel said. "See who wishes to go with you, and bring me a list. If there are more than thirty, I will choose who is to be left behind."

Once the idiot had gone, the colonel sat back. It was certain that only the most reckless, foolish soldiers would want to embark on such a venture. And with the troublemakers out of the way for weeks, he would get some much-needed peace. And in truth, if they never came back it would be no great loss.

* * *

Calais, France

In the end the swords did not arrive the next day, or the day after that. Or even that week. Or the next. While Gabriel fumed and tried to discover the cause of the delay, the smugglers, accustomed to such things, enjoyed themselves drinking, playing dice and cards and spending time in the huge choice of brothels that could always be found in a port.

To their combined astonishment and amusement, only two of the Highlanders would accompany them on their sexual excursions, the others all saying they preferred to either stay in the tavern or explore the town or countryside around it.

"I know you're all Papists, with you going to church and all on Sundays, but you're not monks, are you? Do Papists all take a vow of celibacy?" Paul, one of the smuggler gang asked. All the Highlanders liked him because he was a great source of amusing or fascinating stories, but one of the reasons for that was because he was genuinely interested in everything and asked endless questions. Which could be awkward if you were trying to reveal as little about yourself as possible.

"Ye do an' you value your marriage," Dougal said.

"Aye, and if ye value the equipment God gave ye, if your wife finds out," Simon added, to laughter.

"But your wives won't find out, will they?" Paul said. "Not unless you tell them."

"Have you ever had the French pox?" Alex asked.

"No," Paul replied. "I don't go with cheap whores."

Alex snorted.

"That doesna signify at all, man," he said. "Rich men get the pox just as poor men do. It's no' poverty that gives ye the clap, man. The more women ye swive, the more chance ye have to get it. And rich men can afford to have a whore every night if they want. And whores have to swive hundreds of men, for it's how they earn a living. It's a matter of time, no' money, an' ye go wi' whores regularly."

A short silence followed this sombre announcement.

"It's no' about our wives finding out, it's about respecting them. If ye love a woman, ye'll be faithful to her. And ye willna risk her life, just for a wee bit of pleasure," Duncan added softly, seriously.

Half the men in the room immediately looked uncomfortable, which told the observant Alex exactly who was married and who wasn't.

"Aye, and I wouldna risk my life for it either," Dougal said. "For she'd castrate me an' I gave her the pox as a present from France!"

This comment lightened the atmosphere, as Dougal had intended it to, and the men who were going prepared to leave, polishing their shoes with their sleeves and smoothing down their hair.

"You can buy a condom if you don't want to give the pox to your wives, or catch it yourself," Gabriel put in as they all headed for the door. "You all know that, if you've been with me for any length of time. Abernathy is right. You might want to think on it."

The uncomfortable atmosphere returned and the men, ready or not, left hurriedly.

"They willna think on it," Alex observed. "Yon things are no' cheap. Ye could buy a whore for the cost of one. I've used them myself in the past."

"You have? Is it true they take away the pleasure?" Michael, one of the few smugglers who'd stayed behind asked.

"Aye, a wee bit. But what ye lose in the sensation, ye gain in knowing ye're no' going to die of the pox."

"Or die of the mercury cure," Gabriel said, and shuddered. "My…an acquaintance of mine died of that. The physician said it was the pox, but he just had a chancre and his hair fell out, no more. The physician told him it could be easily cured with his medicines. Paid a fortune for them, he did. When he started having spasms and lost his sense of smell, I told him to stop, but he was so terrified of his family finding out, he ignored me. He died soon after. I'm sure it was the cure that killed him, because I've known lots of men with the pox in my time, and it doesn't kill that quickly, or that way."

"Is that why ye tell your men to buy condoms?" Duncan asked.

"Yes," Gabriel said. "He was a close acquaintance." He wiped his hand across his face, the first sign of true emotion Alex had seen in this normally tightly controlled man.

"I'm sorry," he said.

Gabriel nodded.

"I'm fair in my dealings with the men," he said. "If they're injured while working for me, I'll make sure they don't starve until they heal. If they can't work again I'll pay them enough for them to survive on, and their families, if they have one. That's why I thought so well of you, Abernathy, when you came to me over White, for it seems you have the same way of thinking. But I'll not pay a penny if they get the pox. I've told them that, and I mean it."

"But they dinna listen to ye," Duncan said.

"That's their concern. They all know I'm a man of my word. Some of them do. Others live for the moment, because a smuggler's life is dangerous and we're not known for making old bones."

"I didna think it was so dangerous," Dougal said. "Did ye no' say that everyone is involved, and so ye're no' likely to be convicted?"

"I did. But there are risks at sea, the weather and the navy sinking you, risks of being peached on, particularly if you're a member of a known gang. If you're caught and you're a gang leader or a known smuggler, they'll try you in London, or another place where they know the judge and jurymen won't be sympathetic to you. And then there are the other gangs, who want to take your area. I'm sure as Highlanders you have a lot of dangers that I wouldn't think of. It's the same for us."

"Aye, I can see that," Alex said. "But if I'm going to die young, I'd prefer to do it wi' a sword in my hand than from a pox. I dinna see the sense in adding another danger to the ones ye already face, when it's avoidable."

Gabriel laughed.

"I agree. I think all of us here do. The ones we need to convince have just gone out to court that danger. So, I've been told the swords will finally be here in two days. That suits me, because your men need time to get to Burghead from wherever they are, and Jim needed to ride to wherever they are to tell them. So I'm thinking that would be three weeks, maybe, depending on the weather?" he asked.

"The weather wouldna signify. No' in March. But aye, three weeks would make sure they're waiting on us," he said. "They'll wait as long as they need to."

"Good. So as soon as the weapons arrive you can examine them, make sure you're happy with them, although I've never had a complaint about the smiths' work. I think you'll believe they're worth the wait," Gabriel said.

"Aye. Our lives might depend on it one day," Alex replied.

"True," Gabriel agreed. "So we'll load everything onto the ship, which should take us a day, and then, weather permitting, we'll leave immediately. When we load, I'll tell you all about the ship and what you'll be doing on board, as none of you are sailors. There'll still be plenty you can do though. It's easier to explain when we're actually on the ship than sitting here."

"It'll be good to be doing something," Duncan said. "I've seen all I want to of Calais now. I'm ready to leave."

"Aye, me too," Iain agreed. "It's a bonny town though. But I'm missing M…my wife," he amended, making his slip sound like a stammer.

"I am too," Dougal agreed.

* * *

They were a strange crowd, Gabriel thought later, when everyone else was in bed and he was running through the logistics of the operation in his mind, something he did on every trip. He never committed anything to paper, because paper could be used as evidence against you, but no one could use your memory against you unless you allowed them to.

It was clear to him that Abernathy or whatever his name was, was the men's leader, for they looked to him for everything. Did that make him the chief of whatever clan they were? And Gabriel would wager his ship that the seasick youth Jim was Abernathy's brother, because they looked so alike.

They were clearly all hard men, hard-working, expert in weapons, ruthless, and would not hesitate to kill if necessary. They were all loyal too, to Abernathy and each other, and Gabriel would also wager that they were trustworthy. In the weeks they had been together, none of them had asked one question that was not necessary, that was prying for information they didn't need to know.

And yet, as hard and ruthless as they were, they were open about feelings that most men would never admit –to missing their wives, to loving their bairns, as they called their children. They would weep unashamedly on hearing a sad song, recite poetry with real feeling.

He realised that he had never felt as relaxed about a venture as he did with this group of strangers. He had not expected that, had expected the opposite in fact, to be tense and watchful the whole time, waiting for them to turn on him, waiting for Abernathy to maybe challenge him for the leadership, or at least to question him continuously in an attempt to maintain his authority as a leader.

But he hadn't, not once. Because he had no need to. He had utmost confidence in his men, in their loyalty to him and in his ability to lead them. He had no need to strut around proving his superiority, because he did not feel inferior and so had nothing to prove.

What was more, he respected Gabriel as an equal, as a man who felt exactly the same way.

Which Gabriel Foley took as a great compliment, because he both admired and respected this Abernathy man enormously, and would be happy to work with him at any time.

Abernathy could be a friend, he thought, *if I wanted such a thing.*

However, he did *not* want such a thing, had not wanted such a thing since he had been betrayed by a so-called friend, many years ago. He would never have a friend, not while he worked in the free trade at any rate.

I'm growing soft, he told himself, *wanting friends. Better alone. Safer alone.*

He drained his tankard then and stood, extinguishing the candle and his sentimental yearnings, and went to bed.

CHAPTER ELEVEN

Scotland

Now he was with the other clansmen, Angus enjoyed the next part of this adventure, his natural optimism and good humour returning almost immediately. The loneliness and tension of the ride through England were now replaced by a conviction that he'd done the right thing in relieving the fool Highmore of his gold. When the man had time to think he might even consider the crucial lesson he'd learnt worth the loss of his money, for it would certainly have been lost anyway, probably along with its owner's life.

Yes, it had been a good thing to do, both for his victim and for the clan. However, Angus knew his brother well enough to know that Alex would not see it that way —not until the clan were in desperate need of the money, anyway. It should be safe in the cave. He had hidden it in a place where it was unlikely to be discovered accidentally. All was well.

With that he forgot all about it and threw himself into the current venture with the other MacGregors, walking all day and sleeping under the stars at night after cooking whatever food they'd either brought with them, foraged or caught, and sharing stories of other trips, or making light-hearted fun of each other.

Although Kenneth, with his great sense of humour and easygoing nature would normally be a source of much good-humoured ribbing, for the first day at least he hadn't joined in any of the conversation, preferring instead to wrap himself in his *fèileadh mór* and sleep, or pretend to sleep, the moment the meal was over.

The men knew that Kenneth and Jeannie were not happy together, which was a surprise to everyone. Jeannie had always had a mind of her own, and had set herself on marrying Kenneth from being a small child, to the clan's amusement. She had worshipped him, and he had finally grown to love her too, passionately and tenderly. It had seemed a match made in Heaven. And in fact they *had* seemed truly happy together, until a few months ago.

No one had any idea what had happened to sour things between them, apart from the conspicuous lack of children. Given such a situation where one of them was hurting, the men would normally endeavour to comfort him in that indirect rough way men do, either talking about their own wives' annoyingly assertive behaviour, or making fun of women in general to encourage him to do the same and lighten his mood.

But you could not do that with Kenneth. If anyone said even the slightest word against his wife, he would go for them. No matter how she behaved, he would not tolerate anyone saying anything against her. And as no sane person would risk a man of Kenneth's size going for them, no one said anything, showing their consideration instead by talking about any topic that did not include the female sex.

The following day he seemed to have shaken much of his moroseness off, and laughed and joked with them as normal, although an observant man would have noticed that his smile did not reach his eyes. Relieved, they all lapsed into normal behaviour, although wisely did not mention his marital issues.

Back at Loch Lomond, the clanswomen had no such reservations. Far from standing in solidarity with their sister, while they were washing clothing down by the loch the next day they all made it clear to her, both in words and behaviour, that they thought she did not deserve such a wonderful man.

"What the hell's happened to ye?" Janet asked, who was the same age as Jeannie and had been her childhood companion. "Ye never had eyes for anyone except Kenneth, and he was a good catch for ye, for any woman."

"Ye're wanting him for yourself, are ye?" Jeannie shot back, instantly defensive, which told Janet that she knew she was in the wrong.

"Ah, no, ye'll no' bait me that easy, lassie," Janet replied calmly. "But I'll tell ye this. If I *had* married him, I'd love and respect him, for he adores ye, and he deserves to be loved as much as any man, and more than some."

"Which is more than can be said for you, at the minute," Peigi, who was wringing out a sheet nearby, put in.

Jeannie flushed scarlet, opened her mouth to retaliate, and then closed it again. Instead she stood up, heedless that the shift she was washing landed in the mud as a result.

"Ye'd never understand," she said. "Ye'll be happy just to live here your whole lives, owning only one dress, working yourself to death, never seeing anything outside this wee bit of land. Ye're too stupit to dream of more. I've the reading, and the writing. I'm wanting more than this."

"We've *all* got the reading and the writing, thanks to Alexander," Peigi retorted. "Ye had that before ye married Kenneth. That isna the reason, and we all ken it. Ye need to think on what ye've got, no' on what ye canna have."

Jeannie flushed even more scarlet at that.

"Who says I canna have it? Ye'll see, one day," she spat. Then she turned and marched away, kicking angrily at a clump of heather that had the temerity to be in her way.

Silence fell as the two women watched her go, stamping off into the distance.

"She's doing something she shouldna be," Peigi said finally.

"What kind of a thing?" Janet asked.

"I dinna ken. Yet. But she's away off walking most days, has been for a time now. I just thought she was restless, for she's always been fiery and impatient. I thought it was because she hadna quickened wi' a bairn, but I'm no' sure of that."

"Aye, well, there's one way to find out, and that's to follow her next time she's away," Janet said.

"Ye mean have one of the bairns follow her? Wee Rory could do it," Peigi suggested.

"No, I dinna want any of the bairns to see if she's doing something…something she shouldna be. My hut is close to hers. If wee Rory watches for her leaving and tells me directly, I'll follow her myself. I havena any bairns as you have, so it's better I go. If I find anything out I'll tell ye, and we can decide what to do then."

Peigi thought for a minute. It didn't seem right to spy on one of your own, somehow. But this was about Kenneth. Everyone loved Kenneth. There was nothing about him not to love. And he had been like a second father to all of them when they were small.

"Aye," she said. "That's a good idea."

* * *

The men made good time, mainly because they pushed themselves, reasoning that arriving early and then resting and waiting for Alex and the others would be a lot better than dawdling and arriving late. Because of that they arrived at Burghead in the early afternoon of the fourth day after leaving home.

Or at least they presumed it was Burghead.

"Iain tellt me there's an old fort of some kind, very old, just earthworks and some stone walls, and this seems such a place," Angus said. "And it was a promontory, which this is."

"Aye," replied Alasdair Og. "It's a good place for a fort, or a castle. Ye can see a long way, and ye can only be attacked frae one side."

Standing on the top of the hill, they all looked out across the sea, but primarily to the right, as that was where Alex's ship would sail in from, coming from France as it was. They could indeed see a long way, but there was no sign of a ship of any kind at all.

"Should we sleep here the night?" Rory asked. "The walls are shelter from the wind, and I dinna think we'll be disturbed. And if a ship comes in we'll see it in plenty of time."

"Aye. I've the dark lantern that Gabriel tellt me to bring. If we see him and light this, he'll see it for miles at night," Angus said.

"If it's night ye willna see the ship coming in, ye loon," Alasdair Og pointed out. "And if it's day he willna see your dark lantern."

Everyone laughed at this, including Angus.

"How will ye ken it's his ship and no' another?" Rory asked.

"I'm no' *that* stupit," Angus replied. "No' quite that stupit," he amended, seeing everyone preparing to question this. "He tellt me he'd fly a red flag from the top o' the mast, and a yellow one underneath it, so I'd ken it was him. For no other ship would do such a thing."

"I'm thinking we shouldna stay here," Kenneth, who had been

exploring the man-made mounds and walls, said. "No, I canna feel any ghosts. I never like to sleep at the top of a mountain, for though it's true I can see a long way, people can see me from a long way away, too."

"People can see ye from a long way away wherever ye are, man," Alasdair Og said, provoking more laughter.

"Aye, but I dinna want to spend the whole time on my knees to be the same height as ye all," Kenneth replied, grinning. "It'll no' be dark for a few hours. Shall we see if we can find yon cave ye mentioned?"

This was a good point.

"Is it a long way from here?" Alasdair Og asked.

"I dinna ken. Gabriel said it was a wee distance from the fort," Angus said. "To the right. It's in a golden rock, wi' another one next to it."

"Ah, well, if a Sasannach thinks it's a wee distance, I can likely piss on it frae here," Kenneth commented. "If we find it today, then we can rest and wait, for they'll be coming in at that wee bit of shore, will they no'?"

"Aye, I think so."

As there was no chieftain to decide, they took a vote on it, and then headed down the hill and along the shore, occasionally having to climb up to the gorse-covered cliffs to reach the next bay. It was a lovely day and felt almost like spring, the sun a little warm on their faces as they strolled along. Having walked a few miles without seeing anyone at all, they all started to relax a little, laughing and joking with each other, and gazing across the ocean every few minutes in search of a sail.

When they saw it, Angus knew at once that this was the cave Gabriel had referred to. It was indeed set in a golden rock, or rather a golden-coloured rock, with another adjacent to it that was more like a tunnel in the cliff face leading to the pebbly shore overlooking the sea. But also there was a fine sandy beach along the seafront, and the bay seemed wide enough to them to allow a ship to sail in and then land, after which it would only be visible from a very few points.

"This would be a good spot to rest for a few days, if necessary. There's a well no' so far back up yon hill, too. Is the water deep enough, d'ye think?" Alasdair Og asked Angus as they strolled along the sand towards the cave.

"I didna see the ship. I only rowed in the wee boat they went to Calais in. Ye could bring that in here. I havena a notion if a ship would make it. I'm thinking Gabriel will though. He does it all the time," Angus replied.

On reaching the cave however, they were all disappointed to discover that it wasn't satisfactory at all.

"I hope yon Gabriel man kens more about ships than he does caves," Alasdair Og observed.

In fairness, to most people it would have seemed ideal. It had a wide entrance, a reasonably flat sandy floor, and was deep enough to sleep all of them with plenty of room to spare. At the back it grew very narrow and was a dead end, unlike the other cave which was really just a short tunnel, open at both ends to any weather. It would provide good shelter only on a still day. The golden cave, as they all immediately named it, would give very good shelter, and as its floor was bone dry, it seemed unlikely that when the tide came in it would flood.

But these were Highlanders, and for Highlanders shelter from the weather was not their priority.

"I wouldna feel safe sleeping here," Kenneth said after they'd examined it and gone back outside to sit on the beach and eat a bannock, washed down with whisky. "I'd have felt safer sleeping at yon crumbling fort."

"Aye," Alasdair Og agreed. "Shame it isna like our cave at home. It's the opposite."

It was. Their cave at home had a very narrow entrance that led along a tunnel before opening out into an enormous cavern. This meant that one or two men could defend it against any number of attackers, and if anyone lit a fire outside in the hopes of smoking them out, it could burn for years before it would pollute the air inside the cavern enough for that.

This was, however, the opposite. A rival clan could storm the place and if there were too many to defeat, the MacGregors would have nowhere to go except the narrow passage that was a dead end. If a good fire was lit at the entrance and the smoke fanned into the cave, anyone in there would be coughing and choking in minutes.

No.

This time they didn't even vote. Instead they carried on, climbing up from the beach to the headland again. From there they could see for miles, past Burghead on their left and out to the horizon on their right. Added to that there were several clefts in the rocks where they could shelter from wind if not rain, and would be unlikely to be observed. It seemed perfect. If a ship with a red and yellow flag appeared on the horizon, they could signal to it and be down on the golden cave beach long before it arrived.

Rory went off with all their leather flasks to get fresh water, while the men made themselves at home under an overhang of rock facing the sea, lighting a small fire to cook their oatmeal on and to warm them when it grew dark, as it would only be visible from the sea. In time Rory returned and they all settled, stretching their legs out.

They were here, and before their chieftain, in a safe, sheltered place. When he arrived they'd be there for him.

All was well with the world.

* * *

This happy sentiment was not shared by the next group of men when they reached Burghead, two days later.

The soldiers had had a horrendous trip. They had set off from Inversnaid in high spirits, headed by their unofficial leader Private Harold Morrison, who marched at the front feeling very important indeed.

It was true that he would have felt even more important had he been *riding* at the front of the twenty-four men who had agreed to go on this venture, or rather this leave, as Colonel Walker had reminded them several times it was. But the colonel had also refused to allow them to take horses with them.

"You can take a cart for your baggage, which will be pulled by one horse, and two others to relieve the first and so that if you are in dire need for any reason, which I cannot imagine as you are only going on *leave* for a few days, someone may ride in search of help," he had told them.

Even so, the thought of seeing a little action and of killing some of the verminous Highlanders, who they blamed for them being in this shithole, had given them all purpose, which had carried them over the snow-covered mountains surrounding the barracks with hardly a complaint. They had reached Fort William cold and wet, but still enthusiastic for the action to come.

This enthusiasm had not survived several days of toil to Inverness however, in spite of the fact that they were now on a proper military road rather than a muddy track or open country. This was because it sleeted for a good part of the way, the wind blowing the icy rain in their faces, and the inns they encountered along the way were both scarce and filthy. Much of the time they found themselves crowded together in one icy room, having filled their stomachs with unsatisfying meals whose ingredients they deemed it wise not to enquire about. They were hungry, and there was nothing else on offer. Better to just shovel it down and not inspect it too closely.

On reaching Inverness they had found a slightly better tavern, and most of them had wanted to stay for a few nights here, so that they could dry their uniforms thoroughly and recover from the trials of the journey.

"After all," Private Henderson had said, "the Highlanders couldn't travel on the roads, could they? They'd have been questioned, maybe arrested if they had, a group of them. So we have time. They won't be here for days yet!"

This was a good point. After all, even though the Highlanders had set off a full day before them, they would have had to battle through bogs and over precipitous mountains. Even so…

"I agree, but what if we're wrong and they made good time?" Morrison said. "After all, they know the land better than we do. There might be short cuts they could have taken. It would be a great disappointment if we arrived there and they'd already unloaded the ship and gone. Wouldn't it be better to just spend the one night here, and then when we've dispatched them all or arrested them, we can bring them here, put them in the tollbooth, and then we'll really have something to celebrate for a few days!"

It had taken him the whole evening to persuade them, because even though he thought of himself as the leader, as without him they wouldn't have known about the smuggling trip, and it was his smooth tongue that had persuaded the colonel to allow them to go, he wasn't. He was just a private like the rest of them, and if he'd tried to order them to continue, he'd have been laughed at.

He had in the end succeeded though, with the result that his companions had blamed him for the horrendous condition of the muddy, rutted path that wound along the coastline from Inverness to Burghead. It was true that the rain had stopped, but the wind was vicious, and it seemed that whoever had made the path had had a strange sense of humour, for several times it snaked down from the cliff to the sand through gorse-filled ravines over loose rocks, only to almost immediately snake back up to the top of the cliff again.

By the time they reached Burghead two days later they were all in an absolutely foul mood.

"I'm not going one step further," Private Jones stated categorically. "I know you said we've got to find some caves you were told about 'near here', but that could be miles away. Let's camp here tonight. If the Highlanders are already at the caves, we don't want to stumble on them when we're exhausted. We want to make a good show of ourselves."

Harold could not dispute this, and in any case his current standing with the others was not particularly high, so he agreed. After all, if the Highlanders *were* already here and they succeeded in killing them and capturing the weapons, it would be a great feather in his cap. So they unpacked the cart and set up their tents on the top of a mound which seemed to have been a settlement of some kind, perhaps a Roman one? At any rate it was very old and crumbling now.

Then they lit a fire and ate a somewhat frugal meal of charred mutton and stale bread washed down with the last of their ale, before settling down in their tents for what they hoped would be a good night's sleep.

CHAPTER TWELVE

Calais, France

When the long-awaited swords finally arrived, the Highlanders agreed that they had been worth the wait, for they were indeed very fine swords. Every one of them said they'd be proud to have one at their side, and a general wish (accompanied by alcohol) was made that it would not be long before they had the opportunity to wield them in battle, too.

As the swords were the last thing they'd been waiting for, the next day, accompanied by a number of heavily laden carts, they all headed down to the port, where the cutter *Josephine* awaited them.

"I'm thinking the weather will hold," Gabriel said conversationally to Alex as they walked side by side at the front of the group of men, "so once we've loaded the ship, I'd prefer we all sleep on board tonight."

"Aye, we thought as much when ye tellt us to bring our belongings with us," Alex replied. "Unless the landlady's suddenly taken to thieving as well as cooking fine meals!"

Gabriel laughed.

"Marguerite was a great find. She was…er…unhappy in her last situation, so I rescued her, and I've never regretted it. She's a wonderful cook, trustworthy, and she even knows a bit about healing. Or about tending wounds, at least."

"I would imagine that's a useful skill. I canna imagine a man in your trade would be wanting to explain to a physician how ye came by some of your injuries."

"Ah, well, that's the pity of it. Here there's no problem in telling a physician the truth, although I'll admit I'd trust

Marguerite to tend a wound without it festering more than most of the quack doctors in Calais. But in England of course, that's not the case. I've tried to persuade her to cross the channel, but she'll have none of it. She told me that English food is all *merde*, and no doubt the ingredients you can buy there are all *merde* too. And when I offered her a goodly sum to come anyway, she told me that she pukes if she even looks at a ship."

"If a woman's set her mind to something, ye canna change it," Iain commented from behind them.

"Ah, married, are you?" Gabriel asked.

"I am, and I love her dearly, but she's stubborn when she's made her mind up," Iain replied.

"So are ye expecting thieves to maybe try to take the cargo?" Alex asked. "Is that why ye're wanting us to sleep on board?"

"Yes, partly. It's a possibility, although unlikely. I am known here," Gabriel said. "But also I'm hoping to leave at daybreak, and if we're all on board we can just head out quietly while you're still asleep. I've eight men, which is more than enough to sail the ship. I won't need your help with that."

"It's my first time on a ship," Dougal said. "I'm no' expecting to sleep when she leaves port!"

A chorus of agreement with this sentiment came from all the other Highlanders within earshot.

Gabriel sighed.

"You'll probably be awake, because the noise and movement will be new to you, but you'll need to stay below deck while the sails are being set, for you'll be in the way otherwise. So I'm sorry, but it won't be safe for you to be on deck until we're on course and under all the sails we're likely to use."

"Will we no' be sleeping on deck, in the fresh air?" Duncan asked.

"No. Everyone sleeps below deck, "Gabriel told them. "There's plenty of room down there. In wartime a cutter like mine could have up to eighty men on board, and we'll only be twenty, so even with the cargo you'll have a lot more space than you did in the room at *Le Chat D'Or*."

"We'll sleep below deck," Alex said firmly, cutting off the anticipated objection from his men. He knew Gabriel well enough by now to know there would be a good reason why men didn't sleep on deck. In fact, he *had* slept on deck a few times, when he'd crossed the Channel to be a student, and had thought to do so on this voyage. But Gabriel was the captain, and not a man who felt the need to prove his superiority by uttering silly commands.

"And here we are," Gabriel said proudly, as they arrived on the quay. "This will be your home for the next few days."

As one all the men stopped and looked at the ship Gabriel was pointing at.

"It's bigger than I expected," Duncan observed. "I was thinking it would be more like the fishing boats."

"No, we couldn't get all the cargo and twenty men on a fishing boat!" Gabriel replied.

"Aye, I should have realised that," Duncan said, laughing.

"She has only the one mast," Alex commented, omitting to say that unlike his brother, he had expected the ship to be a lot bigger. But that, he realised now, was because as a student he'd sailed to France on a much larger ship with three masts, and for no good reason had been expecting Gabriel's ship to be similar. "Ye said she's a lot faster than the navy ships because of her sails, so I expected more than one mast, that's all," he added.

"Ah. One mast, but we have more than one sail. We can have four or more if we need them, but we shouldn't for this voyage. We've ten cannon too, although I'm *really* hoping we won't need those!" Gabriel said. "Come on, let's go on board and I'll show you around, and then we can start loading her."

The Highlanders all followed him on board, while Gabriel's men busied themselves onshore unloading the carts of their cargo.

"So on a cutter there's no fo'c'sle as there would have been on the ship you sailed on, Abernathy," Gabriel said, "just one deck from bow to stern. When the crew are raising the sails to leave port, and adjusting them as we set the course, they'll need to move quickly, and as you don't know what they'll be doing, if you're on deck you'll likely get in the way. So it'll be better if you're down below then. But once we're on course you can come up. You'll want to, for it gets dark and stuffy down there after a time."

"Yon wee rowing boats," Iain said, pointing to the two small boats under the main boom. "Are they for if the ship sinks?" Everyone turned to look at them in alarm.

"We would use them for that, yes," Gabriel said. "But on this voyage I'm expecting to use them when we reach Scotland. The water won't be deep enough for me to sail right in, so I'll anchor offshore and we'll take the cargo and men ashore in them. Can you all swim?" he asked.

"We can," Alex answered. "We live near a body of water, and it's a useful skill."

"Aye, and fun too," Dougal answered. "We all learnt as bairns."

"Good. Not because I anticipate us sinking," Gabriel added hurriedly, "but as you're not accustomed to the motion of a ship, if one of you falls overboard then we'll have a chance to rescue you. Have you ever fired a cannon?"

This question received a universal no by way of answer.

"Well, if there's time you can learn a new skill then!" Gabriel told them.

They all followed him down a hatch, which led into a large, dark space below deck.

"We'll string our hammocks up here," he said. "They're very comfortable. I prefer them to a bed myself. The galley stove is down here too. We'll mainly eat biscuit and peas porridge with salted pork, and we should only be at sea for maybe four days. Right. Shall we load the cargo, and then we can eat and relax?"

It took them a few hours to load the cargo of weapons, brandy, soap, tobacco and various other provisions, as loading a ship and securing everything was very different to haphazardly piling it into a room. They were shown how to string up a hammock and then get into it. By the time they'd succeeded in doing this they were all both tired and hungry from the loading, and in good humour from the hysterical attempts at getting both in and out of their new beds.

"It's an awfu' shame that Jim's seasick," Duncan said to Alex later as the two of them waited to climb back up onto deck with their bowls of green porridge. "He'd love all this, learning new things, especially if we do have a chance to fire yon cannons. No' in battle," he added.

"He'd have loved Calais, too," Alex agreed.

"Aye, or the whorehouses at least," Iain put in from behind him. "Were ye both as obsessed wi' the lassies at seventeen? I ken I wasna. I suppose ye didna have the opportunity, living where ye do," he added, careful not to give away the location, just in case anyone was listening.

"I had the opportunity," Alex replied. "I was away, ye ken. But no, I wasna like Jim. But then he has more free time than I did at his age. And there's no harm to it, for he wears they sheepskin things so he shouldna get the pox. I'm hoping he's enjoying leading the men to Burghead, though. He hasna acted for me in such a way before."

"He hasna been there though, has he?" Dougal said. "Is that no' why ye wanted…er…John to go to Scotland?"

"No. John kens the area better than us, but Jim's been to Inverness wi' me once, and that's no' so far from Burghead. Ye just keep the sea on your left, so ye canna get lost. They'll be there when we arrive, I'm thinking, for they've had time, wi' the swords delaying us," Alex said. "It'll be good for him to have a wee bit of responsibility."

They climbed up on deck and sat, eating their food and chatting together companionably, while the sun set over the town. This was pleasant, and Alex felt exhilaration rush through him, knowing that this time tomorrow he would, God willing, be well on his way to Scotland.

"I'm sorry ye willna see home," Duncan said softly, reading his brother's mind, as he often did. "I ken ye're awfu' heartsick for it."

"I'll no' deny that," Alex said. "But I'll see the men, and hear the news, and at least walk on Scottish soil for a day. That will be enough."

It would have to be enough. They both knew that. The task that kept him in London was too important for him to give in to homesickness. And in London he *was* still following his heart, although in a way he'd never imagined.

The hammocks were, as Gabriel had said, remarkably comfortable, once you grew used to the position you lay in and the swing of them when you moved. The Highlanders had all stayed on deck for as long as possible, knowing that they would have to remain below in the morning until the cutter was well under way. By the time they all went down, the crew, who would be woken early, were fast asleep and snoring, the air already warm and stuffy from the combined heat of the bodies and the galley stove.

They climbed into their hammocks as quietly as possible in the dark so as not to waken their shipmates, their considerate gesture somewhat spoilt by laughter when a sudden crash and flurry of Gaelic curses told them that Dougal had fallen out of his hammock. They settled down to sleep, still giggling quietly to themselves.

Ah, but this had been a bonny adventure so far!

* * *

At dawn they were woken by the sound of the crewmen getting up, although they only knew it was dawn by the faint grey light spilling through the hatch as it was lifted for the men to go up on deck. Then the hatch was closed and they were all plunged into darkness again.

Now awake they lay, alternately chatting and listening to the sound of feet running nimbly across the deck above their heads. Then they heard Gabriel shout, "Stand by to raise the mains'l!"

"What's a mains'l?" Jamie asked.

"The mainsail," Alex replied. "I watched the sailors do it when I sailed to France and back. The ship wasna like this one, so I could stay up on deck to watch them. It's the biggest sail, so it'll be the one on the mast, I'm thinking."

There was more movement, and then Gabriel shouted, "Hoist away!"

"Does that mean we'll be away now?" Dougal asked.

"I dinna ken how many sails they need to hoist, but we'll ken when we leave, for the ship'll move about," Alex told him.

Dougal cursed in Gaelic and then there was a thud.

"Christ man, did ye fall out again?" Duncan asked, laughing.

"No I didna!" came the indignant reply. "I *climbed* out now, because I dinna want to try it when the room's swaying about!"

"Ye'll have to, ye wee gomerel, unless ye're thinking no' to sleep until we reach Scotland," Alex replied. "The ship'll be moving the whole time, no' just when we sail out of port!"

The laughter and comments that followed this drowned out any further commands from above, then suddenly the ship did indeed start moving, and the laughter stopped. There was silence for a while as they listened to the ship's timbers creaking, the noise of the men above shouting to each other or moving across the deck, and other, unidentifiable sounds.

"I wish I was up there now, wi' the wind in my face," Duncan murmured with such feeling that Alex wanted to reach across and comfort him, for he knew that of all the men, his brother loved to be outdoors most, and always had. Even in the depths of winter, when most Highlanders stayed indoors as much as possible, Duncan would find reasons to go outside, no matter how wild the weather.

"Gabriel will tell us when it's safe," Alex said, "then we can spend as much time as we want on deck, as long as we dinna get in the crew's way."

It seemed like forever before the hatch opened and Gabriel climbed down the steps to tell them that they were now on course and could all come up whenever they wanted, by which time they were all out of their hammocks and were practising walking up and down the hold without staggering about.

"It's a wee bit different to a rowing boat," Iain said in response to Gabriel's quizzical look.

"Ah. You'll get the hang of it soon enough," Gabriel told them. "This trip won't be long enough, but on a long trip, when you reach land you have to learn to walk again, because you become so accustomed to being on board! If you're ever in a port when a ship comes in, watch how the sailors walk when they come off the gangplank and you'll see what I mean."

Once on deck they stood for a time watching the sea and the birds, something they hadn't had the luxury of doing on the journey from England to Calais, which they had mainly spent focussing on the oars and trying to keep time with the other men.

After a while however, being men of action they grew bored, and so Gabriel set them to cleaning the deck, and then preparing the food for everyone, as the crewmembers had enough to do.

"If we continue with this wind and fine weather, we could be there in two days," he told Alex later that day as they ate their meal. "So your men won't have time to grow too restive."

"In a bad winter we'll have days where we canna stir from the hearth," Alex said. "They're no' truly bored, but they find it hard to sit about chatting when your men are working so hard. They ken they havena the knowledge to help wi' the sails and such, though, so it's good ye're giving them tasks they can do."

"That's always a problem on the navy ships," Gabriel said. "A ship this size might have sixty men or more in wartime. You've seen how many are needed to actually sail it. The others are there for battle, when they're needed to fire the guns and fight, and to replace sailors who die."

"I canna imagine sleeping below wi' sixty other men," Alex commented. "It would be awfu' crowded. The air was sour wi' just twenty of us by morning."

"Exactly. Imagine when you've been living like that for weeks, with the same food every day, and enduring the same irritating habits from the other men. A good captain makes sure there's a lot to do so the men are too weary to mutiny, and keeping the ship spotless is one of the tasks."

"So were ye telling the men a lie when ye said cleaning the deck helps to stop it leaking, and keeps the mushrooms from growing?"

"No," Gabriel said, laughing. "Although we won't grow mushrooms on a two day voyage! The saltwater makes the planks swell so they're more watertight. Any water that gets through goes into the bilge, which we can pump out if we have to. I showed you the pumps yesterday. There's always some water down there, but we don't want too much. And pumping is hard work, and tedious."

"Have ye been in the navy, then?" Alex asked. "Ye dinna have to answer, an ye dinna want to."

"No. I've never been so stupid as to volunteer, and until now I've escaped the press gangs, although it's been a close thing on more than one occasion. But I know men who weren't as fortunate as me, and some of the stories they've told me make me even more determined never to be pressed. I'll show you all how to use a cannon later," he said. "That'll be more interesting for them than cleaning the decks!"

It was. Gabriel was a good teacher, Alex thought, watching him as he explained the parts of the cannon to the MacGregor men, and then how to prime and fire it.

"These are only small guns," he told them, "with a three pound ball. But that's enough to drive through a hull, if you're close to the enemy. "Different amounts of powder are used to carry the ball further, and the powder's in a canvas and paper cartridge. We prepare them and store them below, so I'll show you one later. None of you have seen a cannon fired on land?" he asked.

"No," Alex replied. "We hope to in battle, if James lands. I've seen Mons Meg, though. She's in Edinburgh, at the castle. She isna fired now, for the barrel burst a long time ago. I was tellt that she could fire a four-hundred-pound ball about three miles. She was given to the king as a present."

All the men stopped for a moment, trying to imagine this.

"Four hundred pounds?" Gabriel exclaimed.

"Aye. The man who tellt me wasna one to exaggerate, either," Alex added, seeing the smuggler's sceptical expression. "It's an awfu' big cannon."

"Christ, that would be a sight to see," Dougal said wistfully. "Can we fire this one?"

"I thought about it, but I'd rather not, for the sound will carry a good way and we don't want to attract attention if there are any other vessels within earshot," Gabriel said. "And now I really don't want to, because if you're thinking of a four-hundred-pound ball travelling three miles, this would be a big disappointment!"

Everyone laughed at this.

Gabriel talked a bit more then about the difficulties in aiming the cannon, because you had to take the anticipated rolling of the ship into account in addition to all the normal factors, and because of that motion also had to insert a wad of oakum after the shot, to keep the shot right up against the charge, which you didn't have to do on land.

"Have ye fired the guns in battle, then?" Jamie asked, when he'd finished.

"Not on this ship, but yes, I have," Gabriel said. "And I hope never to have to do so again. I'll let you go to prepare the food now," he added, so quashing any further questions.

* * *

For the rest of that day and the start of the next, the weather was perfect, with the result that Gabriel told Alex they should reach Burghead that evening.

"Or rather the cove near Burghead. That's where you told Jim to take your other men?" he said.

"Aye. The one ye tellt me about, wi' two caves. They'll be there, or verra close by," Alex said.

"Good. If I can't land there for any reason, then I'll continue towards Burghead. But if they're there they'll see us in plenty of time to signal if it's clear. Evening is the perfect time to land. Then we can take the weapons ashore under cover of darkness, store them in the cave and carry on to Burghead. If your men are willing to come on board and travel with us that would be good, because they can help to unload the rest of the cargo and load the whisky, all while it's dark. After that I'll take your men back to the cave, and you can row in with them and spend a few hours on land if you want. I know how homesick you are."

"Aye, I'm not ashamed to admit that I am," Alex replied.

"No more should you be. As long as you're back on board before daybreak, so we can be on our way back to Calais."

* * *

The sun had just set and the light was starting to fade from the sky when a sudden call came from the man on lookout at the top of the mast. Gabriel cursed, then called up to him.

"Are you sure?"

On receiving an affirmative answer he ran up the rigging with incredible speed for such a brawny man, standing there for a minute or so before returning to deck, followed by the lookout.

"There's a storm coming, and fast," he said.

"What do we do?" Alex asked.

"Well, we need to head back out to sea, because we do *not* want to be pushed onto the rocks, so that means unless we're very lucky we won't be landing this evening. Then we need to shorten sail…reduce the sails, and we need to start now. You'll all need to go below, and keep the hatches closed. We'll need to pump the bilge continuously, but if the hatches are open enough water could get in to sink us anyway."

"My men'll no' want to do that. Can we no' be of help on deck?" Alex asked.

"No. When a wave hits, it'll travel the whole length of the deck, and anyone who has no experience of sailing through storms could easily be swept overboard. Sorry, but you need to get them below now and they'll need to hold on to beams, and I need to prepare. Take a lantern. You can pray," he added, and left Alex then, trusting him to deal with his men.

Alex looked across to where the east coast of Scotland could now clearly be seen, as could the ominous mass of heavy cloud, and sighed. Then he went to command his men to go below, which they did with extreme reluctance.

Once down, with the hatches firmly closed, they all sat in the stuffy dimness, the only light the flickering candle in the lantern, which Alex kept hold of. As they had when leaving port, they listened again to the sound of running feet and incomprehensible orders, the only difference being the edge of panic in the crew's voices. Not in Gabriel's though.

He's a damn good leader, Alex thought admiringly, listening to the calm measured cadence of his voice as he gave the men their orders.

A distant booming sounded, one that all the men picked up instantly, as it was a familiar sound among all the unfamiliar ones, and they tensed instantly.

Thunder.

"I'm sure all will be well," Alex said now, with far more reassurance than he felt. "Yon Gabriel's certainly sailed through storms before, and kens exactly what to do. We'll just be a wee bit late arriving, that's all. Ye'll need to brace yourselves, and hold on, for Gabriel tellt me the boat will rock a good deal, and ye dinna want to be thrown across the hold and injured."

They all moved then, leaning against the sides of the ship and holding on to beams, or the ropes which held the cargo tightly in place, their faces tense in the lamplight. They needed something to do to take their minds off the sound of the increasing wind and the water sloshing past the sides of the ship, which reminded all of them, himself included, that they were in a small boat on a mighty ocean, and their lives were now in Gabriel's hands.

Alex considered then rejected relaying Foley's suggestion of prayer, which would not reassure the MacGregors at the moment. Another clap of thunder sounded, closer now, and everyone jumped. The movement of the boat became more violent. Much more violent.

Alex felt the terror thrill through him, and saw his men were feeling the same way. They were all looking at him intently and with a huge effort he kept his expression calm. His brother would be aware that he was trembling slightly because he was sitting right next to him, but then Duncan often knew what he was feeling anyway, sometimes even before he did. Duncan would remain calm, though, no matter how his chieftain was feeling. The others would take their lead from him.

The boat pitched suddenly, and someone cried out above. Half the men crossed themselves instinctively.

"If we were away to fight wi' another clan, ye'd no' be feart, would ye? Ye'd follow me without hesitation," Alex said, speaking slowly and calmly.

"Aye, we would," Duncan replied, and the others agreed.

"Well, we've all been wi' Foley for weeks now, and in all that time he hasna put a foot wrong. He's a chieftain to his men as I am to you, and the sea is his battlefield, and the weather his foe. And I have no doubt at all that he's as capable of steering this ship through a wee storm as I am leading ye in a wee skirmish," he said.

"That's true. But this doesna feel like a wee skirmish," Jamie said.

"That's because it's no' a fight we ken how to win. But Foley does, and he'll win it. I'm sure a wee stramash wi' another clan that we wouldna think about, would terrify yon silk-clad Sasannachs in London, if they were in the middle of it," Alex added, causing them all to laugh, for they had all seen the type of Sasannachs he was referring to. The tension eased, just a little. "Everyone's afeart of unfamiliar things," he continued. "I ken that better than many, for I face them daily in London. But that doesna mean they're any more dangerous than the risky things ye dinna even think about at home. Ye've dealt wi' many new experiences in the last weeks, and I'm proud of ye all. And ye'll deal wi' this, as will I."

They let out a cheer at this, spoilt a bit by another violent movement, which caused Dougal to retch suddenly, then swallow frantically a few times.

"Christ," he said when he'd regained control of his stomach, his face pale and sweaty in the lamplight. "I'll no' make fun of Angus again!"

"Aye, ye will," Jamie said. "If he was here he'd have puked himself inside out by now!"

There was more laughter, and then another clap of thunder sounded, which seemed to tremble through the ship.

"*Ifrinn,*" Iain cursed softly. "That was close. D'ye think—"

He never finished his question, for at that point the ship lurched again, water began cascading down on them from above, finding its way through every gap, and Dougal lost control of his stomach, causing several others to follow suit.

And then, as the icy water soaked them and the ship pitched about, the men stopped talking and instead concentrated on keeping a firm grip on whichever part of the ship they'd braced themselves against.

And prayed.

This state of affairs continued for what seemed like hours, broken only by momentary pauses when the ship stopped lurching as violently and everyone looked up hopefully, as though the deck was made of glass and they would see what the weather was doing through it. Then another clap of thunder would sound, the waves crashed against the side of the hull, and as one, the men hunkered down and continued to pray, for it was the only thing they could do to ward off the unaccustomed sense of helplessness that they were all feeling.

When the third such hiatus came, Alex felt Duncan tense, and then shift.

"I'm sorry," he muttered, low enough so that no one but Alex could hear him. And then he stood and staggered across the deck to the nearest hatch, letting in a welcome rush of clean air as he opened it then made his way up the steps, closing it behind him.

"What's he doing?" Dougal asked.

Alex thought rapidly. He knew exactly what Duncan was doing. But he could not tell the others that.

"He's gone up to ask Gabriel if there's anything we can do to help," he lied. "I'm thinking that everyone will be too busy to come down and ask us, and maybe they're needing to hold on up there, as we are. He'll tell us if we're needed, and if not, when it's safe to go on deck. Until then, we stay here. All of us," he added, in a tone which none of them would argue with.

And then he waited for the ship to start pitching again, and prayed that Duncan was wrong.

* * *

In the end they did not wait for Gabriel to come and tell them it was safe to go up, for, after what seemed like days, the cascade of water pouring in from above became a trickle and then stopped, and the motion of the ship became more like that they were growing accustomed to. Alex waited for a short time in case it was just another hiatus, and finally stood, stretched, and then made his way over to the hatch Duncan had disappeared through earlier.

"Wait here," he said when the others made to follow him. "I'll tell ye either way in a minute."

He went up then, and seeing that the storm had indeed passed, a few stars now visible through breaks in the cloud, he beckoned the others to come up and bring the lantern with them, as there were none currently burning on deck. They all stood for a moment breathing in great lungsful of crisp sea air, a welcome contrast to the stale air they'd endured for the last hours, made fouler by the stench of vomit.

Then Alex made his way across to Gabriel, who was at the helm, taking the lantern with him.

"Well done, man," he said when he was close enough. In the light of the lantern Gabriel was white, exhaustion written in every line of his body. "It was bad, then," he added.

"Yes. Although I've sailed through much worse in my time," the smuggler said. "But usually with more men. I didn't call you up," he added, seeing the question forming on Alex's face, "because if I had, I'm sure that some of you would have gone overboard and drowned. Two of my men almost did, and they're experienced. I would not risk that, not unless I had no choice. Your man Murdo is pumping the bilges," he continued. "He used his petticoat to tie himself so he wouldn't be blown overboard. You could relieve him and the other man now, if you want. I'll stay here until we reach land. The rest of the crew can take turns to go below and rest for a short time."

"It doesna smell so good down there right now," Alex warned Gabriel.

"I doubt they'll care. But they can leave a hatch open now. It's passed. I don't think there's a deal of damage. Nothing to stop us landing, anyway. I'll know more when it's light."

"Thank you," Alex said simply then, knowing that would be enough. And then he turned away and went to find his brother.

Once Dougal and Jamie had taken over from Duncan and Paul at pumping the rest of the water out of the bilge, Duncan wrung his *féileadh mór* out, and then dressed himself as best he could while standing and bracing himself against the movement of the boat, thankfully now gentle. Then he joined Alex, who was standing at the bow gazing in the direction of Scotland, although it was too dark to see any land as yet.

"I'm sorry," he said again. "I tried to stay down. But I couldna do it. I truly thought we were going to sink. Did ye no' think that too?"

"Aye," Alex said. "I did, more than once. Ye dinna need to explain, man. I ken why ye came up. I wanted to as well. But I couldna."

"I should have stayed wi' ye," Duncan replied.

"No. Ye did right. Ye've asked me before, if we're together when ye're dying, to make sure ye're outside if it's at all possible, or at least to open a door or window so your last breath is a sweet one, for ye've a horror of dying inside."

"Ye mind that? We were bairns when ye promised me ye would," Duncan replied.

"Aye. But I've a good memory, as ye ken well, and I dinna forget a promise. If it's in my power ye'll die wi' me by your side, outdoors, and your last breath will be of the pure air of the Highlands, if possible."

"Thank ye," Duncan said, reaching across and squeezing his brother's hand with such emotion that it was painful.

"I should have made an excuse for ye to go up," Alex said. "I'm sorry I didna. I ken how important it is to ye. If I can, I'd like to die in the fresh air too. No' wi' your passion, but even so…"

"I ken that. But being chieftain is more important to you than that. I ken that too."

"It is. And if I die before ye, ye'll be chieftain in my place, and if ye are—"

"I could never be the chieftain ye are, and I pray it never happens, but if it does, I swear to ye now that it will override everything else," Duncan interrupted.

Alex smiled, and nodded.

And then they both stood, holding hands as they had sometimes as boys when in need of comfort, and stared across to the dark horizon.

Homeward.

CHAPTER THIRTEEN

North-East Scotland

Alasdair Og slid back down into the sheltered spot the Highlanders had chosen to wait in for their chieftain. They'd made it quite comfortable now, having furnished the floor with a thick covering of heather which made a soft bed for them to lie on. In one corner of the spot formed by the overhanging rock they'd placed all their remaining foodstuffs, which they were now rationing out equally. If Alex took a long time to arrive, one of them would go into Elgin with the small amount of coin Angus had brought and buy more provisions, as it was too early in the year to forage for all their food. But for now they were snug, especially as the rain had stopped, and although the wind was fierce and gusty at the moment, it was coming from the land rather than the sea, so the overhang sheltered them from it.

"There's a wee fire on yon hill wi' the old fort," Alasdair Og said, pushing his wildly tangled hair back off his face. "Now it's dark I can see it easily, and I can see the shapes of people passing in front of it. I canna see what they're doing, but they're moving around a lot, so I'm thinking there's either a lot of them or they're very busy."

The rest of the men abandoned their pastime of watching the stars slowly appear in the sky and climbed up to the top of the cliff to see this new sight of interest.

"Are ye thinking it's some clansmen from whoever's land we're on?" Simon asked after they'd observed the bright orange flames for a minute or two, the only thing now visible as night had descended fully and there was no moon.

"If it's Highlanders, aye, for they must be feeling awfu' safe if they dinna care that everyone within miles will ken they're there," Kenneth replied.

"Could it be other smugglers, guiding a ship in wi' a fire?" Alasdair Og asked. "And if it is, d'ye think Alex might think it's us and head there?"

"No, I dinna think so," Angus said. "When Gabriel tellt me how to signal when we see the ship, he tellt me it was important that no one else saw the light. That's why I've got this dark lantern. He said only an idiot would light a fire, for if they did the revenue men or other people would see it too and they'd all come to see what was amiss, which is the last thing a free trader wants.

"He tellt me that they only light a fire if they're wanting to distract the revenue men, so that while they're all away off to the fire the ship comes in somewhere else and unloads. So he'll ken it's no' me, for I tellt him I'd use the lantern, and he said the caves were easy to find, so he'll be expecting us to be here, no' cavorting in full sight on the hill there."

"Well, whoever they are, they're no' coming here the night, so we can sleep easy," Kenneth said. "We can watch out for them the morrow, and see which way they go."

This was sensible, so they all went back under the shelter of the overhang and continued their evening of stargazing, chatting, or looking to the horizon for a sail, even though they knew the chances of them seeing one was remote, when they could hardly distinguish where the sea ended and sky began in the pitch dark.

Finally they settled down on their heather mattresses in their snug hideaway, heedless of the wind roaring behind them, warmed by a dram of whisky and lulled to sleep by the rhythmic lapping of waves against the shore below.

* * *

The Highlanders sat on the cliff the following day, watching as the men who had announced their presence last night by means of fire straggled along the path, heading in their direction. The wind was still gusting fitfully and it had started to rain again, with a lot more promised for later judging by the dark grey clouds looming on the horizon behind the scarlet-clad soldiers.

Although the MacGregors instinctively took care to make sure they could not be seen while observing this sight, in truth they could probably have danced a Highland jig on the cliff without being observed, so absorbed in their misery were the redcoats.

It had been a horrible night. The wind had demolished their tents three times during it, and one of them had been set on fire by a stray ember blown from the carelessly attended fire. John and Arthur, who had been lying, although luckily not sleeping, in the tent at the time, had just managed to scramble out, upon which, relieved of their body weight, the wind had saved them the trouble of trying to extinguish the blaze by blowing the tent down the hill into the sea.

As a result of all this damn Scottish weather, none of them had slept for more than an hour or two, so, as the MacGregors had seen, they were not in a particularly observant state, nor in a particularly good mood. Most of them were wishing they had not volunteered for this ridiculous endeavour and had instead stayed in the garrison, which now seemed like a place of warmth and comfort rather than the virtual prison they had thought it to be for the last few months.

To add to their misery, this bloody path was probably suitable for primitives, but for civilised soldiers of the British Army it was completely impractical. Not for walking on, although even for that it left a lot to be desired, so rutted and meandering was it; but for the cart it was virtually impossible, with the result that the redcoats spent more time pushing or pulling the cart out of some muddy hole than the horse did pulling it along the track.

The Highlanders watched this with great amusement and not a little perplexity, Kenneth stifling a guffaw as the idiots dragged the reluctant horse on the steep descent to the beach that they remembered well, having traversed it themselves a couple of days ago.

"The horse has more sense than they do," Simon said in bewilderment. "What the hell are they taking it down there for? Why do they no' just cut a way through the gorse and broom and come along the cliff edge?"

"We didna do that," Alasdair Og commented.

"We didna have a cart. And we wanted to see if it was a good beach for the ship to come in at, or we would have done," Angus said. "I canna wait to see how they manage to bring the cart up the wee path again," he added, laughing.

"I'm wanting to see how they react when they find out they've half a league of soft sand to drag it over, and then an even steeper path back up to the clifftop," Kenneth said.

"Will we away to the cliff edge and watch them?" Simon asked. "I'm thinking we'll learn an awfu' lot of Sasannach curse words if we do."

As they had nothing else to do, and there was still no sign of *any* ships on the horizon, let alone one with a red and yellow flag, they all agreed with this fine suggestion, and running along the cliff path they found a good spot where they would not be visible from the beach or the path, and lay on their stomachs, looking down on the pandemonium below.

"Christ, why do they need so much baggage?" Simon commented on seeing how heavy the cart was. It was so laden that it had come to a standstill in the soft sand, the redcoats now trying to contrive a way to hitch the two spare horses to the cart in the hopes that their combined strength would pull it free.

"My grandda tellt me that redcoats canna sleep without tents and yon wee mattresses, and pillows and blankets, for they're no' accustomed to sleeping outdoors as we are," Alasdair Og said.

It was on the tip of Angus's tongue to say that he could understand that, as he'd found it harder than normal to do so on his way to Scotland, after only a few months of extreme comfort in London. But he did not want to be the butt of every joke for the next week, so he kept silent.

"I canna think why they dinna just unload the cart and carry everything up the path, for that would be quicker, and the poor horse isna going to drag that up the steep track anyway," Kenneth said. "If they left the cart there, and just put their tents on the horses, they'd already be on their way."

"Where are they going, d'ye think?" Simon asked, growing bored of watching the men below make such a huge endeavour out of what seemed obvious to them. "What's to the east that redcoats would want to travel to?"

"I havena a notion," Angus replied. "All I ken is that France is to the east and Alex is coming from there. Maybe they're wanting a wee stramash wi' the Gordons?"

This comment resulted in a good deal of hastily stifled

laughter, as the Gordons were an enormous clan, and would pay less heed to this bunch of fools than they would to a cloud of midges.

"I'm thinking that they'd lose a wee stramash against our bairns, no' mind the Gordons," Alasdair Og said. "Ah, it's a pity the wind's blowing out to sea, for I canna hear a word they're saying."

In truth their body language and hand signals, and even a brief fight breaking out between two of the men, conveyed the frustration and ineptitude of the soldiers better than any language could. After an extraordinarily long time, during which the MacGregors had grown bored and were preparing to head back to their shelter, the men finally figured out what Kenneth had seen instantly, and uncoupling the horses from the cart they started to unload it, distributing the baggage between themselves and the three mounts.

Then they set off trudging along the sand again, until they discovered that they could not get any further without swimming and would have to clamber back up to the cliff edge, upon which another scuffle broke out, on which the MacGregors set off back to the shelter, tears of laughter streaming down their faces at the men's antics.

"I canna imagine why James is waiting for King Louis to give him an army," Simon observed as they settled back under their shelter, Angus having volunteered to keep watch to see if the soldiers passed them when they finally reached the cliff path. "If that's the calibre of the redcoats, the loyal clans could wipe them out without breaking into a sweat."

"They're no' all like that, though," Kenneth said. "Alasdair tellt me many a tale about the redcoats. They're a fearsome enemy when they're organised, he said, and he's seen more battles wi' them than anyone. I'm thinking there's a task that no one else is wanting to undertake from Inverness, maybe, and yon wee gomerels have been ordered to do it, for if they fail, they'll no' be any loss."

* * *

By the time the soldiers, whose situation if not their place of origin Kenneth had unknowingly so accurately described, had managed to struggle back up the path, burdened as they were, and then saw the caves on the next beach ahead of them, the sun had already set and the light was fading.

"Those are the caves the woman told me about!" Harold exclaimed, pointing down the mercifully gentle incline that led to them.

"Are you sure? Because you've been sure about a lot of things, and they've all gone wrong," another man said nastily.

"Not least that this would be fun, and that after a stroll along the roads we'd get to see some action against the Highland scum, and share the spoils of the smugglers between us," John added.

"I couldn't predict the weather!" Harold said defensively, with some justification. "And I thought Colonel Walker would have told us how far away it was from Inversnaid. None of us knew that. But those are the caves. She told me there were two. And that's a good beach to land a ship on, isn't it?"

The men all looked at the beach cluelessly. None of them had had any dealings with ships, apart from seeing them in port once or twice.

"Do you think the Highlanders will already be in there?" James asked. "Because if they are, I've no wish to fight them now. All I want to do is sleep. After I've eaten."

They all stood observing the caves apprehensively for a while, then, after seeing no sign of life at all apart from the gulls wheeling round above, they made their way down to them.

"See? I told you we'd get here before the Highlanders!" Harold said when they arrived, buoyed up by being right at least once. "They'll still be struggling over the mountains. And this cave looks ideal! It's lovely and dry, and deep. We can all fit in here, and the horses too with room to spare. It's perfect!"

He was right. The soldiers sighed in utter relief, dropping all their baggage near the entrance, then unpacking the mattresses and examining the meagre supply of food they had left with some dismay.

Still, at least they would not be disturbed here, nor would the weather try to burn them alive or blow them off a cliff. Small mercies.

They lit a small fire to cook on and to give some light, then they settled down, examining their feet for blisters, which several of them had, and eating the provisions. By that time the cave had started to become a bit smoky from the fire, so they extinguished it, carefully this time, and after voting unanimously that Harold should take the first watch of the evening as it was due to him they were all here, they settled down, falling asleep almost immediately.

* * *

"*Bàs mallaichte,*" cursed Angus, jumping down into the shelter and narrowly missing landing on Kenneth's outstretched legs. "They've stopped at yon golden cave for the night."

"Aye, well, I'm no' surprised after all the work they did to travel half a league," Simon said. "Does it matter? They'll no' find us here."

"They couldna find their arses without a guide," Kenneth added disparagingly.

"No, but if Alex's ship comes in, even they'll notice that," Angus pointed out.

"Ah. Will we attack them?" Alasdair Og asked hopefully.

A short silence followed in which Angus tried to think as his chieftain brother would, profoundly wishing Alex was here with them rather than out on the ocean somewhere.

"I dinna think Alex would," he said finally. "The ship might no' come in the night, and in the morning they'll likely continue on their way. They're no' hunting us. Maybe they've an issue wi' a local clan, or are being sent to another place for some reason."

"Aye, I agree. We dinna want to draw attention to ourselves unless there's need," Kenneth said, to Angus's relief. Kenneth knew Alex well and would have spoken honestly if he thought Angus wrong. "The poor wee gomerels'll likely save us the trouble by killing themselves, the way they're behaving."

Everyone agreed with this.

"I'm thinking one of us should go down there and observe them a wee bit more, though," Kenneth added. "Just in case. We ken there's twenty-five of them and three horses but no cart. They've likely only the normal weapons, but we dinna ken what was on the cart. Maybe they're sitting around the fire blethering about what they're here for?"

"I'll go," Alasdair Og offered, and climbing out of the shelter disappeared silently into the dusk.

He returned about half an hour later, carrying two flasks of brandy, which he offered to the others, grinning.

"Christ, man, we didna think ye'd introduce yourself to them!" Simon said.

"Och, if Grandda was here, we could away down there and have a wee *ceilidh* while he played his fiddle, and they wouldna be any the wiser," Alasdair Og informed them, grinning. "They're all sleeping like wee bairns. They're sleeping in their sarks and their uniforms neatly laid out to dry. Their swords are in their scabbards, which are wi' the muskets, stacked at the left side of the cave."

"Jesus, Mary and Joseph, we wouldna have been so stupit when we were wee bairns," Simon gasped.

"I should think not, wi' me teaching ye how to fight," Kenneth put in.

"Well, in fairness, they have got a man on watch, and he *is* fully dressed and has his musket with him," Alasdair Og added. "He's sitting against the wall at the entrance, snoring, and cradling his gun as if it's a lassie. The three horses are in there too."

"Aye, well, as long as no one's cradling the horse as if it's a lassie," Angus said.

Everyone started laughing.

"Most of them are awfu' young too, a good deal younger than you, Angus," Alasdair Og said. "They canna be more than sixteen, I'm thinking."

Angus was not offended, although he himself was only seventeen, would turn eighteen the following month. But a Sasannach sixteen and a Highland sixteen were, after all, totally different things.

"I'm thinking if they *are* after some clansmen, they'll no' live the night if they're that careless, for they'll surely have been seen by them," Angus said. "Although we havena seen anyone else."

"I'm hoping yon ship comes over the horizon tomorrow, after yon loons are away, for I'm a wee bit bored o' counting stars now," Kenneth said. "No' bored enough to kill a gang o' raw bairns though. No' unless they give me cause to."

Everyone agreed with this, and so they settled for another evening of talking, enlivened by the brandy Alasdair Og had brought them. During breaks in conversation they stargazed until the sky clouded over, after which they watched the distant flashes of light on the horizon, hoping that the storm was not heading this way, although they should escape the worst of it if it did, as they were sheltered here.

CHAPTER FOURTEEN

Simon had the last watch of the night, and had moved out of the shelter to sit on the clifftop, partly because he was tired and thought the fresh sea breeze up here might keep him alert, and partly because he enjoyed watching the sun rise over the sea in the morning. He knew that once this adventure was over and he returned home he might not view such a sight for a long time, if ever, living as he did on the west coast.

He yawned. It was good to be alive on days like this, although he was missing his sweetheart Janet something fierce. She would likely still be asleep now. He closed his eyes for a moment, imagining sitting with her on the banks of the loch, the warm weight of her as she leaned against him. He smiled, and when he opened his eyes again, he saw it. A shape, just slightly lighter than the ocean it was floating on.

For a moment he wasn't sure; it was still very dark, only the slight lightening of the sky near the horizon indicating that it would soon be sunrise. He gazed out across the expanse of darkness, narrowing his eyes in an attempt to focus better. And saw it again, enough to ascertain that it was, indeed, a vessel of some kind, one with sails. More than that he could not determine at the moment, but it was enough for him to slide down the gap into the shelter and rouse the others from their slumbers.

Once awake, they all stared out to sea. By now the sky had lightened a fraction more, and they could see that it was, indeed, a tall ship, sailing silently in their direction. What they could *not* see was whether it had red and yellow flags raised on the mast.

"What d'ye think?" Simon asked Angus. "Is it their ship?"

"I havena a notion," Angus replied honestly. "I didna see the ship in harbour, for it was in Calais. But it's the only ship we've seen since we've been here, and it seems to be sailing into shore. I dinna want to signal it yet, though, no' until we're sure. It could be a revenue ship for all we ken."

"*Bàs mallaichte,*" Kenneth muttered under his breath. "If it *is* them, what do we do about yon redcoat bairns down in the cave?"

"Will I away down and see if they're awake and have seen it?" Alasdair Og asked.

"Aye, I'm thinking the ship will be a while reaching shore yet, although I dinna ken how fast they travel," Angus said.

Alasdair Og disappeared silently. While they were waiting, the others all watched the tall ship's progress intently as the sky lightened, waiting for it to be light enough to see any flag. After a short while Alasdair Og returned, breathing heavily in his rush to be back.

"They're all still fast asleep, snoring. They dinna look to wake for a time yet. I'm thinking they maybe had a lot more of that brandy than we did," he informed them.

"I canna blame them. It was awfu' good," Simon said.

It had been. But they had measured how much they drank, knowing that if the ship came in they would have to be instantly alert. And they wanted to keep some to toast the chieftain landing on Scottish soil again, when he did.

"Christ, it's moving quickly," Kenneth said. "I'm thinking we need to decide what we'll do now, if it is Alex, for we havena much time."

"We've two choices, have we no'?" Alasdair Og said. "Either we signal them no' to come in wi' yon dark lantern, or we signal them to come in and attack the bairns in the cave while we're waiting for them to land."

"D'ye think the redcoats ken there's a ship coming in frae France?" Simon asked. "It seems awfu' strange that they're here at the same time we are."

"How could they ken?" Kenneth said. "Nobody does except us and Foley's men. If Foley's a good free trader as Alex tells us he is, he wouldna tell anyone where he's landing, except those who need to ken. And we certainly havena."

"Aye. And who would send the dregs o' the army to take it, in any case?" Alasdair Og added.

This was true. Capturing a ship full of Jacobite weapons and the Jacobites smuggling them would be a huge feather in the cap of a commanding officer. No, it was certainly coincidence. They hadn't known the whereabouts of the caves either, as they had shown by their comedic trek down to the previous bay with the cart.

"I'm thinking we wait until we ken if it *is* Alex," Kenneth suggested. "If it isna, we do nothing. If it is, then we signal him to come in, and while we're waiting we away down there and deal wi' them. I could likely kill them all myself, if ye're no' in the mood for a fight."

As one they all looked at him to see if he was serious, not least because anyone who'd seen Kenneth fight when his blood was up knew that he was speaking the truth, not boasting. Then they saw the glint in his eye, and realised he was joking. Maybe because, by the soldiers behaviour yesterday he was not taking the threat very seriously, and so his blood was not up.

This decision voted on and unanimously agreed, they ate whatever they had to hand which needed no preparation, and waited until they could see the flags, which, within a few more minutes they could all see were, indeed, red and yellow.

This was it, then. A wave of excitement and anticipation shot through them like lightning, and they all grinned, moving as one to strap on their swordbelts and pick up their targes, while Angus lit the lantern, shining it out to sea as arranged. A brief flash of light from a similar lantern told them the signal had been seen. And then they set off, moving silently down the sandy track from the clifftop to the beach, arriving there a few minutes later, so quietly that even the horses inside the cave made no sign of having heard them.

The young soldiers were, indeed, still all asleep, although the sky was lightening rapidly now, and an orange glow on the horizon heralded the imminent appearance of the sun.

The Highlanders sat at the bottom of the path, from which they could clearly see the sleeping sentry, and hear the snores of the slumbering youths.

"Christ, it doesna feel right to kill them," Kenneth murmured. "No' unless they actually make a fight of it. What was their chieftain thinking, sending such innocents alone through clan territory? I could gladly kill that bastard, if I find out who he is."

"Even so, we canna leave them here wi' the ship coming in, can we?" Alasdair Og said. "It'll be them or us, so we havena a choice."

"We havena much time, either," Angus added, seeing a lot of activity on the ship, which was now close enough for them to see the people clambering around on deck lowering the sails, although it was not possible to identify individuals yet.

"Ye tellt us their weapons are stacked against the walls, and the horses are in there too?" Kenneth said softly to Alasdair Og.

"Aye."

"So I'm thinking, why do we no' give them a Highland charge?" Kenneth said, grinning. "An' we do that, the puir wee gomerels'll be so afeart they'll shit themselves and surrender, I'm thinking. They'll no' have time to ken where they are before we're among them. Wi' luck we'll no' have to kill them at all."

A broad grin spread across the face of every MacGregor at the thought of taking part in an authentic Highland charge, albeit a miniature version as there was only a handful of them. It was the manoeuvre which had made the clansmen the most feared warriors in the land, which had caused whole armies to flee without a drop of blood being shed.

"Ah, that would be a fearsome sight," Angus breathed.

"Aye, it will be to them. And they canna run away, for they'll be trapped in yon cave, which is why we didna sleep there," Simon said.

A very soft masculine giggle ran round the assembled clansmen, and then they backed away a little, just far enough to be able to get up enough speed to terrify the slumbering soldiers.

* * *

On the ship Gabriel was issuing various commands to the exhausted sailors, which resulted in the sails and anchor being lowered and the ship coming to a stop a short distance from the shore.

"I can't get any closer without risk of being grounded," Gabriel explained once this was done, coming to the rail, where the MacGregors were looking at the beach. "We'll row in on the longboats. It'll take a little longer, but it means that if there is any trouble we can be back on the ship and sailing away in no time. Can you see your men?"

"Aye, they're away a wee bit up the cliff path," Alex said, squinting to focus better, then pointing.

Gabriel, who prided himself on his excellent vision, stared in the direction Alex was pointing, yawning. He was *very* tired. They all were, after the night they'd just had. Even so there was work to be done, so sleep had to wait. Everyone was working slightly slower than normal, but there was no hurry now. The sea and the shoreline seemed to be completely deserted to him.

"I can't see anything," he admitted after a minute. "Are you sure? I mean, I know they're there, for young Jim, if it was him, signalled as I told him to, but..." He gazed intently at the beach again, then shook his head. Alex grinned.

"That's a good thing," he said. "Ye'll see them when they move." He turned away then. "Are we lowering yon boats?" he asked. "If so, we'll row into shore, and I can greet my men and tell them what we'll be doing. Ye can come in wi' your men and some of the goods then. Or are ye thinking to sit here until the gloaming? Dusk," he added, seeing Gabriel's look of incomprehension.

"Christ, no. It's true I'd hoped to come in at dusk last night, but the squall stopped that. No, I want to be away from here as soon as I can. If we put the goods in the cave, then your men can take them away at dusk, but we'll sail back out to sea, sleep as much as we can, for none of us got any rest last night, and come in at Burghead this evening to load the whisky. I assume you'd like to spend some time with your men before you sail back to France with me?"

"I would, but I dinna expect to as we couldna land last night," he said.

"Well, Burghead isn't far away, so if you'd prefer to walk there rather than sail, you could spend the day with your men and then meet us at Burghead later, if you want. It makes no difference to me, and I trust you enough to know that you won't let me down," Gabriel said.

Alex smiled, his blue eyes lighting up at the thought of spending a whole day in his homeland. God, but he was homesick!

"I appreciate that," he said. "That's considerate of ye, and aye, I willna let ye down."

The first boat was now lowered, and the clansmen climbed down the rope ladder, sat down, and raised their oars. Alex, the last to go, was halfway down the ladder when an almighty roar from the shore made him twist his body to look back, just in time to see the MacGregors on shore charge down the path in the direction of the cave, raised swords glinting in the morning sun.

He leapt down the remaining few yards into the boat, causing it to rock alarmingly, then threw himself down on a bench, grabbing an oar.

"*Àrd choille!*" he roared, and as one the MacGregors set off, rowing to shore at an incredible speed, watched by the astonished smugglers still on board the ship.

"What the hell?" Gabriel said, watching the men on shore, who seemed to have magically materialised from nowhere, charging full tilt at the cave, and then at the Highlanders in the boat, rowing at a speed he didn't know was possible towards them.

"What did he say?" Michael asked, moving next to Foley and watching the unfolding scene with equal bewilderment.

"I've no idea, but whatever it was I'm very glad I'm not whoever is in that cave," Gabriel replied.

"You think the revenue are waiting there?" Michael asked.

"Someone is, that's certain," Gabriel said. "If it's the revenue, I doubt they'll be prepared for *that* reception. If it's another gang of Highlanders wanting the weapons, then we're about to be spectators to a Highland battle, I think."

"Should we lower the other boat and go to their assistance?" Paul asked, somewhat reluctantly.

Gabriel considered for a moment. Abernathy and his men were almost at the shore and the others were already inside the cave, from which a horse had just bolted, charging along the beach in panic, closely followed by another.

"Yes," he said, wondering if he was being foolhardy. Normally he would have stayed on the ship, preparing to lift anchor and flee if it did turn out to be a formidable enemy. But there was something about this Abernathy.

Maybe the fact that if their positions were reversed, he wouldn't hesitate to go to Gabriel's aid. Having been with the man for a few weeks now, Gabriel was sure of that. He sighed.

"I'll go in with the best fighters. Michael, you stay here, because you know how to command a ship. If it goes badly head out to sea, and come back in this way later on your way to Burghead, just close enough to see if there's anyone worth rescuing. Come on, then."

Inside the cave, absolute pandemonium raged. The youths, abruptly woken from their drunken dreams into the worst nightmare they'd ever had, managed to do no more than sit up groggily before they were either stunned by a fleeing panicked horse, a glancing blow to the head from a targe, or stopped from moving any further by a blade being held at some part of their anatomy.

Harold, who was the only one with a weapon in his arms and the closest to the mouth of the cave, didn't even manage to shoulder his musket before a numbing blow to his shoulder rendered his right arm temporarily useless, the musket clattering to the ground, where it was kicked away by his attacker.

He looked up, to see the most enormous man he'd ever seen in his life glance down at him, then nod, assured that he was no threat, before assessing what was happening in the rest of the cave. Harold blushed at the insult, but had neither the ability or the desire to respond to it. Although the oldest of the redcoats, he was only nineteen and had a great wish to see twenty, so he stayed silent.

All of the youths who were still conscious seemed to have the same wish as Harold, so that by the time Alex and the rest of the MacGregors arrived at full tilt, swords drawn and ready for battle, which terrified the British soldiers even more, it was all over, to their mixed relief and disappointment.

Alex took in the situation; a number of unarmed youths lying or sitting on the cave floor dressed only in their shirts, eyes wide and faces white with terror, their muskets and swords thrown carelessly in one corner. Then, to the boys' utter humiliation, he clapped the red-haired giant on the shoulder and started laughing, saying something to the monster in that Irish gibberish the savages used to communicate with each other.

One word, however, Harold *did* understand. *Cináed*. Kenneth. Jeannie's husband. *This* was the old, feeble man she'd told him she was married to? No. It couldn't be. There must be more than one Kenneth in the clan. Then he remembered that she'd mentioned once how lovely his soft brown wavy hair was, how different from her husband's tangled mass of orange, a perfect description of the hair this giant standing over him had. She had never actually said he was feeble, Harold realised, only that he was old. And this man *was* a lot older than Jeannie, that was certain. It was also certain that if he knew what he'd done, this Kenneth creature would tear him limb from limb. And if he did, no one could stop him.

To his horror, Harold's bladder emptied immediately. If he survived this, which he doubted he would, he would never, never go within a hundred miles of that bitch again.

CHAPTER FIFTEEN

By the time Gabriel and his men arrived the youths had been stripped of their shirts and were blindfolded, their hands and feet tied with strips of cloth, and were sitting in a pitiful group at the narrow back of the cave. They sat there shivering, partly because it was a cool day and they were naked, and partly from sheer terror, because they had no idea what the Highlanders were going to do with them.

They had heard all sorts of terrible stories from the older soldiers at the garrison. This included various versions of the tale of the Scotsman Sawney Bean, who had lived in a cave with his family, had murdered anyone who passed by, and had roasted and eaten their bodies. When the Bean family were discovered there were body parts all over the cave, and bones that the children had gnawed. There were lots of Scots like that, the soldiers had added, just looking for some young, tender meat to put in the pot.

At the time they had thought the veteran soldiers were making fun of them because they were new recruits and had dismissed the tales, but now, sitting helplessly surrounded by terrifying clansmen who were speaking in a brutal unintelligible tongue, the stories came back to them. Perhaps this was the very cave that Sawney and his family had lived in? Perhaps these were descendants of Sawney?

When the next boat arrived the cannibals suddenly started speaking English, which was a great relief to the soldiers, as at least they now knew that the topic of discussion was not the best way to butcher them, but rather the best way to bring the goods in and be on their way. Even so, when they were talking together the Highlanders still spoke their own tongue, so perhaps they were discussing culinary matters then?

They sat, enduring the most miserable, terrifying day of their lives so far, completely ignored by their captors, who were focussing on more important matters.

The boats were rowed back and forth, bringing in the weapons and a few other supplies Alex had paid for, necessities like soap and salt, and some luxuries that the MacGregors would love; tea, claret, cognac, lace, and another roll of silk for the clanswomen to make dresses with that they could wear at weddings or *ceilidhs*, which would make them feel beautiful. It was not as fine as the exquisite chiné silk that Maggie was currently labouring over in London, but it was lovely, nonetheless.

The only problem Alex could see caused by his generosity, was that now everything was unloaded it was clear there was too much for the men to carry back to Loch Lomond. The weapons would have to come first, no doubt. But it would be a shame to see the rest wasted.

"Dinna fash yerself about that," Angus said when Alex voiced his disappointment. "I ken where there's a cart sitting on the sand, lonely and waiting for such a task as this."

At that the rest of the clansmen who'd come up from Loch Lomond all started laughing, to the bemusement of the others. Angus then told them about witnessing the humorous escapade yesterday, to the amusement of the smugglers and MacGregors and the added humiliation of the redcoats, after which he set off with a few others to retrieve the cart, while the rest finished unloading the ship.

In time the cart was brought to the cave along with the added bonus of one of the horses, which had stopped once it was well away from the pandemonium of the Highland charge and had been found grazing on the headland.

They all sat down then to discuss their options, the situation having been complicated by the redcoats' presence.

"What will you do with them?" Gabriel asked.

"What would you do?" Alex replied with a question.

Gabriel thought for a moment.

"It's irrelevant," he said finally. "They're your responsibility. Your men captured them, and while they might have seen some of *their* faces, they haven't seen any of my men because they were blindfolded before we arrived and none of us have said anything in their hearing that could identify us. All they know is that we're smugglers bringing in goods, no more than that. It makes no difference to me what you do."

"I'm thinking it would be a shame to kill them. They're just bairns, in truth," Kenneth put in, causing Gabriel to look at him in surprise, for, like many people meeting the giant for the first time, he expected Kenneth to be as fierce as he looked. "It was bad luck they decided to sleep here last night. They dinna deserve to die for that."

"Aye, that's the crux of the matter," Alex replied. "I've no' lived as long as I have by believing in coincidence. I'm needing to talk to them first. The one that was still dressed, bring him out to me. Ben there," he added, nodding in Alasdair Og's direction in case the others had forgotten his alias, "tellt me he thought he was their leader?"

"Likely, aye. He's the oldest, and when we were watching them wi' the cart he was trying to give the orders, although the others didna heed him," Simon answered.

Kenneth returned from the cave a moment later with the unfortunate Harold over his shoulder, dumping him unceremoniously on the sand in front of Alex.

"Leave him blindfolded," Alex said in Gaelic. "He doesna need to see me. Right then, laddie," he continued, switching smoothly to English, with a softer Scottish accent than he usually had, "ye need to tell me the truth, for that will decide the fate of yourself and all your men. Will ye do that?"

Harold nodded, the lump of fear in his throat strangling his speech.

"Why are ye here? This isna the route to a military barracks. Were ye waiting for us?" Alex asked conversationally.

Harold thought frantically, fighting to overcome the paralysing terror that had him in its grip, trying to stop the trembling in his limbs, wanting to appear unafraid, or at least defiant. And then behind him Kenneth said something in the gibberish to the man addressing him, and all thoughts of defiance vanished, along with all thoughts of telling the truth. If he told the truth he would die.

There was no doubt of that. For if he told them about the information he'd learnt, they would want to know who had told it to him. And then...

"We're on leave," he blurted out, "from Inverness, and we thought to visit Elgin, for the older men told us it's a fine place, with a cathedral and...and...lovely houses. So we came together. We thought it would be fun," he added sadly. This at least was true. He did not think that any more, that was certain.

"I can't imagine what's in Elgin that a boy would want to see. I only wanted whorehouses and taverns when I was his age," Paul said. "There are few of those in Elgin that I know of."

"That's what they told us!" Harold said, grasping this straw desperately. "We thought it would be good to see the sights by day, and then the...other sights by night. The men make fun of us a lot, because we're young," he added bitterly, slightly reassured by the sound of an English voice, with a dialect close to his. "They tell us all kinds of tales. They told us one about a man called Sawney Bean—" He stopped abruptly, suddenly remembering who he was surrounded by, even if he couldn't see them.

He couldn't see the grins that had appeared on the clansmen's faces at this slip either. If he had he would probably have emptied what was left in his bladder on the sand, although unknown to him it was this slip that saved his life, for although Alex would kill if necessary, he was not in the habit of killing young boys coldbloodedly if it could be avoided. There was no way that this boy would have mentioned the grisly tale of Sawney Bean to them deliberately, as whether true or not, it insulted the Scots, implying that they were savage cannibals. So whatever this Elgin tale was, it was unlikely to be a complete fabrication.

He sat and pondered for a minute, thinking as the others had earlier. If the British army had somehow known that a cargo of weapons was being smuggled in from France they would have sent a whole regiment of soldiers, expecting a mass of clansmen to be waiting on the shore for it. No commanding officer would send twenty-four bumbling recruits on such a mission.

It seemed that their presence here *was* a coincidence. Or it seemed it enough for Alex to give Harold the benefit of the doubt.

"Take him back," Alex said to Kenneth.

"What will you do?" Gabriel asked, when the boy had been

thrown over Kenneth's shoulder like a sack of barley and carried away.

"Load the cart up with some of the goods and cover them wi' heather, which we'll say we're collecting to roof our homes in the unlikely event that anyone stops us to ask. Then we'll leave it all in the cave with a few men on guard, and the rest of us will come to Burghead at dusk to help ye load the whisky. Then we'll sail back here wi' ye and the men will start for home while it's still dark. D'ye need Murdo today? For I'd like him to walk wi' me as well. He's missing his homeland as sorely as I am."

"No, you take all your men to Burghead on foot if you want," Gabriel replied. "I trust you all to meet me there this evening. I meant what will you do with the soldiers?"

"Well, we'll add their swords and muskets to our pile, and if ye'd be so good as to give all their uniforms a watery grave somewhere on the way to Burghead, I'm thinking to leave them in the cave tonight, naked and bound. If they've any sense of survival at all, they'll manage to cut through their bonds wi' a sharp stone, in time," Alex said. "But I'll wager it'll take them a goodly amount of time to do that. And another while to argue about the matter, and then they'll no' be wanting to walk around the countryside naked, so they'll only move by night, which means they'll be very slow, for they're Sasannachs and they dinna ken the paths, from what my men tellt us. By the time they reach Inverness we'll all be far away, either out on the sea or in the mountains. I canna have their deaths on my conscience when there's no need. If ye have a different view tell me, for I respect your opinions."

Gabriel thought for a minute, weighing up Alex's plan.

"No," he said finally. "I think you're being generous, but I can understand that. I wouldn't want to have their deaths on my conscience either. If they were older, seasoned men, that would be a different matter. But these are raw lads who've either believed the recruiting sergeant's story about excitement and travel, or who've had a shilling dropped in a tankard of ale bought for them, then told they've enlisted when they've pulled it out."

"Is that how they recruit redcoats?" Alasdair Og asked, shocked.

"Yes. To enlist you need to take the King's shilling," Gabriel said. "If you do that, it's binding. There are no rules as to *how* you take the shilling, and the recruiting sergeant is paid by the number of recruits he gets, so he'll come up with ingenious ways to make innocent lads take it, if they're not persuaded by his wild stories of the glories of war. It's the same with the press gangs for the navy, except they'll take men by force, because you can't desert from a ship as you can from land."

Once the decision had been made, Gabriel and his men, who were all red-eyed and yawning hugely with fatigue, rowed back to the cutter and headed out to sea, intending to get some sleep once they were out of sight of land. Not that there was much risk of them being discovered by revenue men in this remote region of Britain, but Gabriel Foley had not lived as long as he had by being needlessly reckless.

The MacGregors who'd slept on land the previous night loaded the cart and prepared everything so that when they returned from Burghead later they could head off immediately, while the ones who'd come in on the ship and not slept at all due to the storm settled down in the cave for a couple of hours' rest, after which they lit a fire and cooked a meal of oatmeal porridge for the men who had not eaten their familiar staple for weeks, and peas porridge and salted pork for the men who'd come up from Loch Lomond with Angus.

"It looks awfu' strange," Kenneth said, casting a dubious eye over his bowl of green porridge dotted with cubes of pink.

"Be adventurous, man," Iain said. "Ye canna spend your whole life eating the same things."

"I dinna see why. It's done me no harm so far," Kenneth replied. "I'm no' exactly scrawny, after all."

Everyone laughed at this, not least because if the fussy Kenneth could best be likened to a human mountain, the adventurous Iain resembled a human cranefly and never put on weight, even now when he had access to a wide variety of foods as Sir Anthony's footman.

"It isna so bad," Duncan said, relishing his own bowl of oatmeal, which tasted like home to him, enhancing the joy of being on Scottish soil surrounded by his clansmen. "I wouldna want to eat it for months though, as sailors do. And yon horrible hard biscuits."

"Gabriel tellt me that when they go on long voyages, sailors often get scorbutic, which is a terrible thing. It rots your gums and makes your teeth fall out, and then your blood goes black and putrid. He said it kills many sailors, and they dinna ken why. But if ye eat yon green porridge a lot ye dinna grow sick," Alex told them.

"Christ!" said Angus. "And I thought the sea sickness was bad. I didna ken ye could die just by being on the ocean!"

"No' so much if you're *on* it," Alex replied. "If ye're under it ye're in trouble though."

The roar of laughter at this set the young prisoners, forgotten at the back of the cave, trembling again. It was terrible not to know what your captors were talking about!

"Gabriel was talking about sailing across the world, though, no' a few days as we have. He said it doesna happen till ye've been at sea for a long time, a month maybe," Alex added.

"I'm thinking it'll taste a lot better washed down wi' some of yon fancy wine ye brought," Kenneth put in hopefully.

Alex had intended for the wine to be taken back to Loch Lomond as a treat for the others, but the mood was good and he felt relaxed and truly at home for the first time in over a year. Looking round he could see that Duncan, Angus and Iain, the three who had spent so much time in England with him, were feeling the same way. To hell with it. He could get more in London and send it to Loch Lomond. This feeling was worth opening fancy wine for!

So it was that by the time they set off later on the short walk to Burghead to meet up with Gabriel and his men, the MacGregors were all a little tipsy and in wonderful spirits. Alasdair Og and Simon had stayed behind to keep an eye on the prisoners and the cargo, while the rest of them strolled along the headland, chatting together in the intimate way that family does, making good-humoured fun of each other, sharing news of the small happenings of their daily lives, commenting on the views and the landscape, which was not as mountainous as their own part of the country.

Alex had been watching his brother, had seen the difference just a few days in the clean fresh air at sea, and a few hours in

Scotland had made to him. Alex was missing Scotland dreadfully, but he was sure that if he could see his own face it would not be glowing as Duncan's now was, his eyes sparkling with happiness.

He realised now that a good part of his own unhappiness was due to the odious job he had in London, rather than London itself. But that was not the case for Duncan. He made no secret of the fact that he considered the capital city of England to be a stinking cesspit with no redeeming features, but he was not one to complain about how miserable he felt living there. His brother, his chieftain needed him, and that overrode any personal discomfort.

"Duncan," Alex said now, suddenly decided, "would ye like to go back down to Loch Lomond wi' the other men, rather than sail back to France wi' me?"

He saw the joy flame in his brother's eyes for a moment, before he regained control of himself.

"I canna do that," he said. "Ye're needing twelve men to row yon boat back from Calais, and I ken how to do it now. No one else does. Who were ye thinking to replace me?"

"No one," Alex told him. "Gabriel tellt me that by the time we get back to Calais there'll be other men in his gang there to help unload the whisky, which is good as when he comes back to England he wants his right-hand man to come with him. So I asked if the right-hand man could row. And he can, of course."

"Ye were thinking to go back home wi' the men yourself then," Duncan replied, and it was not a question.

Alex sighed. He should have known he could not fool this brother who knew him better than anyone ever had, than anyone ever would.

"Aye, I was," he admitted, then held his hand up to stop Duncan continuing. "But I've watched ye the last days, and today especially. Ye need it more than I do. I can cope wi' the city, the smell, the noise, the crowds. I dinna like them, but I can cope. But it's wearing ye down. I kent that in my heart, but I've really seen it now."

"The clan needs its chieftain," Duncan said. "They'll be overjoyed to see ye if ye go. Ye've no' been home in a long time."

"Aye, well, if I had to choose a man to replace me, it would be you. Ye can do everything I can do."

"No, I canna."

"Ye can do everything that needs doing right now. Ye've my trust and they all ken it. I'll need ye back in London wi' me before too long, I'll no' deny that, but ye'll be a lot more use to me there if ye're refreshed and in good spirits again. Ye're pining dreadful, and I can see it now. So if ye spend a few weeks at home, ye'll be helping me too."

Receiving no reply to this, Alex turned to see his brother wearing a deeply sceptical expression.

"I'm no' lying to ye," he insisted. "I *do* want to go home, and the day I can I'll no' hesitate. But ye need it more than I do. Ye help me every day in London, man. I dinna think I could keep going without you beside me. Angus, Iain and Maggie too, but ye give me something they canna. Ye always have. Ye do that for me, though it's costing ye dearly. Let me do this for you."

Duncan nodded then, his grey eyes warm.

"Thank you," he said then, and gripped Alex's arm for a moment. "I'll no' be away for too long, though," he added. "I'll bring Angus back down wi' me too. It's a miracle he didna get himself in trouble this far. Best no' tempt fate."

Then he went back to join the others, leaving Alex to deal with the relief that his brother had agreed so easily to his suggestion, mingled with the sadness that he himself had no idea when he would see Loch Lomond again.

CHAPTER SIXTEEN

Loch Lomond, Scotland, March 1743

Wee Rory took both the responsibility of watching Jeannie and his solemn oath not to tell anyone what he was doing very seriously, which was both heartwarming and amusing, for the little boy was barely six years old. Every time Janet saw his face appear round her door, his solemn expression due to the gravity of his task made her want to laugh and hug him. She did neither, knowing that she would hurt his masculine feelings if she did. Instead she made sure to have some sort of small treat for him; a slice of apple, a bannock with honey, no easy feat in March when food stores were low.

This was made even more difficult due to the fact that Rory's little face appeared round her door every single day, regardless of the weather. Every day Janet stopped whatever she was doing, gave him his little reward and hared off after Kenneth's black-haired wife, slowing only when she had her in her sight.

After a week of this, Janet was regretting having volunteered to follow her neighbour. Not least because every day Jeannie would briskly walk to a clearing a couple of miles away, pace around it for an hour or two while Janet crouched in the undergrowth or hid behind a tree growing wetter or colder or both, after which she would walk home again, face like thunder.

"She's waiting for someone," Janet told Peigi after one particularly wet excursion, as she sat as close to the peat fire as she could, sipping a cup of hot water with whisky to warm her up, while Peigi stood at the doorway wringing out her friend's arisaid.

"Who could she be waiting for?" Peigi asked, returning and

spreading the arisaid across the floor in the hope that it would dry a little before Janet had to return home.

"I havena a notion, but I'm certain of it now. I canna think of any other reason why she'd go out in weather like this wi' no intention to do anything useful, and then walk around a muddy clearing gazing off into the trees every few minutes."

"Which direction is she looking in?" Peigi asked.

Janet thought for a minute.

"North," she said.

"Well, one thing is certain," Peigi commented, "it's no' one of our men she's thinking to meet."

"Of course it isna," Janet replied. "For one thing they're all away wi' either Alex or Angus. And for another, bonny as Jeannie is, no man who kent Kenneth would touch her, even if she were to beg him to."

This was true. What Kenneth would do to any man who cuckolded him didn't bear thinking about.

"Aye," Peigi agreed. "Whoever it is doesna ken Kenneth, and doesna ken Jeannie either, I'm thinking."

Janet looked quizzically at her companion over the rim of her cup.

"As ye said, she's awfu' bonny but she's a temper on her too, and a tongue like a knife. Her ma and da let her have her own way in everything, and Kenneth does the same, the fool."

"Aye, well, he loves her, always has," Janet said.

"No, he hasna," Peigi countered. "I was only a bairn when she set herself on him, but I remember. I thought she was wonderful then, ye ken, no' just because of her looks, but because she seemed free, somehow. She did what she wanted, and she always got what she wanted. I used to watch her carefully, for I wanted to learn how she did it, so that I could be like her too."

"I didna ken that," Janet said.

"No, well, I'm four years younger than ye, and that's a lot when ye're a bairn," Peigi said, reddening a little. "I dinna want to be like her now, that's certain. But I watched her wi' Kenneth, for I loved him. He was like a da to me."

"Aye, he was to all of us. He is to the bairns now. It's a sadness that Jeannie hasna quickened."

"She wanted him. So she put everything into getting him. And now she wants whoever she's hoping to meet in the trees, or whatever she thinks they can give her that Kenneth canna. So she doesna want Kenneth any more."

Janet thought for a minute. She loved Jeannie too. It was hard not to, for she was beautiful, always laughing and had a glorious voice. It lifted your heart just to hear her singing as she passed your door. But she couldn't argue with Peigi's description of her either. Jeannie was selfish, and could be cruel when she didn't get her own way. She just hid that side of herself well.

Clearly not from Peigi though.

"Who do ye think it could be?" she asked.

"I havena a notion. Hopefully ye'll find out one day before Kenneth comes back. And Simon. For ye willna be able to disappear for a few hours every day once he's home, no' without him learning of it. For he watches you as I watched Jeannie. When are ye going to marry him then?"

"Christ! I havena decided whether I *am* going to marry him yet!" Janet protested.

"Aye, ye have. Ye're just afraid to do it. But ye should. He's a good man and he loves ye. Maybe Jeannie'll take him from ye if the man she's wanting doesna appear."

"Pffft," Janet replied. "I'm no' feart of *that,* even if she wasna married already. He doesna like her, he tellt me so. He thinks she's too high an opinion of herself. I'm thinking I'll be taking a walk to yon clearing every day, either until the men return or the idiot Jeannie's waiting for appears."

* * *

Janet did indeed end up walking to the clearing for another week, but with no success, because whoever this person was that Jeannie was so anxious to meet, he did not seem to share her passion, or not enough to show up anyway.

And then Jeannie seemed to give up, for she stopped her daily walks and instead occupied herself around the settlement as all the other women were doing while the men were away. Except they laughed and chatted together, while Jeannie remained silent, her face like thunder, snapping at anyone who enquired as to what was amiss.

"What do we do now?" Peigi asked one evening, the two of

them sitting around her fire again, her four-year-old having just gone to sleep in the boxbed she normally shared with her husband Alasdair Og.

"Ye'll regret that, when Alasdair's home, for he'll be wanting to sleep wi' ye still," Janet observed, glancing towards the bed, the doors of which were slightly ajar.

"No, Jamie kens he can only sleep there when his da's away," Peigi told her. "He's a comfort to me too, for I miss Alasdair sorely when he's no' here. I've a piece of news for him when he comes back too," she added, blushing.

"Have ye? Can ye tell me?" Janet asked.

Peigi considered.

"Aye. I shouldna, but I'm desperate to tell someone, and I ken ye'll no' tell a soul," she said after a moment. "I'm wi' child again. I didna say anything before he left, for I wasna sure, and I didna want to raise his hopes and then be wrong. But I'm sure now."

"Oh! That's wonderful news!" Janet cried, then clapped her hand over her mouth, looking towards the box bed. Silence fell as both women listened intently. From the bed came the soft snores of a deeply sleeping child. After a minute, both women relaxed.

"I trust ye no' to say a word to anyone," Peigi said softly. "What will we do about our other secret though?"

"I dinna see what we *can* do," Janet replied. "All I could say in truth is that she walks round a clearing every day and looks north. If we confront her she'll deny she's meeting anyone. She'll likely say she's missing Kenneth, and looking for him to come home."

She glanced up and caught Peigi's look, which was so sceptical it made her laugh.

"Aye, I ken," she added. "But we couldna say a word against it if she did, for I havena seen her meet anyone. And then we'd never ken what she's up to, for she'd be warned."

"That's true," Peigi mused. "And we canna tell Kenneth, either."

"No. He wouldna believe us. So we'll have to wait, and keep watching out for her. If she's meeting someone, we'll find out. If she isna, or isna any more, then we'll have to keep the secret forever. I wouldna grieve Kenneth for the world, unless we've no choice."

* * *

A few days later the men returned from their trip north, accompanied by a new cart, a horse and Duncan, who greeted everyone, announcing that he was only home for a few days and promising to tell them all the news from London that Angus hadn't already told them, that evening.

Then, while the other men went to their homes to embrace their wives and children or their sweethearts, he headed straight for the loch, whose waters were sparkling in the late afternoon weak sunlight.

Once there he stood for a few minutes with his eyes closed, listening to the wind rustling through the branches of the trees, the soft murmur of the loch against the shore, the distant sound of the clan going about its daily business. The sounds of home.

Then he opened his eyes and looked across the loch to the mountains edging it on the far side, green turning to blue in the distance. The water was icy, but clean and clear. He had not seen clean, clear water in all his time in London. Certainly not in the Thames, which was a cesspit in his view.

He inhaled deeply, breathing in the scent of crisp, pure air, air which somehow smelt different to the air he'd breathed on his walk home with the other men. Different because it was the smell of home. Something in him shifted and settled, and he was completely Duncan again, not Murdo as he had been for too long.

Suddenly decided, he unfastened his swordbelt, letting his kilt fall to the ground before pulling his shirt over his head and dropping it carelessly on the shingle. Then he strode into the ice-cold water, gasping for a moment with the glorious shock of it. And then he cried out in pure unadulterated joy at being home again, the only place in the world where he was truly complete.

Kenneth, who unlike all the others had *not* gone immediately home to embrace his wife, instead unloaded the cart and so heard the uncharacteristic whoop of joy from the lochside, which made him smile. For one moment he contemplated joining Duncan in the loch, but then realised he could not put it off forever.

He pushed his hair back off his face, sighed, then headed home, his smile fading as he walked. He half expected her to be out on one of her walks, as she had not come out to meet the returning men as every other clan member had. But when he opened the door and walked in she was there, sitting on a stool near the fire. She looked up.

"So, ye're back then," she said indifferently.

"Aye," he replied awkwardly, not knowing how to respond to this. In the past, even in the very recent past, she would have jumped up, grey eyes shining, and run into his arms, telling him how she'd missed him. Then she would have told him any news of what had happened while he'd been away, and demand to know everything that had happened to him. And then they would have gone to bed, regardless of the time, desperate to make love. What had happened to turn her against him?

"Jeannie, we canna go on like this," he began. "We must talk about—"

"The broth isna ready yet," she interrupted, "so I hope ye're no' hungry. Ye were away longer than I expected."

His heart lifted at this. Had she missed him?

"We had a lot to bring back, no' just the weapons," he explained. "We couldna carry it all, so we brought some back in this wee cart we found, but we couldna travel as fast because of it. It's a fine tale of how we came by the cart—"

"So ye brought a lot back. Did ye bring me a present?" she interrupted, her voice cold.

How the hell could he have brought her a present? He hadn't been anywhere where he could have got one for her. As she well knew. He felt suddenly weary.

"Alex bought a good roll of silk when he was in Calais," he told her. "Enough for all the womenfolk to make a bonny gown. Duncan's come back wi' us, for Alex couldna, and I'm sure he'll show it to ye all this evening. We were thinking to have a wee *ceilidh* at the chieftain's house."

"So Alex bought me a present, but you didna," Jeannie shot back. "Are ye happy wi' that?"

He held up his hands in surrender.

"I'm no' arguing wi' ye, woman," he said. "I ken that's what ye're wanting, and I dinna ken why. If ye're wanting to talk to me, tell me what's amiss, then I'll listen. Until then I'm weary, and I'm away to my bed."

He lay in the bed, praying that she would come to him, nestle beside him as she used to, and tell him what he had done to make her take against him so. Whatever he had to do, he would fix it, for she was everything to him. But he couldn't fix it until he knew what it was.

After a few minutes he heard the door close, and knew that instead of wanting to mend what was between them, she'd gone out for another of her walks.

He sighed, and turning over in the bed he closed his eyes, allowing sleep to take him.

CHAPTER SEVENTEEN

Inversnaid Garrison, Scotland, late March 1743

Colonel Walker stood in the square in front of the barracks and looked at the group of shivering men standing in front of him with absolute disgust.

"Dear God," he said. "You look like beggars!"

They smelt like beggars too, worse than beggars, in fact. He wrinkled his nose in disgust, heartily glad that there were too many of them to fit in his room. He would have had to have the place fumigated to get rid of both the stench and whatever vermin they were carrying if he'd interviewed them there.

He looked over them, taking in the assorted filthy rags that barely covered their emaciated bodies, their tangled greasy hair, their swollen blistered feet, most of them wrapped inexpertly in more filthy rags in place of shoes.

"What the hell happened to you?" he asked.

The men, who had all been looking at their throbbing feet now looked at their commanding officer, as they had been asked a question. Who would answer it was another matter. An uncomfortable silence fell as each man waited for another to put his head in the lion's mouth.

"Well? Have your tongues all been cut out?" the colonel shouted. "Morrison. Answer me."

Private Morrison closed his eyes in horror for a moment, then attempted to pull himself together.

"Sir, we were ambushed. By an army of Highlanders, sir," he added.

Colonel Walker looked the men over again.

"Ambushed. By an army," he echoed. "How many were in this 'army'?"

"Er…a lot, sir," Harold replied, having waited a second in the futile hope that someone else would answer this time. "Too many to count."

"I see. And yet, as soldiers of His Majesty I assume you put up a good fight against this army of savages?"

"Oh yes, sir, we did!" Harold said emphatically. Several others murmured agreement with this.

"That's gratifying to hear. And as you are all present, and none of you appear to be badly injured, can I assume you were victorious in your battle?" The sarcasm dripping from every syllable was obvious to even the dimmest soldier, and they all returned to examining their feet, except for the unfortunate Harold, who flushed beetroot instead.

"Um…we tried, sir, but there were too many of them," he ventured. "We were overpowered."

Colonel Walker nodded.

"Overpowered. And what happened to your uniforms?"

"We were made to surrender them, sir," Harold replied in a low voice.

"You were. So you are trying to tell me that you put up a brave resistance to an army of clansmen, were captured and stripped of your uniforms, and yet *not one* of you is dead or injured? Before you fabricate your next answer," he added, holding up his hand, "let me remind you that I have seen Highlanders fight, have in fact fought them myself, and whilst they might be barbarian primitives, they are also formidable, ruthless warriors. If you had put up any sort of resistance at all to an army of these men, you would be in no fit condition to stand in front of me telling me a tissue of lies. In fact it would be very unlikely that any of you would have survived to tell me anything at all! Go and clean yourselves up. Get something to eat and find some clothes. I'm assuming you all have at least one civilian outfit. I'll deal with you later."

A sigh of relief passed through the men at this announcement. They would feel better with a hot meal inside them, and some clean clothes on. And while they were eating and washing they could come up with a plausible story. They should have done it on the way home, they realised now, but it had been all they could do just to survive the nightmare journey.

"Not you, Morrison," the colonel said as they all made to go. The rest of the men's shoulders slumped, telling Walker a great deal, both of what they thought of Morrison and what they thought of the adventure he had led them on. Whatever balderdash they'd intended to invent while cleaning themselves up had been scuppered by him keeping Morrison back. He smiled nastily.

"Now," he said, once the rest of the men were out of earshot. "Tell me what really happened. Did you reach the beach where your whore told you the arms were being brought in?"

"Yes, sir," Morrison replied, frantically thinking of how to put a positive spin on this. If he couldn't, his military career was dead, and he would spend the rest of his life as a private rotting in shitholes like this.

"You did? Well, that's something, at least. And were the arms brought in?"

"They were, sir."

Colonel Walker raised his eyebrows. What, there really *had* been a landing of arms for the Jacobites? Shit.

"Morrison. I warn you now. If you are lying to me about this, I will have you flogged until I see bone. You are sure of this?"

Morrison blanched at this threat. He had seen men flogged, had seen their agony, and never, never wanted to experience it personally.

"Yes, sir. I wouldn't lie about that," he said urgently.

"Tell me then, what manner of arms? How many? And I will need descriptions of the men involved, and the ship. As much information as you can give. Did you hear any of their conversation?"

"They spoke in the Irish tongue, sir. I couldn't understand them," Harold replied, desperately grasping at the one question he could answer truthfully without telling the shameful truth of how they'd been overcome.

Colonel Walker waited, allowing the silence to stretch, until Harold could stand it no more.

"We…er…we slept in the cave when we arrived, sir. They ambushed us in the night, while we were asleep," he said.

"I see. And did you not post a sentry, who could warn you in advance of such an ambush?"

"They came from nowhere, sir. We had no time to do anything before they were on us," Harold said.

"So, did you have a sentry?"

"Yes, sir."

"And who was it?"

Harold could not lie now, because he knew the others would all say who the sentry was.

"It was me, sir. But it was a very wild night. I didn't hear anything unusual until they suddenly were there. As you said, sir, they're formidable. We had no chance. I'm so sorry."

He really did look sorry. And, knowing Highlanders, the colonel knew it was distinctly possible the fool had heard nothing. The clansman's ability to blend into the undergrowth and move silently was remarkable. He sighed.

"Go. Get clean and eat, and then come to my room. In one hour," he said.

At least he would be able to get some descriptions of the men, he thought as he went back to his room. Maybe some names even, and some idea of the weaponry being brought in. Who would have thought that a woman would find Morrison appealing enough to divulge her clan's secrets to? The man must be hung like a horse!

* * *

An hour later Morrison appeared in Colonel Walker's room, dressed somewhat haphazardly in grey breeches, a voluminous shirt which he'd clearly borrowed from a much larger man, and a waistcoat from a smaller one. His lower legs and feet were bare, and looking down at them the colonel could understand why. The man's feet were a mass of suppurating sores. How the hell he'd walked all that way with them was anyone's guess. Desperation, probably. The natives between here and Elgin were not known for their welcome to British soldiers.

"Sit down," Walker said, pointing to the chair on the other side of his desk. "Right, tell me about the arms first." He dipped his quill in the inkpot and then waited, quill poised over the sheet of parchment in front of him.

Harold flushed scarlet. He had talked with the other men over bread and meat, and they had all agreed that he could not invent descriptions for everything. The colonel would no doubt question all of them, and any discrepancies in their story would be severely punished. Better to tell the truth, as shameful as it was.

So Harold, almost purple with shame, and stammering with embarrassment, confessed that they had been stripped, bound and blindfolded before the ship ever arrived.

The colonel put the quill back in the holder and looked at him.

"So you are telling me that you went all the way to Burghead, and that a ship full of weapons was landed and carried away in your presence, and you can tell me *absolutely nothing useful at all* about what was landed, who landed it, or which direction they took it?"

"No, sir. I'm sorry, sir," Harold said.

Colonel Walker blew out a breath, then glared at the ridiculous excuse for a soldier in front of him. He thought for a moment.

"Are you still fucking this bitch? When are you meeting her again?" he asked.

Harold was so shocked at this question that he looked straight at his superior, his mouth open.

"I...er...I was supposed to meet her again, but I didn't because I was away, and now I...I won't see her again, sir," he said fervently. "I've learned my lesson."

"Yes you will see her. Didn't she tell you where they store the arms?" Walker asked.

"Yes. At Stronmelochan."

"Where at Stronmelochan?"

"I don't know, sir. I don't know where Stronmelochan is."

Neither did the colonel, but he would find out.

"Morrison. I have no idea what the hell this woman finds attractive about you, but she clearly does see something. Enough to tell you the truth about this landing. If you are to salvage anything of your career from this pathetic shambles, you will find out exactly *where* at Stronmelochan these weapons are stored. And to do that you will have to meet this bitch again. Do whatever you need to, but find this information out. If you do, I might look on you a little more favourably. And keep her sweet. She could be useful. Do you think you can at least manage that?"

Harold thought of the red-haired giant who had slung him over his shoulder as though he weighed nothing. Who was the husband of this woman he now wished he had never seen. A woman he never wanted to see again.

A woman he would have to see again. Maybe many times. He had no choice. He had to at least manage that, and pray to God that Kenneth never found out. He just had to hope that Jeannie hadn't lost patience with him not showing up and was still going to the clearing every Wednesday as they'd arranged, in the hopes of meeting him.

* * *

The following week Jeannie did not go to the clearing, because she was angry with Harold for not making the effort to either meet her or somehow let her know that he couldn't. And she was angry with Kenneth, because no matter how hard she tried she couldn't make him lose his temper and say all the horrible things she wanted him to say to her, things that she could then use to justify her adultery in her own mind.

Every time she tried to argue with him he would leave, or if he couldn't leave for some reason he would refuse to answer her, no matter what she said. It was impossible. She could not make him justify her decision to run off with another man.

By the time the next Wednesday came round she had given up trying to provoke him. He was pathetic, she decided. He didn't deserve her. Harold didn't deserve her either, but at least with him she would have a better chance of improving her life, of travelling, of having beautiful clothes, not just one silk dress that she would have to sew without any help from the other women because they disapproved of her attitude to Kenneth, even though it was none of their business. And that meant it would look dreadful, because she was a dreadful needlewoman.

Harold had told her he would buy her dresses sewn by a professional seamstress, with embroidery and spangles on! And she would be able to go to places that justified wearing a lovely gown, not just the chieftain's house, which should be her house anyway, if Kenneth had any ambition whatsoever.

So on the first Wednesday of April, while the other women were taking all their washing down to the loch to make the most of the first fine weather and the men were gloomily gathering implements to start the peat cutting, a job they all hated but which was crucial to the survival of the clan through the next winter, Jeannie slipped off unnoticed and headed to the clearing.

Or rather she *thought* she had slipped off unnoticed, but wee Rory, still wanting to impress Janet and Peigi, to say nothing of receiving an edible treat, appeared down by the loch a minute later, locating Janet and speaking earnestly to her.

"Aye, come on then, laddie," Janet said, somewhat wearily. "We'll walk back together. It's a secret between us," she told the other women, who were looking at her with curiosity. She tilted her head towards Peigi and put her finger to her lips, which told the others that it was some sort of surprise for Peigi's imminent birthday.

Then she set off back to the house with Rory.

"Which way did she go?" she asked.

"The same way she always does," the boy replied. "She must like walking a lot."

"Aye, she does. Here ye are, then, for being such a bonnie sentry," she said, taking a precious honey cake that she'd saved to get her through the laborious task of laundering all the clothes and handing it to him, smiling as his eyes widened with joy. Then she was gone, striding off in the direction of the clearing, cursing Jeannie under her breath.

"So then," said Peigi that evening when Janet appeared in the doorway. "He's away out at the peat still. The both of them are," she added on seeing Janet looking for Peigi's husband and son. "I'm thinking ye didna spend the whole of this fine washing day making a wonderful treat for my birthday then?"

"No, but I'll have to now or the others will wonder what I was really doing," Janet said, sitting gratefully on the stool Peigi pointed to. "Christ," she continued. "I wish I hadna seen what I've seen today, for no good will come from it, I'm sure."

Peigi put the oatcake she'd been shaping down.

"What? Ye saw who she's been meeting, then?"

Janet nodded.

"I did. They'd been there a wee while when I reached the clearing. I canna imagine what Kenneth would do if he found out."

"So he's swiving her, then?" Peigi asked directly.

"Aye, and I'm thinking they've been doing that for a good time, for there was no shyness between them. They were as cosy together as I'm sure you and Alasdair are. And that's bad enough, but…I'm thinking he's a soldier, Peigi."

"A soldier! He had a redcoat uniform on?"

"He didna have a lot on when I arrived. Neither of them did. And no, he didna have a silly scarlet coat wi' all the stupid ropes on. But he did have the black leather boots they wear, and a good horse. And he was a Sasannach. I couldna hear what they said when they were lying together, though they blethered on for a good while, but when he came back to the horse to leave he tellt her he'd try to come back next Wednesday, and he spoke in the English. I canna think of anything else he could be but one of yon soldiers from the garrison at Inversnaid."

"What the hell is she thinking of to do that at all, wi' such a fine man as Kenneth for her husband? He worships her! And wi' a redcoat! An enemy! I'd thought it was maybe a wee flirtation wi' a laddie from another clan, but this…this is something different," Peigi said. "What will we do? Will we tell Kenneth?"

Janet blanched at even the thought of that.

"I canna tell Kenneth. I couldna bear it. And I ken how gentle he is, but we all ken how he fights when the rage is on him. No. I couldna live wi' myself. And I wouldna ken how to tell him in the right way, so he didna…" Her voice trailed off as she thought of all the terrible possibilities.

"So he didna tear the both of them limb from limb, and then the garrison after it," Peigi said, standing and going to the press, where she filled two cups from one of the small tubs of claret Alex had brought back from Calais. "Here," she said, handing one to Janet. "I'm thinking ye need this. I do, just hearing of what yon fool Jeannie's doing."

Janet accepted the cup, taking a deep draught of the rich wine.

"I'll wager he's filled her daft head wi' promises, so she'd agree to swive him.," Peigi mused angrily. "She's been walking round like a queen for weeks now."

"We canna do this. It's a matter for the chieftain," Janet said now. "It's no' a simple thing. It wouldna be anyway, but wi' a redcoat…no."

"But Alex isna here, and willna be here for months perhaps!" Peigi said. "We could have tellt Duncan, for he acts as chieftain for Alex, but he's gone now too, and he didna say when he'd be back either."

Janet buried her head in her hands.

"Then we'll have to keep it a secret, Peigi, until one of them returns."

"Holy Mother of God. How will we do that?" Peigi murmured.

"I'm thinking it'll be easier to do that than to tell Kenneth," Janet replied.

Silence fell as the two women, both forthright and honest, contemplated keeping such an enormous secret, possibly for months.

"We canna tell Kenneth, that's true," Peigi said after a time. "But we can tell Jeannie."

Janet looked up.

"Tell *Jeannie?*" she said. "She'll deny it."

"She canna deny it. Even she canna do that, no' when ye tell her ye saw them naked. They *were* naked?"

"Almost. Enough for there to be no doubt what they were doing," Janet agreed.

"Well, then. We go together, tomorrow, while the men are at the peat, and we tell her what ye've seen. And we tell her that we'll be watching her, and if she goes to meet the bastard again, then we'll tell Kenneth. No, we'll *take* Kenneth to see what she's doing."

"We couldna do that!" Janet said, aghast.

"Aye, we could. If we dinna, and the redcoat gets her wi' child, it'll be much worse. How could we tell Alex then that we kent about it for a long time, and didna do anything? At least this should stop her."

"She could already be wi' child," Janet pointed out.

"Aye, well, we willna think of that now," Peigi said, her hand automatically moving to rest protectively on her swelling belly.

"I meant we couldna take Kenneth to see that," Janet clarified.

"Aye, we could. I could, anyway. I love Kenneth. Maybe she'll wake up and see what she's got when we confront her. If she doesna, then she deserves whatever he does. Are ye agreed?"

Janet wiped her hand across her face, then picked her cup up and took a deeper draught of the wine.

"Aye," she said then. "About telling her we ken, at least. We canna do nothing. Ye're right in that."

CHAPTER EIGHTEEN

After her two unexpected visitors had left, Jeannie sat in the house for a long time, staring into space, unable to think of *anything*, let alone a solution to the enormous problem they had dropped in her lap. Then she stood and went to the door, looking at the sky to assess the time. She had an hour, maybe two before Kenneth came home from the peat with the other men, and by that time she had to at least be acting normally.

She scraped her hand through her hair, closed the door and sat down again. Would they do it? If she met Harold again would they really bring Kenneth to *see* what she was doing? Yes, they would, she thought, because they knew he wouldn't believe such a terrible thing if he didn't see it with his own eyes. He could see no wrong in her, never had been able to.

But if he *did* see it with his own eyes…dear God. No. She couldn't imagine what he'd do. She'd never seen him when the red mist took him, but others had, and talked about it on dark winter's nights when they told stories of battles they'd fought. And if he caught her with another man, the red mist *would* take him. Of that she had no doubt.

She could not meet Harold again. That was certain, for she'd had no idea Janet had been following her, and she couldn't get a message to Harold to change the place or the time, unless she went to Inversnaid. Even if she did they might not let her speak to him. And Janet might follow her there, too.

She was trapped.

Now she would never have beautiful dresses, dance in gilded rooms under one of the huge lights with thousands of crystals that Alex had told them the rich people had. She would never have a house of her own with a chimney and big windows with glass in.

And all because Janet was jealous of her!

That was it, Jeannie thought spitefully. That was why she *still* hadn't agreed to marry Simon, even though they'd been courting forever. Janet was hoping to take Kenneth from her, and knew well she never could, because she wasn't beautiful, and she sang like a frog. And because Kenneth would never look at another woman while Jeannie was alive.

She would spend the rest of her life living in this hovel with a giant of a man who had no ambition to do anything except cut peat and watch over the bairns when they played in the loch.

Christ! Jeannie put her head in her hands, feeling the despair crash down over her. She could not live like this for the rest of her life. She was worth more than this.

She would wait for as long as it took, until everything had settled down and Peigi and Janet were no longer suspicious. She'd be kind to Kenneth. It wouldn't take much to have him worshipping her again. And then she'd go to Inversnaid and persuade Harold to take her in.

Or maybe…

He had been different yesterday, unsettled somehow. And she'd expected their lovemaking to be fierce and passionate, after weeks apart. But it hadn't been. In fact for the first time in their affair he hadn't grown hard enough to really pleasure her, even when she stroked him and kissed it, which usually made him shoot to attention, as he'd said laughingly in the past.

Maybe he had another woman. Maybe that was why he hadn't met her for so long. He'd seemed very reluctant to talk about what he'd been doing in his absence.

No. She wouldn't go to Inversnaid. If she was going to leave, she might as well do it properly, and go to Stirling, or Edinburgh even! She knew she was beautiful, everyone had told her that from her being a child. And she could do the reading and the writing too, and even the numbers! There were lots of men in Edinburgh. She would have no problem finding one there. Someone better than Harold, anyway!

She would have to plan this, though, and take the time to do it right. She would need money, for one thing. And she would need to be friendly with the other women, so that they would help her to sew her silk dress, so it would look fit to be worn in Edinburgh. And then she would just disappear one day.

She was worth more than this, more than a hut with a dirt floor, more than a man who couldn't give her children of her own, even though she didn't really want them, noisy, smelly things who ruined your body and tried to kill you when you were birthing them.

It would be different having babies in Edinburgh. She would have women to help her, and servants to look after the babies too. And a chandelier! That was the name of the huge crystal light!

She could be intimate with Kenneth, friendly with all the stupid, unambitious women, if she knew it was only for a short time. She sat then, smiling into the fire, dreaming of her beautiful home and the *ceilidhs* she'd have, with crystal glasses and silver cutlery, and flowers on the table.

And while she was doing that Kenneth came home. She looked up at him as he came over to her, dressed only in his shirt, which was soaking wet from a dip in the loch and clinging to his body, heavily muscled from a lifetime of work and weapons training, his *féileadh mór* folded over one arm, his long auburn hair loose on his shoulders. She had to admit that Harold looked like a child, *was* a child compared to her husband, who was looking down at her sitting by the fire, smiling uncertainly, his blue eyes warm, gentle. Loving. And in that moment she realised that however her life turned out, no one would ever love her like this man did, or even come close.

And she suddenly found she could not be intimate, not even friendly with him, for if she was she might weaken, and then she would never have all the things she so desperately craved.

She stood, and turning from him went into the bedroom, leaving him standing there alone, the warmth fading from his eyes, to be replaced by confusion. By sadness.

* * *

Loch Lomond, Scotland, April 1743

It was evening when Duncan finally reached the top of the hill and saw the waters of Loch Lomond below him. He smiled then, but not with joy as he had last time he'd seen his home, although in spite of everything, a thrill of happiness did run through him at seeing the place which held his heart.

He stopped then and sat down on the grassy summit, looking at the loch, at the mountains surrounding it, at the numerous small islands dotted along its surface. It had been a clear sunny day, the sky the pale watery blue of spring, the blue now deepening as gloaming approached. A light breeze brushed his cheek as he sat, playing with his hair, which was loose, not scraped back and tied with a leather thong or a ribbon, as it had to be in London. He would not tie it until he either reached London again, or had to from necessity to prevent it obscuring his vision in a fight. It was childish, but he wanted everything about him to be unrestrained while he was in Scotland, even his hair.

He did not expect to fight while he was here, although he did expect to do violence. Great violence. And that was why, instead of rushing down to the loch crying out for joy as he had less than a month ago, he was now sitting on a hill staring across it, trying to work out the best way to deal with this dreadful problem, his mood as dark as the distant mountains were slowly becoming in the deepening dusk.

Duncan had never thought he would dread going home, always thought he would leap at any chance to go back. But here he was, looking down on his beloved home, wishing with all his heart that he could be anywhere, even London, rather than here.

Less than a week ago Alex had told his brothers that he needed to meet them, urgently. Duncan and Angus were staying in a cheap room in a maze of filthy alleys between the Strand and Drury Lane, while Alex trained them to be servants at the home of Sir Anthony Peters. They were almost ready now, and once their ridiculous and uncomfortable velvet outfits were finished they would be exchanging this stinking, vermin-infested hovel for much more luxurious quarters in the house the baronet was renting.

That night they had not gone to Alex's workplace though, instead meeting in a disreputable tavern where people minded their own business, knowing that if they did not they could bleed to death on the floor while everyone continued drinking and chatting as though nothing out of the ordinary was happening.

Mainly because nothing out of the ordinary *would* be happening. When they were there he had told them the news that every Highlander dreaded to hear.

One of their clansmen was a traitor.

Alex had told them that he'd received a letter from Donald MacGregor, telling him that the cache of arms stored in the cave at Stronmelochan had been discovered by British redcoats. One of the clansmen who had been there had hidden and observed them, and had told Donald that it was clear the soldiers had known exactly what they would find, and were pretty certain where the cave was, only needing to look around its vicinity briefly before locating it, although it was well concealed with rocks and plants.

"I'm certain now that someone in the clan is passing information to the enemy," Alex had told his white-faced brothers later that evening back at their lodging, having decided even such a tavern as that was too risky to discuss a topic which would mark them as traitors to the Hanoverian crown.

"When ye captured yon wee gomerels at the cave near Burghead, I wasna certain their being there was a coincidence. But I couldna imagine why any commander would send such an ill-trained group to deal with such an important task, so I didna pay heed to my instincts," Alex continued regretfully. "And even then it could have been one of Gabriel's men who was the traitor, but Gabriel himself wasna suspicious, so I dismissed it. I didna think even for a minute that it could be one of ours. But now I ken it must be. For no one outwith the clan kens where the arms were stored. No one."

They had sat in silence for a time then, sick with the horror of it. For Alex was right. And the punishment for betraying your clan, whatever the reason, was death. It had to be.

Highland life was in the main a matter of surviving. In a land that was largely inhospitable, bad weather or a hostile neighbour could wipe out your harvest, your livestock, your homes and even your people. For a Jacobite clan life was even more dangerous, because you were classed by the authorities as traitors.

Not that the Jacobite clans, or any clans for that matter, paid much heed to what the authorities thought, as it was pretty difficult for those authorities to impose their will on large groups of hardened warriors who could only be reached by travelling across the most impossible terrain in ever-changing weather. But even so, it was an extra danger.

If you were a MacGregor the risks were multiplied even further, because the whole clan was illegal. They were prohibited from using their name, from carrying weapons, for existing. They did not have to break any laws, commit any crimes to be executed. Just *being* a MacGregor was a hanging offence.

Because of the profound precariousness of their existence, the Loch Lomond MacGregors stood together, no matter what. They might argue and fight, dislike each other, even hate each other. But faced with an enemy of any kind, they stood together, fought together, and died together when it came to it. Their survival depended on it, because they had nothing else but their fighting skills, their survival skills, and the loyalty of the clan members to each other.

So to discover that one member of that clan had betrayed them to the enemy, not once but twice, was unimaginable. And it could not be tolerated, could not be excused. Once could be a slip of the tongue perhaps, but twice was deliberate.

It was the clan chieftain's job to discover who the traitor was, and to judge and execute them, once discovered. No one would try to stop him doing his job, but it was the worst possible task a clan leader would ever have to do.

But Alex, the chieftain, could not do it, because his job in London was too important for him to leave again so soon, even to deal with something as serious as this. So Alex had asked Duncan to find the traitor and dispatch him.

And as much as Duncan did not want to do this, it never occurred to him to refuse, even though Alex would have understood if he had, would not have commanded him to as he could, being his chieftain as well as his brother. They had been through a great deal together, both as children and adults, and the bond between the two of them was total, beyond any clan allegiance. Because of that Duncan had agreed immediately and had left the next morning.

He sighed, watching as the stars began to twinkle above him, and then he stood. By the time he got home it would be very late, and everyone except for those watching for enemies would be in their homes, and most of them asleep. Hopefully he would be able to get a good night's sleep himself, or at least *some* sleep, for he was exhausted both in body and spirit, and needed to gather all his strength before starting his task.

Tomorrow he would call the clan together in small groups and tell them there was a traitor in their midst. Then he would watch their reactions closely, hoping that whoever it was would betray themselves, either by a facial expression, a movement, or even by trying to escape. If they did he would act quickly and coldly, partly to give a clear warning to the whole clan that such betrayal could not be tolerated, and partly to get it over with. He so desperately wanted, needed to get it over with.

He had spent the whole journey north trying to think of who it could be, to at least come up with some names. But he could think of no one. Nor had Alex been able to. But he would find out, would not leave until he had, no matter how long it took.

He set off down the hill, consoling himself with the knowledge that although he couldn't take Alex's other burdens from him, at least he could take this one. At least he could do this for the brother he adored.

That would be something to hold on to in the days to come.

CHAPTER NINETEEN

Janet had just fallen asleep and was beginning a very pleasant dream, when she was suddenly awake again. She lay for a minute in a drowsy stupor, wondering if whatever had woken her was real or just something in the dream, which was already fading.

Then the knock came again, and, suddenly awake, she leapt out of bed, grabbing her arisaid and wrapping it round her as she ran to open the door.

Peigi was standing there, as close to the door as possible, trying to shelter under the overhang of the heather roof from the sudden downpour. She pushed past her friend to get out of it, moving to the fire as Janet closed the door against the weather.

"Why did ye no' just come in? What's amiss?" she asked urgently as she poked the embers back to life. "Is someone ill?"

"No," Peigi replied. "I'm sorry. I didna want to frighten ye, but I needed to tell ye something. I've been awake wi' Jamie. He cut his leg today and he tellt me it was paining him so, and he couldna sleep. I spent a time comforting him, and then I said that if it was so bad, then he'd need a dose of the medicine for healing it. He's sleeping now."

"Medicine? What kind of medicine?" Janet asked, yawning. "It must be awfu' good."

"Aye. Barbara made it for me. It's a kind of medicine that makes your face turn inside out, it's that bitter. Awfu' good for deciding if bairns are truly hurting or just wanting their own way. I dinna think it has any other properties," Peigi said wryly. "When ye've bairns of your own, I'll give ye some. Ye'll no' need more than one dose for each bairn. After that, just showing them the bottle is enough."

In spite of her crossness at being dragged out of a lovely dream for what seemed to just be a chat about children, Janet started laughing.

"So ye've come through the rain in the middle of the night to tell me what wicked mothers you and Barbara are?" she said.

"Ah. No," Peigi replied. "No. Duncan's here."

"Duncan? Alex's brother Duncan?" Janet said.

"Who else would it be? We've only the one Duncan in the clan!"

"But he only left a few days ago, and he tellt us he'd be gone for a long time. He was awfu' sad about it too. Are ye sure? If he'd come back, the whole clan would ken about it."

"Aye, they would, if he'd come back in the daylight. But I was standing by the door, waiting to be sure the wee monster was really asleep before I went to bed, and I saw him going into the chieftain's house. I'm thinking he's just arrived."

"If he has, he'll be wanting to sleep," Janet said. "Are ye thinking to go and talk wi' him about Jeannie in the morning?"

"No. I'm thinking to do it now," Peigi said. "If we do, no one will see us, and we'll no' have to find a time when he's alone, and everyone wondering why we need to see him. It'll save a lot of awkward questions. I'm thinking he wouldna come all the way back from London so quickly, unless something has happened. Alasdair sleeps heavy, he'll no' wake while I'm gone unless Jamie calls for him, and he'll no' do that, no' wi' the bitter medicine still on his mind."

Janet thought for a minute. It seemed a shame to disturb Duncan if he was wanting to sleep, but this *was* important, and it had been very hard to keep their secret from everyone else, even Alasdair and Simon. It would be wonderful to be rid of the burden. And Duncan would understand that. Duncan was very understanding.

"Aye," she said, standing. "I'm no' going in my shift though. Give me a minute to dress, and then we'll go together."

* * *

"Mother of God. Wi' a *redcoat?*" Duncan said half an hour later. "Are ye sure?"

The three of them were sitting round the table, on which an

open bottle and a candle stood. Otherwise the room was cold and cheerless, as Duncan had gone straight to bed without lighting a fire on arriving, although he hadn't been asleep when the knock on the door came.

"Aye. I couldna follow her because of wee Jamie, but Janet did," Peigi said.

"She's no' been herself for months now. We all ken that she's no' happy wi' Kenneth. She's awfu' harsh wi' him," Janet explained.

"I kent that, aye," Duncan said. "But Kenneth doesna talk about it. I just thought it was a passing thing."

"So did we, for he's a good man, and they were happy together. We all thought it was because she hadna quickened," Peigi said. "But then we saw she was going walking, in all weathers, which seemed awfu' strange, and she kept telling us that she's wanting more than this."

"So when the men were all away up to bring the weapons back, we decided to follow her, for we thought she was maybe meeting wi' someone from another clan who's been promising her things." Janet said. "She's awfu' wilful, always has been, and vain, and kens how bonny she is."

"So she was meeting wi' the redcoat the whole time Kenneth was away?" Duncan asked. "Why did ye no' tell me when I was here last?"

"Because she didna meet wi' the man," Janet told him. "She went every day, and it was awfu' taxing having to stop what I was doing and run after her then hide in the bracken while she walked about for hours. But it was clear she was waiting for *someone*, so I followed her for two weeks, but no one came, so she stopped going."

"We didna tell ye, nor anyone, for what could we say?" Peigi continued. "And we didna tell Kenneth, for we wouldna hurt him if we didna need to. We thought maybe it was over and she'd see sense, for Kenneth's a fine man, and he loves her dreadful."

Duncan scrubbed his face with his hands, for he needed to think clearly and he was very tired.

"I'm sorry," Peigi said immediately. "It was my idea to come. I thought ye'd want to ken, and in truth it's been hard no' to tell anyone. Will we go?"

"No," Duncan replied. He thought for a minute. "So when did ye see her wi' the man then?"

"In the first days of April," Janet said.

"And she only met wi' him the one time?" Duncan asked. "Did ye hear what they talked about?"

"No," Janet said. "I saw what they did, though. It sickened me. They talked a lot, afterwards, but they were too far away for me to hear what they were saying. They were speaking in the English anyway, for he was a Sasannach. She was waving her hands about, though, as she does when she's excited, so I'm thinking he promised her some wee trinket for betraying Kenneth. I didna dare try to move closer in case they saw me, and I wouldna have understood much of what they said anyway. I canna remember a lot of the English I learnt."

"And she hasna met him since?" Duncan asked, watching with interest as both women flushed scarlet in the flickering candlelight. "What have ye done?" he added.

"Aye, well, we couldna bring ourselves to tell Kenneth, and we didna ken when Alex or yourself would come back, so we tellt Jeannie we'd seen her, in the hope that she'd stop," Peigi admitted.

"We tellt her if she met him again, we'd take Kenneth to see what she was doing," Janet added.

Duncan closed his eyes in horror for a moment, envisioning what could have happened if they had.

"So she hasna met the man since, then," he said, and it was a statement, not a question.

"No. So we're thinking it worked and she saw sense, although the pair of them dinna seem any happier together," Peigi said sadly. "No' yet, anyway."

"Have ye tellt anyone else?" he asked. "Anyone at all?"

"No," Peigi said. "We were hoping we wouldna need to, except for Alex, who should ken, being chieftain. And yourself, for you're chieftain when he canna be."

"What will ye do?" Janet asked.

"I dinna ken yet," he replied honestly. "I need to sleep. Promise me ye willna tell anyone else, no until I say ye can."

Both women promised, then stood to go, because they could see how tired he was. How shocked he was.

"Janet," he said suddenly as they reached the door. She turned back. "Did ye see the man? Can ye describe him?"

"Aye, I did, when he was dressing, for I was no more than the length of this room from him then," she said. She went on to describe what he looked like, making it clear that although she'd forgotten most of the English she'd learnt as a child, having no use for it, there was nothing wrong with her memory otherwise.

Then they were gone, leaving him sitting at the table alone, and, unusually for one who loved his own company, feeling desperately lonely. Right now he would have given almost anything to have Alex sitting opposite him to share this burden.

Because Janet had just described, exactly, the sleeping guard in the cave near Burghead. The wee loon that Alex had interrogated and then dismissed, thinking the redcoats must be there by coincidence, as no commanding officer would send raw youths on such a task. And he had agreed with his brother. Coincidence.

Duncan didn't know why such a group of idiots would be sent to intercept a band of Jacobite Highlanders, but he now knew that their presence was no coincidence.

And he also knew, God help him, that the traitor in the clan was Jeannie MacGregor. And that she'd betrayed the clan not once, but twice at least, telling the man both the location of the landing *and* of their hiding place.

He shook his head, trying to clear the fatigue, trying to fight off the dark loneliness that threatened to unman him. He could not give in to it. Alex must feel this way often, but he didn't give in to it. He must sleep, but had no idea how he would with such knowledge fresh in his mind.

He would lie down anyway, close his eyes, try to think of something pleasant and relax, even if he could not sleep.

He went to bed, dreading the long night ahead, and was asleep as soon as his head touched the pillow.

* * *

In the end he slept long and deep, and by the time he awoke it was broad daylight and the clansfolk were about their daily chores. So deeply had he slept that for a moment he didn't know where he was, until he heard someone laugh, and the warm and welcoming sound of the Gaelic as one of the women greeted another.

And then the events of the previous evening came back to him and instinctively he closed his eyes again, wanting nothing more than to go back to sleep, to forget what a horrendous day this was certainly going to be. True, he no longer needed to interview the whole clan in small groups, and watch for signs of guilt. But he would need to tell Kenneth at least that his wife had betrayed both him and the clan.

He lay there for a minute longer, listening to the cheerful sounds of people who knew each other intimately chatting and laughing, so different from the raucous discordant racket of London, and then he swung his legs out of bed and got up.

Once dressed he sat at the table, thankful that Peigi and Janet had kept their promise, not only regarding their secret, but about the fact that he was home. He did not light the fire, as if he did the smoke from the chimney would alert the clan to his presence. Instead he thought, hoping that now he was fully awake some solution would come to him.

No one apart from himself and his brothers, the letter writer Donald, and Davy who'd witnessed the redcoats locating the cave, knew about the weapons being found, because Alex had made them swear an oath to keep quiet. He did not want the traitor to be forewarned and have a chance to slip away, and maybe betray a lot more about the clan to the British soldiers.

For the last days Duncan had planned how to tell the clan about the traitor in a way that was most likely to make the culprit reveal themselves. Although he'd still have to tell them, he no longer needed to worry about how. The evidence against Jeannie was overwhelming.

He had no doubt that Peigi and Janet were telling the truth. But even if he'd had doubts about their story, everyone knew that Jeannie and Kenneth's marriage had suddenly deteriorated, and that it was Jeannie who was the discontented one. Kenneth had mentioned her walks as well. And Janet could not have known what the redcoat in the cave looked like.

So. Now he needed to think about how he was going to go about dealing with Jeannie. Both Alex and himself had assumed the traitor was a man, for no good reason, Duncan now realised. Alex had given him permission to kill the man, if he discovered who he was. But Duncan could hardly be a pedant and use the exact wording of his permission as an excuse to go back to London and ask him what to do.

Jeannie had to die. Of that there was no doubt. She could not be trusted. And she had put her own silly vanities before the lives of her people. Because if the weapons had been hidden on MacGregor lands rather than Campbell ones as they were, he had no doubt that the British army would have already seized the excuse to wipe out the whole clan. Suspecting a clan was Jacobite was one thing; having evidence that they were planning an uprising was another thing altogether.

Stupid, stupid woman.

Duncan sat, staring into space, pondering. He would have to override all his instincts to do this, for he had been brought up, as all Highlanders were, to respect and protect women. Not that the women couldn't protect themselves if they had to, but because it was the man's job as a warrior to keep the women and children safe. Women were the heart of the clan. Without them the men were nothing, and they all knew that, even if they never spoke of it.

Jeannie had put herself outside that protection now, though. All of the clansfolk would agree that, once they knew what she'd done.

Except Kenneth. He would likely not agree, and he was by far the strongest man in the clan. No man could match him in strength. No two men could match him in strength, even when he was calm, which, thank God, he almost always was. He would not be calm, however, if someone was to execute the woman he loved with a strength which matched his size.

Vaguely Duncan remembered standing with his brother as a very small child, watching Kenneth cradling someone in his arms and howling like a madman. And blood. A lot of blood. Alex would remember what had happened. Alex remembered everything. Perhaps it was better that Duncan could not, he thought.

One thing was certain; in spite of him having the power of the chieftain, which was total, he could not order Kenneth to stand back while he executed his wife. Neither for practical reasons nor for emotional ones. Because although it was true that Kenneth would certainly take out a good number of men before he was subdued or killed himself, he was probably, after Alex, the most loved member of the clan.

He was like a second father to everyone under thirty, and had been since they were born. He had taught most of the men to fight, and some of the women too. He was gentle, good-humoured, loyal and trusting. There was absolutely nothing not to like about Kenneth, unless you were his enemy and the rage was on him.

So Duncan had to tell Kenneth this terrible, impossible piece of bad news without rousing his rage and becoming his enemy. That was the crux of it. He sat for a while longer, finishing the contents of the bottle he'd been sharing with Peigi and Janet last night, and then, no closer to a solution, went out to announce his presence to the clan.

Of course, the first person he met on emerging into the sunlight was Kenneth himself, with a peat iron slung over his shoulder, Alasdair Og following with the peat cart.

"Duncan!" Kenneth cried joyfully. "What are ye doing back, man? I thought ye were in London!"

"Aye, I was, but when I got there Alex tellt me he didna need me for the now, and as he kens how I hate the place, he tellt me I could come back for a wee while if I'd a mind to," Duncan said, hoping he sounded sincere.

"And ye'd a mind to, I'm thinking," Alasdair Og said wryly, "for ye must hardly have arrived in London before ye were leaving again!"

"Ye're away to the peat, then?" Duncan stated the obvious, hoping to change the subject.

"Aye," Kenneth said, "There's a stack of dry ones up there now to load, and then we'll cut and lay the next load to dry. That should be enough to keep us through the winter, if it's no' *too* harsh."

"Have ye other things to do?" Duncan asked Alasdair Og, coming to a sudden decision.

Alasdair Og laughed.

"There's always other things to do, ye ken that," he said.

"I'll take your place, then, for a walk in the fresh air and some honest work is just what I'm needing," Duncan offered.

He did not need to offer twice. All the men hated the peat

cutting, as it was tedious and dirty work. Within a minute Duncan had charge of the cart, and he and Kenneth were heading away from the settlement, far enough away that if the rage took Kenneth when he was told about Jeannie, he would hopefully have calmed by the time he was able to act on it. Unless he directed his rage at the messenger.

In which case, Duncan thought, *at least I'll have my wish to die in my homeland, if very much sooner than I'm wanting to.*

CHAPTER TWENTY

They walked along together companionably, the sun pleasantly warm on their faces, a cool breeze fanning them that they'd appreciate later, for peat cutting was hard work.

If they actually *did* any peat cutting.

Kenneth chatted about how much they'd cut so far, how joyously filthy the bairns had got helping to spread the peats out to dry, how most of the land they were putting to oats was cleared now, and Duncan tried to appear interested, natural, whilst at the same time planning how to broach the subject when they reached their destination.

He was so engrossed in his deliberations that he didn't notice Kenneth had stopped until he'd travelled some distance past him. He halted the horse and looked back to see Kenneth eyeing him thoughtfully.

"What's amiss?" he said.

"Nothing," Duncan answered automatically, seeing immediately by Kenneth's expression that the older man was having none of it.

"Laddie," he said, moving forward and laying the peat iron he'd been carrying down on the cart. "I've kent ye since ye were at your ma's breast, your brother too for that matter. Alex wouldna have let ye travel all the way to London if he hadna needed ye there. He's organised. There's a reason he's sent ye back so quickly, and it's paining ye badly. Ye ken ye can trust me. I'm thinking that's why ye've volunteered for the peat. Are ye wanting to tell me something?"

NO! Duncan screamed silently.

"Aye, I am," he said aloud. "Ye ken me too well. Let's get to the peat ground first though."

"Well, I'm sure whatever it is, together we'll think of something that can be done about it," Kenneth said. "And just sharing a worry lessens it. Alex has shared many a problem wi' me when he was a boy, but ye ken that, I'm thinking."

Kenneth smiled then, his eyes warm, honoured to be singled out by Duncan as the person he could share this problem with, whatever it was.

Oh God.

When they reached the peat ground, Duncan took the cart to the peats that had been laid out to dry, intending to load it before stopping for a rest. That would give him more time to think of how to word what he needed to say before having to do it. But instead of joining him, Kenneth sat on the side of the cart, patting the space next to him.

"Come on then, just say whatever it is," he said. "Let's get it done wi', shall we?"

Duncan opened his mouth to object, then closed it again. He could stack peat for the next ten years and be no closer to knowing the right way to word this. He sat down, not next to Kenneth, but on a nearby rock, partly because sitting next to the giant always made him feel like a small boy, not a good idea when he was acting as chieftain, and partly because he had no idea how the man would react to what he was about to say. A little distance could be a lifesaver.

"Alex sent me back because the arms at Stronmelochan were discovered by the British," Duncan began.

"What? Did someone see them?" Kenneth asked, his eyes wide with shock.

"Aye. Davy Drummond was there. It was after the heavy wind and rain, and he was making sure everything was dry, and that nothing was out of place that a passing Campbell might see. He heard them crashing their way up the hill, so hid and watched them."

"Aye, I ken what a noise yon redcoats make," Kenneth said. "I used to wonder why they wore such a stupit bright colour, that ye could see them coming from miles away. But now I ken it doesna signify, for ye'd hear them coming from miles away whatever they wore. But why are ye telling me and no' the whole clan? Why did Davy no' tell us?"

"Davy didna tell anyone because Alex made him swear no' to. The redcoats went direct to the cave, Kenneth. It wasna a chance discovery."

Duncan waited then while the enormity of this registered with Kenneth, watched the horror on the man's face as he realised that there was a traitor in the clan, and knew that if he *had* needed to gather the clan together to discover who it was, it would have been instantly clear that it was not this gentle giant.

"So we've a traitor among us," Kenneth said quietly. "Do ye ken who?"

"Alex sent me to find out, and to kill them when I did," Duncan replied evasively.

"So why did ye tell me first? Are ye wanting me to help ye find the man?" Kenneth asked.

This was it, then.

"No. I asked ye up here to talk about a private matter, for I need to. We all ken there's discord between yourself and Jeannie, and I'd no' interfere in that normally, for it isna my business. She's been taking long walks, has she no'?"

"Aye," Kenneth replied, reddening a little. "She's restless, but she willna rightly tell me why. She thinks I'm no' ambitious enough. I'm thinking it'll pass in time, if I'm gentle with her, and if—"

He stopped suddenly, but Duncan knew by the look of embarrassment on his face what he'd been about to say. *If I can get her with child.*

"Kenneth," Duncan said, resolved now not to drag this out, for there was no use or pleasure in torturing the poor man. "There's no good way to tell ye this, so I'll just say it. She's been meeting another man in the wee clearing over the mountain. I'm sorry."

Silence fell, while a number of expressions crossed Kenneth's face. Denial at first, then realisation, then utter misery. And he hadn't heard the worst of it yet.

"How d'ye ken that?" he asked finally, very softly. "Are ye sure?"

"I am. I wouldna tell ye otherwise," Duncan said. "While ye

were away at Burghead, two of the women watched her, and one followed her when she went out. They thought to find out what she was doing, and try to stop her if it was what they suspected. They did it for love of ye, Kenneth, for we all love ye dearly, ye must ken that. Jeannie didna meet anyone while ye were away, so they thought they were maybe wrong. But then one day when ye were all up here cutting the peat she went out again, and this time she met wi' the man. They didna want to have to tell ye, to hurt ye, so they tellt Jeannie they'd seen her instead, and that they'd tell you if she didna stop."

Kenneth nodded, but his hands were clenched tightly on his lap.

"She hasna walked out when I've been home at least, for a wee while now. I'm thinking she's stopped then," he said.

"Aye, it seems so. They havena tellt anyone, only myself."

Kenneth nodded.

"Did they ken who the man was?" he asked with deceptive mildness.

Duncan shook his head.

"I'll no' ask who the lassies are. It was kind of them to do that. Will ye thank them for me?" he said. "Will we load the peat, then? I'll think on what to do while we do it. I'm thinking if she's stopped, it was maybe just a wee fling, and—"

"Kenneth," Duncan interrupted. "They didna ken who the man was. But it was a redcoat, a Sasannach, likely from the garrison at Inversnaid. She didna meet him while ye were at Burghead because he was one of the boys in the cave there. The guard who Alex spoke with."

And then Duncan saw the rage flare in Kenneth's eyes, his enormous hands clench into fists and his whole body go rigid, and even though he had known Kenneth his whole life, knew how gentle he was, the fear exploded in him and he leapt to his feet, hand moving automatically to his sword hilt.

"Ah, no, Duncan," Kenneth said quickly, holding one huge hand up, palm forward. "I'll no' hurt ye, I swear it. Just let me be a while. Please."

The note of agony in that last word brought tears to Duncan's eyes, and he nodded then walked away, far enough that he was out of both sight and earshot. He sat down again then, looking blindly at the landscape. He should be relieved that it was done, but he was not, because he would have done almost anything not to cause this man, of all men, such pain. And it was only partly done, for he hadn't told Kenneth she was the traitor yet. That was still to come.

He would sit for as long as he needed to, until Kenneth was ready to hear more, even if he had to sit here all week. He owed the man that, at least.

He did not have to sit there all week, or even all day. After a short time Kenneth came into view, walking normally although his shoulders were slumped, and Duncan suddenly saw what he would look like as a very old man. Still formidable, but broken, somehow.

I did that, he thought sadly. *No, Jeannie did that,* he corrected himself. Love was more powerful than time, more powerful than anything. He knew that, for different reasons. But he could not think of that now. He had to have his wits about him, had to break this man more than he already had. Had to try to heal him afterwards, somehow.

When Kenneth reached Duncan he sat down, leaning against a rock.

"Is she sure, the lassie who saw them?" he said then. "Thinking on how she's been, it makes sense. The wee shite's no doubt been promising to take her away to live in his big house in England or some such nonsense. He's likely a farm boy, wi' no more to his name than I have. That'll be why she was talking about wanting a chimney and glass in the windows. If it's just that and it's over, I can deal wi' it. Is it just that?" he asked.

"No," Duncan said then. "It isna just that." Then he saw Kenneth's mouth twist and realised he did not have to spell out who the traitor was after all. "The lassie who saw her doesna ken about the cave yet, and when she described the man to me I didna tell her I kent who it was. But I'm sure of it, Kenneth. I thought on it all morning, for in truth I was trying to find a way to be unsure. But it canna be anyone else.

"I'm thinking the bastard tellt his sergeant or whoever about what she'd tellt him, and he didna believe it, maybe thought it was a clan plot to draw the men out so we could attack them. So they went without permission. The boy tellt us they were on leave. Maybe he hoped to win promotion by capturing a ship full of arms, I dinna ken. But then he meets her again when he's back, and a week later they raid the cave. Alex doesna believe in coincidences, and neither do I. And this is too many of them."

He paused then, giving Kenneth time to process this, saw the tears spill down his cheeks, and felt his own eyes fill. God, this was awful.

"If ye're wanting me to go back to Alex, ask him what he thinks before I…before I act, then I'll do it, and gladly," Duncan said softly.

"Ye'd do that? It's a mighty long way, and ye've just done the trip twice."

"Kenneth, I'd walk round the world for ye, if it'd help ye deal wi' this. I canna tell ye what it's cost me to say this. I ken how ye feel about her. We all do."

"Ye dinna need to," Kenneth replied. "I can see it on your face. Aye, then. I'd like ye to go back to London. No' because I think ye're wrong. Wanting ye to be doesna make it so. I love her, but I ken she isna perfect. She's been awfu' restless lately, hasna been thinking right. She tellt me I should challenge Alex and become chieftain, for she wanted a bonny house to live in! I thought she was havering, but she talked of it a few times, even tellt me I was a coward for no' challenging him.

"She couldna understand why I wouldna do it, why I should be loyal to a man I could kill if I wanted to. She doesna understand loyalty, no' if it stops her getting what she wants. I see that now, but I didna then, didna think she'd be willing to risk the lives of the whole clan for it. Maybe if I could have got her wi' child she'd have settled. Probably no', but I canna do that in any case."

He paused for a while, then seemed to bring himself back from a dark place a long way away, and looked Duncan straight in the eye.

"He met her in yon clearing, ye say, over the hill? Wi' the birches and the wee burn nearby?"

"Aye," Duncan said. "But they havena met since."

Kenneth nodded.

"I'm no' wanting ye to go to London to ask Alex if he agrees Jeannie's the traitor," he continued, and his voice was calm now.

Too calm, although Duncan didn't see that then, tense as he was himself. "I'm needing ye to get his permission to let *me* be the one to kill her. And the permission of her brothers, for they're in London at the minute. They're all the family she has now, and if they prefer Alex to do it, then I'll no' go against them."

Duncan spent the rest of the day trying to get Kenneth to change his mind, to no avail. He was absolutely adamant that unless Alex himself or Jeannie's brothers refused permission, he would do this himself.

"Christ, man," Duncan said finally, wondering as he did why he was so desperately fighting to do a job he had been dreading doing with every fibre of his being. "Ye canna do this. I ken how ye love her. It'll break ye. Let me do it. I'll be quick, I swear it. She'll no' feel any pain."

"Ah, laddie, ye've a good heart. But no, ye'll no' change my mind on this. And nor would Alex, were he here, and we both ken how persuasive he is. Go. Ask him for his permission."

"But even if I leave right now, I'll be two weeks at the least," Duncan reasoned. "Ye canna see her every day, wi' this burden on ye. Even a cold man couldna do that, and ye're the warmest man I ken. And ye canna tell her, canna tell anyone about it."

"No more will I," Kenneth said. "I've no intention to go home. I'll live out on the mountain until ye come back. I'll no' go near the settlement, for ye've the right of it there. I dinna want to see her until…ye ken. When ye get back, come here. I'll watch for ye."

"But it'll be a torment to ye the whole time! Is it no' better to have it over with? And everyone will wonder where ye are. What can I tell them?"

"Nothing," Kenneth said. "Dinna tell them anything. They'll ken when ye come back, and that's soon enough. I'm set on this, laddie," he added, seeing Duncan about to object again. "Now, let's load yon peat for ye to take back, for the day's nearly done."

And so it was that, to the clan's utter bewilderment, Duncan, after returning from the peat without Kenneth, went straight into his house and firmly closed the door. Those who had things to discuss with him thought to let him sleep, for hadn't he just had an arduous journey home, followed by a day doing a horrible task? They'd speak with him in the morning.

But in the morning, although the fire was still burning, Duncan was gone. And Kenneth had not returned from the peat. It was a mystery.

As the days passed and neither Duncan nor Kenneth returned to solve the mystery, the clansfolk tried to solve it themselves, coming up with increasingly outlandish possibilities. Only three people did not take part in these interesting discussions.

Peigi and Janet, because they had been told by Duncan to say nothing about Jeannie's affair, and although they were certain Kenneth's disappearance was something to do with it, they would not break their promise. It was easier to find lots of tasks that kept them from these awkward conversations.

And Jeannie, who, aware that her attitude towards her husband had the disapproval of the whole clan, continued to keep herself to herself. She did not go for walks any more, except occasionally down to the loch. She did not need to go for walks, partly because she dared not meet Harold, and partly because there was no need to keep away from Kenneth.

He had gone. And as days passed with no word, it seemed he was not coming back.

She sat and wondered. Had Duncan sent him on an urgent errand? Had Alex sent Duncan to bring Kenneth to London for some reason, and they'd gone together? If so, why had he not at least come to say goodbye to her?

Or had Janet told him what she'd witnessed?

No, she thought. If she had he would not have quietly gone away. He would have come to her, asked her why, asked her what he could do to make her love him again, begged her to stop seeing the man. Because he loved her, completely. She knew that. Hadn't he told her so, many, many times?

She didn't care, she told herself fiercely. He was a weight around her, dragging her down with his lack of ambition. She would be better without him. She did not need him. She did not love him.

She told herself that, over and over again. But still every night she would toss and turn in bed, missing the feel of his strong warm body next to hers, missing curling into him like a child, knowing that nothing and no one would ever harm her while he was there. In the daytime, whenever the door rattled she would tense, both hoping and dreading to see him come through it, bringing the smell of the outdoors in with him, blue eyes warm with love for her, with joy that she was his, that he was hers.

She did not miss him. Not at all. She did not care, she told herself. Soon she would leave. Soon she would be in Edinburgh, and her life here, her marriage, all of it would fade, washed away by the dances, the plays, the music. And her new man, her rich man would be better than Kenneth, would give her expensive presents, would love and cherish her, more than Kenneth ever had.

She did not know how that was possible, but she would make it so. She could do anything. She was beautiful, and had the learning, and the ambition to rise. She could do anything, given the opportunity.

And she was about to make the opportunity.

CHAPTER TWENTY-ONE

Private Harold Morrison reined in his chestnut mare just outside the clearing, looking around carefully. Then he rode slowly, tensely, round the edge of the clearing, peering through the trees, watching for even the slightest movement in the shadowy areas. He did this for several minutes. Nothing. There was no sign of anyone. He was completely alone here. The tension left his shoulders then, and he started to relax.

He had not wanted to come here today, had thought the meeting in which he had wheedled out of Jeannie the exact location of the cave where the weapons were stored would be their last. But then Colonel Walker had sent a troop of soldiers to the cave and had been elated that she had given Harold correct information not once, but twice now.

"You will continue meeting this woman, Morrison," the colonel had said afterwards to a dismayed Harold. "And you will continue to give her whatever encouragements she needs in order to keep providing you with information. I hope you appreciate what a rare gem she is among her kind?"

For a moment Harold had wondered how the colonel knew what Jeannie looked like, that she was indeed beautiful, sparkling with vitality, unlike many of the ragged, emaciated Highland women he'd seen as he'd travelled through this horrible country. But then the colonel had continued.

"The Highlanders have a strange sense of loyalty, and it's almost impossible to find one who will betray his —or in this case her —own clan. Men and women have been tortured in the past in attempts to discover the details of their traitorous plots, and have died without uttering one useful word. But now a songbird has fallen into our hands. Well, your hands. We must make the best possible use of this opportunity. I am relying on you to do so. I have of course mentioned your name in my despatch to London regarding the considerable discovery of arms at Stronmelochan. Well done, Private. I'm sure you will go far, if you continue to provide such important intelligence."

At the time Harold had been ecstatic, thinking that in spite of the humiliating experience on the northern coast, he might indeed be promoted, one day become a General even! Anything was possible! But his confident joyous mood had dissipated a few days later as he'd left the safety of the garrison behind to head into the wilderness, where a Highland savage could be hiding behind every rock. After all, none of them had seen or heard a thing at the beach until the men had been upon them! They were unnatural, almost certainly in league with Satan.

By the time he'd got to the meeting place he had been a bundle of nerves, jumping violently at every sound. And then she had not even arrived. After enduring a nerve-racking hour in the clearing and another nerve-racking journey back to Inversnaid, he had been relieved. He had done his part, and she had clearly decided not to meet him any more. That would be that.

But the colonel had thought otherwise. This source of information was too important to give up so easily. The woman could have been delayed for any number of reasons. Morrison would go there at the same time every week until it was certain she was no longer interested in meeting him.

This time Harold had deliberately arrived late, thinking that if Jeannie's husband had found out about their affair and thought to ambush him, he would surely have arrived early and be skulking in the undergrowth, probably accompanied by several of his friends. But there was nobody.

There was no sign of Jeannie either, but that did not trouble Harold much. A vague hope of future promotion was not worth the heart-stopping terror of having to ride here alone every week. Not now he had seen Highlanders in action, had seen how adept they were with weapons. Had seen how enormous and powerful Jeannie's ancient feeble husband was.

He remained mounted for a while longer just in case someone other than Jeannie did appear, in which case he would gallop away at full speed. The Highland horses were a joke, small squat creatures that could barely manage a trot. He should be safe as long as he stayed on his horse, and alert.

But you could only stay alert for so long, and after some fifteen minutes of tension, during which time the burn burbled merrily over the rocks, the birds sang, and the sun shone warmly down, Harold told himself he was being ridiculous. Jeannie would never tell her giant of a husband that she was swiving a soldier! She would be insane to do so. And this place was safe. She had told him that, had met him here many times, and had happily taken all her clothes off and coupled with him, completely relaxed. She would not have done that if she'd thought that someone might stumble upon them, for if they had it would have been clear that she was cuckolding this Kenneth monster.

He laughed softly to himself then, chiding himself for his own childishness, and dismounting, wrapped his horse's reins round a birch trunk. Then, after spreading the blanket on the ground in the sun, he reached into his saddlebag, took out the bread, cheese and flask of ale he'd brought with him, then went and sat on the blanket, relaxing completely now. He would eat his food, drink his ale, and if she hadn't arrived by then he would return to the garrison and tell Colonel Walker that she had failed to turn up again. Maybe the colonel would give up then. But if not, Harold determined, he would not be so afraid next time. He was a man, for God's sake, not some puling boy afraid of monsters in the cupboard! He smiled, took another bite of bread.

"Aye, it's a fine day for a wee feast in the sun, is it no'?" a pleasant voice came from directly behind him. "Ah no', dinna leave on my account, laddie. Ye look so peaceful there," the voice continued, its owner stopping Harold's attempt to jump up by means of gripping his shoulder and squeezing, which told the private exactly who was behind him even before the red-haired giant released his grip and moved to squat down opposite the redcoat.

They eyed each other; Kenneth relaxed, smiling, blue eyes cold as ice, razor-sharp dirk held casually in his right hand; Harold pale as death, suddenly cold, and shaking with terror in spite of his attempts to show no fear.

"Right, then, I'm thinking we've a reckoning, you and I, for ye've been intimate wi' my wife, and that isna a gentlemanly thing to do, as I'm sure ye ken, Sasannach though ye are. Were ye hoping to meet wi' her today?" His voice was soft, with no anger, and if it hadn't been for his size and the dirk, Harold might have thought Kenneth *did* actually mean to just talk with him.

"I…er…I didn't know she was married, I swear I didn't!" Harold blurted, belatedly realising that he might have done better to deny it altogether. Too late now. "She told me she was a spinster!"

"Aye, she tellt ye a great many things, I ken that. But she'll no' be telling ye any more, laddie. Ye've had a wasted journey, I'm thinking."

"Yes!" Harold almost shrieked, leaping to his feet. "I'm sorry. I won't come here again, I swear it! She led me on. It's not a thing I'd normally do! If she'd told me she was married, I never would have—"

Kenneth stood smoothly, and Harold glanced sideways to where his horse was, wondering if he could reach it before Kenneth caught him. Fighting him was out of the question; his shoulder was on fire just from the casual squeeze and the man could gut him before his hand even closed round the hilt of his sword. But Harold was the fastest runner in the regiment. He had a good chance of outrunning this hulking mountain of a man, who would surely be slow.

He swivelled on his toes then made a run for it, but took no more than a few steps before Kenneth, who it seemed was not slow at all, caught him by the arm, swinging him round. Harold braced himself to feel the cold iron of the knife between his ribs, but to his horror instead the giant enfolded him in his arms, pulling him against his chest.

"Ah no, laddie, it wouldna be right for ye to ride all this way for an embrace, and go home disappointed."

For one horrendous moment Harold actually thought the man was a molly and that he was about to be buggered. And then Kenneth flexed his arms and squeezed, and thought vanished, replaced by blood-red searing agony as Harold's body was crushed. He writhed for a minute, kicking out and arching backward in an attempt to break the bone-crushing hold, desperately trying to pull air into his rapidly constricting lungs. He felt his ribs crack, and then the pain overwhelmed everything, even the desire to survive, and his head fell forward onto Kenneth's chest. As his limbs grew limp and his vision darkened, the last sound he heard was the giant's heartbeat, strong, slow and steady, although the pain went on for much longer. So much longer that when death finally took him, he welcomed it.

Kenneth held Harold in his grip until he was sure the youth was dead, after which he released him, allowing his body to fall bonelessly onto the blanket. The blanket that he had no doubt swived Jeannie on.

Then he sat down, and reaching out for the bread and cheese broke his fast, for he had not eaten at all today, had eaten very little for the past several days in fact.

After Duncan had left, Kenneth had contemplated then rejected cutting several more loads of peat while he waited, not because it wouldn't be a useful thing to do and much appreciated by the clan, but because he knew that when he failed to return to the settlement people would come to look for him, because they cared about him.

Which was heartwarming in one respect, but right now he could not bear the thought of meeting anyone, of having to either talk as though nothing was wrong or tell them the truth; that all meaning in life had gone, and he didn't know how to continue living. His wife was a traitor, one of the worst things you could be. She had deceived him, threatened the whole clan, made a fool of him. And he still loved her. God help him, he still loved her, and could not imagine being without her, although he would have to be, and soon.

No, he could not see anyone, could not bear to see the pity and contempt in their eyes, not until he had found a way to somehow stop loving her. But he had no idea how to do that.

So instead of cutting the peat he had decided to come to the clearing, because this was certainly a place none of the MacGregors normally came to, unless they were following his wife. He had slept on the mountain overlooking it, and then every day, when the sun was almost overhead, he had settled himself comfortably into the undergrowth, drawing the top part of his *féileadh mór* over his bright auburn hair and blending into the landscape.

He had stayed there motionless until the sun had set, after which he had returned to the mountainside to sleep in the heather, before repeating the whole proceeding the next day, and the next.

This had been the fifth day. There would not be a sixth. Tomorrow he would go and cut peat, because no one would be looking for him by now, and when Duncan returned he would come to the peat stacks and wait for Kenneth to appear. Or perhaps, if his request was declined, Alex would come instead, and tell Kenneth that the deed was already done. And after five days of lying in the undergrowth, he was no nearer to knowing how to deal with that.

But before he cut the peat he had to finish this day. He chewed thoughtfully, washing down the food with ale, and then he wiped his mouth with his hand and sat back, closing his eyes and raising his face to the sun for a moment.

He had never killed like this before, coldly, with no emotion, no pity, no regret. It was a strange, unnatural feeling to erase someone, destroy forever all their dreams, their hopes, their future. It was an act that could not be undone, and normally Kenneth could only do it when the red mist took him and compassion ceased. Most of the clansmen had experienced the red mist to some extent before or during battle. It helped to quell the fear, to give courage, to stop you feeling pain if you were wounded.

But Kenneth was renowned for it, because he *never* killed unless the red mist took him, for he had always had to be careful with people, because it would be too easy for him to injure or kill by accident, so powerful was he. And he was gentle and kind by nature, rarely moved even to irritability, let alone rage. When in extremity the rage *did* take him though, all gentleness was obliterated and he was literally unstoppable.

He had expected the rage to take him when he'd seen the man who had used his wife so casually, who had reported her confidences to his officer, no doubt in hope of praise or glory, and who had risked the lives of everyone Kenneth held dear. Who had effectively condemned Jeannie to death.

But when he'd seen the nervous boy he had remembered the pathetic naked figure shaking with terror when Alex had interrogated him on the beach, and instead had felt nothing. No pity, no rage, just an icy void. Which was good, because instead of killing the boy blindly, he had killed him as he had planned to do. In a way which would not bring the British army down on the clan when his body was found.

And it had to be found. Because he had no idea whether Jeannie had revealed she was a MacGregor, or had told the boy where she lived. If she had, then the disappearance of the soldier would certainly be blamed on them, even if his body was never found.

Kenneth lay back for a minute, running through the next steps in his mind, and then he stretched, yawned and stood.

He put the empty flask back in the horse's saddlebag, taking a few minutes to let the mare become familiar with his scent, to relax so she would not baulk at what he wanted her to do next. Although as a soldier's horse she had no doubt been trained to remain calm around death.

Then he picked Harold up in his arms as though he was a child and gently put him over the saddle, tucking the blanket around his limp form. He was tempted to get up behind him and ride, but he had never ridden a horse such as this, had never ridden any horse in fact, for the garrons were too small for him to ride without his feet trailing on the ground. And if he was seen by anyone on the way to his destination, his story would seem more plausible if he was leading the horse submissively than if he was riding it.

He set off then, walking slowly, taking the long Highland route through the mountains to the Garrison of Inversnaid, although he halted just before the building came into view, having no wish to meet any more redcoats if he could avoid it. So far he had met no one at all, which suited him.

This was a good spot for what he wanted, at the bottom of a rocky outcrop. If he left the corpse here and released the horse, she would make her own way back to the garrison, by which time Kenneth would be a good way away. And the body was close enough to certainly be found before too long.

Any attempt to discover the cause of death would reveal the crushing injuries to the soldier's body, which could have been inflicted by a horse rolling on him, or by falling down a rocky hill, perhaps. But not by another man. No man could inflict such devastating injuries on someone by merely crushing him in his arms.

No one would suspect for even a moment that the youth had been murdered at all, let alone by a Highlander, Kenneth was sure of that. He had never met a man with his strength, knew what a freak of nature he was, knew what a blessing and a curse it had always been. Right now a blessing though.

He knelt by the pathetic remains of the youth then, crossing himself and saying a *Pater Noster* and an *Ave Maria*, hoping that would suffice, because he did not know the prayers for the dead and almost certainly the boy was not a Roman Catholic anyway. But he did not think God would mind.

Then he released the horse, patting her on the rump to get her moving towards the garrison, before heading in the opposite direction. He would go to the peat grounds now, cut some more fuel, and wait for Duncan to return. Or Alex.

CHAPTER TWENTY-TWO

When Duncan returned to Loch Lomond two weeks later he went directly to the peat ground, although he was very tired, having made the four-hundred-mile journey in record time. He could not imagine what Kenneth was going through alone in the heather, without even the company of the clan to distract him from the dreadful ordeal ahead of him. And because he could not bear to make that lonely vigil any longer than it needed to be, once the permission of Alex and Jeannie's brothers had been obtained he'd headed out of London early the following morning, stopping only to sleep and eat on his way north.

As soon as he arrived he knew what Kenneth had been doing to occupy the long hours, physically at least. Enough peat had been cut and spread out to dry to keep the clan warm through the longest winter. He whistled softly, impressed, and then he heard a small noise behind him and turning, saw Kenneth standing there.

"So Alex has agreed then," the big man said simply.

He looked terrible. Not because his shirt was filthy from the peat cutting, his hair wild and tangled around his shoulders and his bare legs badly scratched as though he'd been running through gorse. Duncan had expected that, if he was living wild. But there was something else, something intangible that distressed Duncan, although he could not address it because he did not know then what to address.

"Aye, he has," he said instead. "It's your right. He agrees, and so do her brothers, although they were grieved sorely when they heard what she'd done. But they'll no' blame you, no' speak of it, or of her, again. But—"

"Right then," Kenneth interrupted. "Let's away and be done wi' it. Do the others ken?"

"No," Duncan replied. "They dinna even ken I'm home. I came directly here, for ye've waited long enough. Alex has asked me to bide here a while this time. He said I'm needed more here than in London. He can manage wi' Angus, Iain and Maggie for a time."

Kenneth smiled, nodded.

"I'm pleased for ye, laddie. Ye hate the city, always have. Ye must be glad to be home for a time."

"Aye, I am. Kenneth—"

But Kenneth was already striding down the hill in the direction of the settlement, clearly intent on getting it over with, now he'd been granted permission to do so. Duncan ran after him, gripping his arm to make him stop for a moment.

"Ye still dinna have to do this. I ken ye've the chieftain's permission, but he doesna expect ye to go through with it. He said I can do it, if ye'll agree. I'll gladly take this from ye, Kenneth. Please, let me do this for ye. Stay here and let me get it over with. Then ye can come down."

Kenneth looked down into Duncan's earnest grey eyes. Then he shook his head sadly.

"Duncan, man, if ye do this it will break something in ye, as it would in Alex were he here. It's a mighty thing to kill a woman. We've been taught our whole lives to protect them. She's already broken me. I'll no' have her break anyone else. I ken what it cost ye to say that, and I thank ye dearly. But I need to do this."

They continued down the hill and into the settlement together in silence, for there really was nothing more to be said. When they arrived it was late afternoon and the clansfolk were outside, the women watching over the children and spinning, and the men sitting outside their homes, relaxing after a long day in the fields sowing oats or harrowing the soil. Everyone looked up when they saw the chieftain's brother and the man whose inexplicable absence had filled their conversation for over two weeks. The questions in their minds and on their lips were silenced though as the two men walked past them as though there was no one there, stopping outside Kenneth's house.

There, Duncan put an arm on Kenneth's, the two of them

spoke softly, just for a moment, and then Kenneth shook his head, and opening the door stepped into the house, closing the door softly behind him, leaving Duncan standing outside looking more distraught than anyone had ever seen him look before.

Then they moved towards him, but hesitantly, wanting to help in some way but instinctively knowing that whatever this was it was intensely private, something they could not help with, no matter how much they wanted to.

Barbara was the first to reach him as he stood outside the door, every fibre of his being wanting to follow Kenneth inside, every fibre of his being knowing that he must not.

"What is it, laddie?" she asked simply, looking up at Duncan, her lined face a mask of worry, the pale blue eyes that her son had inherited dark with fear. "What's amiss wi' him?"

She made a move then to go past him, to go to her son, who she had always helped in times of need, and Duncan moved in front of her, barring her way.

"Ye canna help him yet," he said. "Just let him get it over with."

She did not try to fight her way past him then, but stood, waiting for her son to get whatever it was finished.

Except it never would be.

"On yon hill there ye tellt me to let ye get it over with, and it was a kind thought. I'll no' forget that. But I caused this, and I'll end it. It'll never be over with for me, Duncan. Ye ken that, I'm thinking. Away with ye now," Kenneth had murmured before going inside.

And with that Duncan could not argue, for he did indeed ken that. Some things could never be over. They could only be endured, until they became bearable.

* * *

He entered the house so silently that Jeannie, who was in the bedroom, did not hear him until she came back into the main room and saw him standing there, his back to the door. She jumped.

"Holy Mother of God, but ye gave me a fright!" she said, bending to stir the pot suspended over the fire. "Where in hell have ye been these last weeks?" she continued angrily. "The whole clan's been asking me, and it shamed me to have to tell them I didna ken where my own husband was!"

There was no reply, and after a minute she straightened again and turned, to see him looking at her with an expression she had never seen on his face before. An expression of pity, of disgust.

And in that moment she knew that someone had told him what she had done, and that he believed them.

She moved forward then, thinking rapidly. She could deny it. She could talk him round. She had always been able to talk him round, because he loved her, and would believe anything she said, anything to keep his stupid illusion that they were happy together.

"Janet's been telling ye lies about me, then," she said defiantly. "She's been lusting for ye for a while now. That's why she hasna tellt Simon—"

"Enough," he said, very softly, and then he stepped towards her.

She saw his fingers curl into a fist, his arm lift, and instinctively raised her own arm in defence, stepping backwards as she did so, frantically thinking of a better lie, a more convincing lie. She saw his expression change then, saw the love and despair on his face, and suddenly knew exactly what to say.

And then she knew no more.

HISTORICAL NOTE

At the end of my later novels (not Mask of Duplicity) I always write a historical note, giving a little information about some of the events in my book which I think readers might be interested in knowing more about. This has proved to be very popular, so I thought I'd include one here too.

Firstly, this is primarily a book about smuggling, so I thought I'd start with a little bit about that. If you've ever gone through the Nothing to Declare section when entering the country, with something in your suitcase that you knew you should pay customs duty on (which many of us have), then you are a smuggler!

People have always felt justified in getting one over on the taxman or the government, and our eighteenth-century ancestors were no different to us in that respect. What *was* different was the taxation system. At that time there was no income or sales tax as we take for granted we must pay today. Before the industrial revolution there were few laws or records governing employment, and so no way to collect such a tax.

As Britain was an island however, any goods that came into the country or left it had to go by sea, and so it was that as far back as the tenth century kings were imposing a toll on certain items as they entered or left the country, in order to raise funds for their wars. Initially this was a toll on wine. Certain ports were designated as 'toll ports' and all vintners landing goods at these ports had to surrender part of their cargo. In the thirteenth century taxes on other goods were added, including a tax on wool and grain exported from Britain, which proved to be very unpopular. Over time, in order to finance increasingly expensive and lengthy wars, which monarchs were so keen to engage in, other commodities became subject to customs duties too, not just the luxury items such as lace, silk, alcohol and tobacco, but also everyday essentials such as salt, soap and candles.

And so smuggling was born, thrived, and reached its heyday in the seventeenth and eighteenth centuries, when so many products were subject to extortionate duties. Extremely organised and proficient gangs ran huge quantities of goods in and out of the country, often financed by aristocrats and wealthy merchants, and assisted by just about everyone else, from farm labourers to tavern keepers, professional men and even vicars and priests.

Smuggling was so lucrative that gangs could afford to pay extravagant sums to people willing to carry or hide items in their homes or outbuildings, could also afford to bribe poorly paid customs officials to look the other way when goods were coming in, and judges and juries to declare them innocent should they be caught.

At the time this book is set, as Gabriel explains, the chance of being apprehended on the sea, or even on land was relatively small, although it did happen. This was partly because of the geography of Britain, which, with its uneven coastline, has a multitude of small, secluded coves, partly because there weren't enough excise men to patrol the coast, partly because much of the population lived on the edge of starvation, so would jump at the chance of a generous payment for unloading and transporting goods overland, and partly because just about everyone, then as now, got great joy from cheating the taxman and government.

Even those who did not take an active part in smuggling goods would not be averse to buying them at prices so low that they it was obvious they had entered the country illegally.

The South-East of England, where Gabriel's gang is based, was rife with smugglers, due to its proximity to London and to France, which meant that the gangs themselves grew incredibly powerful and increasingly violent and ruthless. By the mid-eighteenth century this had become a real problem, with whole communities being threatened by some of the gangs.

What had originally been a willing collaboration now became a very different thing, and people went in fear of their lives. Anyone suspected of being an informant could be tortured and brutally murdered, and there are numerous records of this happening, often to innocent people. And the gangs were too large and aggressive for the rural authorities to tackle alone. Instead sometimes whole communities would band together and act against a smuggling gang that was threatening them, with some success.

In general, fiction and film portrays smugglers or the 'free trade' as it was known, as a dashing, romantic venture (much as it does with pirates and highwaymen). Indeed I have also taken romantic licence in portraying Gabriel Foley as a courageous, ruthless but fair man, and his gang as loyal to their leader and each other in general, although readers of Mask of Duplicity will have seen another side to the smuggling fraternity, in the character of Joshua White. In my defence though, there *were* men like Gabriel, but many gangs resorted to increasing violence as the criminal underworld took control of this highly lucrative trade.

In my book I have the MacGregors and smugglers rowing to Calais. Rowing boats were sometimes used when crossing the Channel from the east coast of England to France, although a sturdier craft would be needed for longer journeys such as Roscoff to Cornwall. A gang of smugglers could make the journey in a few hours, with virtually no risk of being intercepted by the revenue boats even if they were seen, as the cutters had to rely on the wind and were not as manoeuvrable as a small rowing boat.

On the return trip from Calais to Burghead, the men are in a cutter. These were used by both smugglers and revenue men as they were fast and strong. The revenue cutters were generally clinker-built (using overlapping planks), which made them stronger, something they needed as they would be sailing in all conditions. This did make them a little slower, however.

Some smugglers preferred to have their boats carvel built (with planks laid edge-to edge). This made them less sturdy but faster, which could be crucial when attempting to escape a revenue boat. This was often a wise choice, as unlike revenue men, smugglers could choose when they sailed so did not need to be as worried about the strength of the hull, and had plenty of funds for building high-quality expensive ships, as the monetary rewards for successful smuggling runs were enormous.

Here's an example to show how profitable smuggling was, using tea as an example. Tea cost approximately 7d (3p) per pound on the Continent, but was sold in England by the smugglers for 5s (25p). Legal tea would be far more expensive, so there was a huge demand for the smugglers' tea.

In 1743 a single landing by a smuggler brought in 2,000lbs of tea. He would have paid approximately £60 for his cargo, but could sell it for £500. This is at a time when a farm labourer's wages might be 1/6 (7p) a day. Renting a house would cost about £10 a year. Hopefully that gives an idea of the vast fortunes that could be made from smuggling!

On to other things. I've written about the landing at Burghead. I have not invented the ancient fort at Burghead, which both the Highlanders and Redcoats visit. There are actually the remains of an ancient fort at Burghead, which was an enormous Pictish fort (although in the 1700s it was thought to be Roman). There's a small museum there, which was sadly closed when I was there! Here's a link to a fascinating article about it: https://www.abdn.ac.uk/news/15492/

The beach with the two caves also exists, and the larger cave is exactly as I've described it in my book, set in beautiful golden rock on a lovely secluded beach about five miles away from Burghead. The walk along the coast is glorious, to me, if not to the poor soldiers! The place the MacGregors shelter in while waiting for Alex to arrive is invented, in as far as the overhanging area on the cliffs was not found by me (although it could well be there –I just preferred using artistic licence to possibly plummeting off the cliff as I searched for it).

The Garrison of Inversnaid also exists, and is now a ruin run as a smallholding, and which has lovely accommodation for travellers. I stayed there last year and was treated to a comprehensive tour of the ruins, and told about the routes used by the soldiers and the highlanders in the area, some of which I subsequently walked. I won't comment in depth here, as I've written a blog about it, with photos, on my website. Link here, if you're interested in knowing more: https://juliabrannan.com/2021/08/15/the-garrison-of-inversnaid/

And finally, a few words about the role of the Highland chieftain, especially for anyone reading this book having only read *Mask of Duplicity* so far. This novella introduces a number of characters who feature in later books in *The Jacobite Chronicles* series.

Readers might find Alex's judgement of Jeannie and the clansmen's reactions to it a bit harsh, so I thought I'd write a little about the role of the chief or chieftain of a Highland clan. In essence a clan was a military unit who in the main all held the same surname and considered themselves to be related to each other. Their commander-in-chief was their clan leader.

The Highlands of Scotland until the eighteenth century were relatively impregnable, and it was virtually impossible for the monarch or anyone else to impose their laws on the clans. So in the main they were left to sort out their own problems, although kings would often attempt to exert authority by bribing chiefs of larger clans to act in the monarch's interests, with varying degrees of success.

In general though, unless they caused problems outside the Highlands, they were left to it. When there was a battle to be fought, usually against a rival clan, the chief or chieftain of the clan would lead his men and fight with them to the death, as it was his job to protect them.

It was also his job to ensure that his people did not starve if the harvest was bad, or the winter particularly brutal. He might live in a better house and have more luxuries, depending on how numerous his clan was, but he was expected to consider the welfare of all his clansmen, as they considered him not only to be their leader, but effectively their father. He was not some remote, lofty figure as an English lord might be, living luxuriously while his people, unknown to him, starved. Instead, he was one of them, and was expected to care for them as a father would care for his children, feeding and clothing them, disciplining them when necessary.

Having said that, in a brutal society where the people literally lived from day to day, with possible starvation or violent death only one harvest or one feud away, any person who threatened the safety of the clan would be dealt with ruthlessly, and the chieftain's word was law. He had the absolute power of life and death over them, and wielded that power, fairly or unfairly depending on the quality of the man. In the case of a traitor to the clan, the sentence would have to be death, and no one would or could argue against that.

So, a chief or chieftain was expected to be an accomplished warrior, and if he was not, either due to age or infirmity, then he would have a war chief, usually a close relativesuch as a brother or cousin, who would lead the clan on his behalf. In spite of the general viewpoint of outsiders that the clans were bands of primitive illiterate savages, in fact many chieftains and not a few of their people were not only literate or numerate, but had often attended universities and were well-versed in the classics or in law. As many of them were businessmen, holding vast tracts of land and dealing in the commodities of that land, this is not really surprising.

Although the Highland clans are now thought of more sympathetically than they were in the eighteenth century, as fierce but protective exotically-garbed warriors who were not afraid to show their emotions, it often comes as a surprise to people to learn that they were often highly educated and proficient entrepreneurs!

I really hope you've enjoyed this book. If you have, and have not read the rest of The Jacobite Chronicles, I hope you'll be inspired to read the next book, The Mask Revealed. It's available on Amazon and in Kindle Unlimited. The link to my Amazon page, where you can buy it and my other books is here:

Author.to/JuliaBrannanAmazonPage

If you'd like to read further historical blogs and other information about the period my books are set in, and also learn about future book releases, then if you haven't already, please subscribe to my monthly newsletter (no spam, guaranteed) here:

http://eepurl.com/bSNLHD

I also post a regular historical blog on my website:

www.juliabrannan.com

You can also follow me on Twitter:

https://twitter.com/BrannanJulia

Or on Facebook:

www.facebook.com/pages/Julia-Brannan/727743920650760

Printed in Great Britain
by Amazon